Of Sense and Sensibility

A REIMAGINE OF THE AUSTEN CLASSIC

R. KATZE

ISBN: 979-8-9931528-1-3

Cover design by: Getcovers

Printed in the United States of America

For lovers of Sense and Sensibility who wanted to see Marianne choose Brandon

on her own...

This is for you.

CHAPTER ONE

There was a somber air over Norland Park, the weight of it felt by all who stood within its grasp. Marianne Dashwood's hand was clasped tightly in her sister Elinore's as they watched their father struggle to breathe where he lay in bed. Marianne ran her free hand through her long ebony hair, and she tried not to notice how it trembled. She knew tears were streaming from her warm chocolate eyes, but the sight of her father, her strong, dashing, father, laying in his bed, barely able to move was almost too much to bear.

Her mother, Mary Dashwood, sat in her place beside him, gently wiping the sweat off his brow. Marianne felt her mouth go dry as she listened to his labored breath. It was so unfair, her father had been a champion for species equality, the one who had been instrumental in brokering the peace accords between the Fae and other magical creatures and the humans, and yet he was still brought down by his own body and an illness none could cure.

A loud commotion from the hall pulled Elinor from her vigil, her deep brown eyes turning to the door as it swung open, revealing their half-brother, John, their father's son from his previous marriage. It had taken him longer to arrive than it should have, even accounting for travels on the roads, he should have been there hours before, however...

"John, thank goodness you have come," Mary said softly as she rose from the bed to let John draw near. Her dark hair was drawn back at the base of her neck, but Mary's gray eyes showed the weight of her worry and sorrow.

"Father, I am here," John whispered as he stepped around Mary, ignoring her completely as he moved. In his haste, he tripped over his feet as he scurried closer and had to catch himself on the bed before kneeling beside the bed, taking his father's hand in his.

"John..." Henry Dashwood's voice was labored as his dulled gaze turned to his eldest child. "I am unable to divide my estate... between you and your... sisters." Henry coughed, the sound almost a wheeze as John leaned closer. "The law says everything.... Everything...must go to you..."

John's eyes widened almost imperceptibly, a look of anticipation that was quickly dashed, but not before Elinor's sharp sight caught it. Despite the progress made in peace between the humans and the magical creatures that walked the earth, humans still had a very outdated view of inheritance and the roles of women. It hadn't mattered how much she had protested, fought, or even her attempts to starve herself in protest, there was nothing her father could do. The estate had to be given to the eldest male child and could not be evenly divided between all of the siblings.

"You must... Promise me... promise me you will look after your sisters, your step-mother... John..." Henry's hand tightened against John's, "you must promise me."

"I... promise, father." John's eyes closed slightly; the light brown now nearly hidden behind his lids. It was a sight that anyone else would see as sorrow, but there was a gleam that reflected in them that made Elinor uncomfortable. It wasn't that John had been a bad brother, if she were honest, but he had been an absent one. When you added that to his wife, the harpy Fanny, who had abhorred all the work that their father had done, bemoaning the peace accords and... yes poisoning John against his father.

Henry's eyes closed in relief as he dropped back against the pillows.

A moment later the labored breathing faded, and Mary let out a cry as Henry's hand fell limp. Marianne's hand covered her mouth as she let out a sob, her chocolate eyes full of sorrow and a hint of fear as she watched their mother fall onto the bed, her head on their father's chest as she sobbed. John stepped back, his gaze slightly wide and full of panic as the doctor rushed through the door at the sound.

Elinor began to tear up as she watched as the doctor examined her father, listening to his chest, holding a mirror to his mouth to check for breath, but she pushed them back. There would be time for mourning later; at the moment, she knew she needed to be there for her mother and her sister. She knew there would be much to do; someone needed to think of what came next, and as much as she loved her mother and sister, they would sooner fall into despair than plan and prepare.

Within three days, she had been proven right as her brother's wife, Fanny Dashwood, arrived with their young son Byron in tow, to install herself as the lady of Norland Manor.

Fanny was as different in temperament and looks from the Dashwood sisters as their brother could have gotten. While both sisters had long dark hair, kept in modest but reasonable fashion, Fanny's black hair was shockingly short, the cut skimming her chin. Elinor and Marianne both were known in the parish as being warm, approachable women, whereas Fanny was cutting and direct, two qualities unusual for a woman of their time. Her black gaze missed nothing, judging everyone and everything, and typically found them lacking.

Elinor curtsied to her sister-in-law as the woman swept by her with barely a glance. Given Fanny's... demands for perfection... Elinor, upon notice that the woman would be arriving by the end of the day, had immediately ensured her best presentation. She stood in the entryway in her best black linen dress, determined to honor the mourning period even though Fanny had made it obvious she took it as a slight. Her sister-in-law's slight sniff and lifting of her nose made her feelings quite clear as she passed.

Elinor sighed as she fell in line behind Fanny, listening with a heavy heart as the woman immediately began to discuss the changes she wanted to make to the home: the paintings that simply *had* to be replaced with something more colorful, and wouldn't that wall look marvelous in green? It hadn't even been a full day, and yet everyone was already miserable, a new record for Fanny. Elinor fell back as Fanny continued on through the home, a manservant scrambling after her to take note of her multiple changes.

"Thank you, Ayumi." Mary's voice had Elinor turning to see her mother with a few of her most precious items from the master bedroom carefully cradled against her chest. "Please get the room ready; your mistress will be expecting it."

"Mama…" Elinor stepped forward to help her mother, taking some of the items. "I'm sure there is no need to give up your room."

"No, Elinor, Fanny is the mistress now; she will demand the best and I…" Mary sighed as she led Elinor through the halls, "I have no wish to fight while I am still mourning your father."

"Well, I think it's rubbish that she is now the mistress at all," Marianne huffed as she stepped out of the room she shared with Elinor, where she had been hiding. "It's not fair; where have they been for the past 6 years? Hiding away as far from here as they could in London? Where were they when father fell ill? They don't deserve Norland."

"No, they don't," Elinor agreed, "but that does not matter."

"Elinor," Marianne fumed, "do you not care that they are taking our home from us?"

"Of course I care, Marianne, but that is not how it works," Elinor chastised. "The estate always goes to the eldest son, and it would do you well to stay in Fanny's good graces. Our livelihood is now entirely dependent on John and Fanny."

"And she will lord it over us every day," Marianne grumbled before turning pleading eyes to her mother. "Mama, how long do we need to stay? I cannot stand to be around that woman for long."

"Until we know what our allowance is, we do not know what we can afford, dearest," Mary said quietly as she began to place her items around her new room. "We will stay as long as we must, and we must pray for your brother's goodwill and generosity."

"You mean pray that Fanny is generous..." Marianne muttered under her breath, and Elinor could only nod at her sister's words.

Three days had passed since Fanny's descent on their... her... home, and John had yet to make any decision as to his sisters and stepmother's future. Elinor walked through her father's library, her fingers trailing over the familiar spines with a sense of sadness. She drew out her favorite story, *Candide* by Voltaire, smiling sadly as she thought of the hours she spent in the library listening to her father hem and haw over some correspondence or theory that was proposed in a book. He had given her one of the most precious gifts a father could give a daughter—an education that included more than embroidery or music—and she would be forever grateful.

"John, I do *not* want... them... ruining anything." Fanny's voice echoed down the hall, drawing closer to the library.

Elinor dropped her book onto her father's desk to hide behind the false door. She had been nice and accommodating to Fanny for three days, but lord, she needed a break. If she was seen, Fanny would have some demand or another, and Elinor would sigh, smile, and do what she could to assist.

"Fanny, they are my sisters and my stepmother."

"And we are being hospitable and charitable by allowing them to stay here for the time being, when they do not belong." Elinor sighed at Fanny's cutting words. "I do not understand why they *insist* on staying; if they would like to stay, then they will need to join the servants."

"Fanny, Mary was lady of the house for nearly 20 years."

"And now I am lady of the house, and I say who stays and who goes, John."

"I promised Father that I would look after them."

"And you have been, my dear John; no brother could have been more attentive in their time of mourning."

Elinor stepped back to leave, but stopped as she heard John begin to speak again.

"I have a mind to give them each 1000 pounds."

Elinor's eyes closed as a sense of relief rushed over her. A thousand pounds apiece would let them find suitable lodgings, and still keep the staff who wished to follow them. She should not have doubted their broth...

"A 1000 pounds apiece?" Fanny's voice rose to a screech. "Surely you aren't intending to rob your only son of his rightful inheritance! How would you be able to look him in the eye, knowing you are taking money from dear Byron?"

"Is... is it too much?"

"John, what would three women need with 3000 pounds a year between them? They would not have many expenses, and your sisters will inherit 10,000 pounds upon the death of your stepmother, which is a more than adequate inheritance."

"Ah, then 500 pounds apiece, that should suffice."

"Oh, John, that would be more than generous, and I am sure your father did not intend for you to squander your inheritance from your mother on his second wife and your half-sisters."

"You are right of course, my dear," John signed as Elinor seethed from behind the door. "Then it is set: 100 pounds apiece. I will inform Mary, and they can begin to find their own accommodations."

300 pounds a year... Elinor felt panic begin to rise.

How would they be able to survive on 300 pounds? That would barely cover a home for the three of them, let alone any of the staff. Elinor felt tears well and she forced herself to push them away. She needed to stay strong, to help make sure they would be safe and could afford necessities such as food when they left Norland. She pressed her back against the wall and let her shoulders drop for a moment before pushing off to seek out her mother.

John stood behind her mother in her new bedroom, his face clear of any expression as her mother buried her head in her hands and her shoulders shook.

"This is not what your father would have wanted, John, you know how important family was to him," Mary exclaimed softly, her voice heavy with tears.

"Yes, as long as it was *this* family." John's eyes took on a hard glint as he spun and stalked past Elinor, barely giving her a nod as he stormed out.

"300 pounds..." Mary whispered, dropping onto the bed, "whatever shall we do?"

"We will make do, mama," Elinor responded as she moved to kneel beside her mother. "It is what we do."

"Oh there you are." Fanny swept into the room, a small, unattractive smile on her face. "I was wondering where you were hiding."

Mary's shoulders stiffened as Fanny spoke.

"I have just heard from my brother, Edward; he will be coming to visit us tomorrow, and I anticipate that his stay will be a long one. You have never met my brother, have you?"

"No," Mary said quietly, shaking her head slightly.

"He is the eldest, heir to a considerable fortune, and I must say, the family has great expectations of him." Fanny looked around the room, a hint of disdain visible as she took in the modest decorations. "Well, there is much to do, my brother is quite... discerning in his tastes, and we would not want him to find any..." Fanny's eyes scanned over Mary and Elinor quickly before continuing, "fault with anything." Her lips turned, the look cruel to Elinor. "So please excuse me, there is thus *much* to do."

Mary waited for the door to close behind Fanny and her footsteps to fade down the hall, her hands clenched at her side.

"We will be leaving as soon as we find suitable accommodations." Mary took Elinor's hand as anger deepened her voice. "I will *not* stay around that woman any longer than I must."

CHAPTER TWO

True to her word, Fanny found many things to change or items that simply were not up to her dear brother's standards, sending the house and the staff into a tizzy. Silver that had been polished only days before her arrival were deemed to be stained or tarnished, forcing the staff to meet *her* expectations before they could move to another task, only to have her yell at them for not working fast enough.

Elinor watched out the window of her room when she saw Alicia and Kara struggling with a rug over their shoulders. She quickly ran out of the room towards the nearest exit, not catching up with the girls until they had managed to throw the rug over a line strung between two trees.

"Celia, Alicia, what are you doing?" Elinor asked, eyeing the carpet beater in Alicia's hand. "Weren't these just done a week ago?"

"Beg pardon, miss," Alicia said softly with a small curtsey, "but Mrs. John Dashwood insisted they be done again with Mr. Edward coming."

"These carpets are clean, Alicia." Elinor reached out to gently take the carpet beater. "And if not, I will take care of it for you. Please, go and see to your other work."

"Thank you, Miss Elinor." Alicia smiled as she curtseyed again and hurried into the house.

Elinor turned to the rug, the one she knew should be laying on the floor in her father's study, the beater in her hand. All of her anger and frustration at the situation began to bubble up, and her grip on the beater tightened. Elinor couldn't help herself, grabbing the beater with both hands, winding back and smacking the carpet as hard as she could, wishing that it actually were her sister-in-law's face.

She took a step back, shaking out her arms as she turned... and came face to face with a man's chest.

"Good morning." A rich tenor voice had her lifting her gaze, deep brown meeting cobalt as the man smiled at her.

"Oh, umm, forgive me, I was j... just..." Elinor stammered, her eyes going wide.

"Beating carpets?" the man teased, laughter dancing in his eyes.

"Oh... ummm..." Elinor looked sheepishly between the carpet and the man. "Yes."

"Edward Ferrars, how do you do?" Elinor continued to watch him warily, unsure of what to make of him as he took his hat off, his black hair long for the fashion of the day, tied back at the base of his neck. "My horse threw a shoe, so I came this way by way of the stables."

"Elinor Dashwood." Elinor dropped into a small curtsey, and as she rose she saw a small smile turning Edward's lips.

"Would you like any help?" he asked, and Elinor tilted her head slightly, unsure of what he was asking. His smile grew as he gestured towards the rug with his hat. "With your... carpet beating?"

Elinor found her lips twitching with amusement for a moment, before she shook her head slightly, a blush forming on her cheeks.

"Oh um... no, thank you." She turned her head briefly towards the house then back to him. "I should... take you back to the house to see your sister."

Elinor moved towards the house, pausing for a moment as she and Edward started towards the same opening between the rugs. Edward stepped back with a small bow, holding out his hand to let her go first.

As they walked back to the house in silence, Elinor could not help but notice the differences between Edward and his sister. He had been warm, charming, nothing at all like the cold, cunning and calculating Fanny. Her eyes darted to him as they walked side by side. She couldn't deny that he was attractive, tall and lean, dashing in his black coat and pants, purple vest and white cravat.

Elinor snuck a look at his boots as they ascended the stairs to the front door; she had learned from her father that one could tell a lot about a man from his boots. If they were new and shiny, the man just wanted to pretend to fit in, but Edward's were scuffed and worn. They were not the boots of the high society lord-to-be that Fanny had painted him as when she spoke of him. This was a man who held the door open for her with a smile, whose cobalt irises shone with intelligence, curiosity, and not with the indifference of the lords who had visited her father from time to time from London.

He puzzled her.

He intrigued her.

"Edward!" Fanny jumped to her feet as Elinor led him into the parlor, dashing away from the table where she sat with Marianne and Mary. "Look at you, why are you dressed like... *that*? Where are your things?"

"They are on their way here from the inn. The weather was nice, so I felt like taking a ride and enjoying the fresh country air."

"And how long are you planning on staying?" Marianne's voice was full of distrust and resentment, but a side look from Elinor had her going quiet.

"Well, that would entirely depend on Mrs. Dashwood." Edward held his hat before him as he smiled first at his sister then Marianne before turning to Mary's. "I would not like to overstay my welcome; I am dependent on your hospitality." Elinor watched her mother give her first real smile since the death of Elinor's father as she nodded to acknowledge the courtesy and respect that Edward had given her.

Elinor watched Edward with her mother and sister, answering their questions easily with a smile as he ignored the dark looks and hisses from Fanny. He was not at all what she expected him to be. More than once he turned back to look at her, laughter and genuine amusement in his eyes, and she could tell he was laughing with, not at, her family.

When Fanny finally had enough of being ignored, she forcibly grabbed Edward's elbow, dragging him away from the three women. "I cannot believe you showed up looking like... like *this*," she seethed, her voice carrying down the hall. "You have more sense than this, Edward, and it's time you start..." Her voice finally dropped off, and Elinor was unable to hear any further... complaints from the woman.

"I like him," Mary said with a soft smile on her face. "He is a proper gentleman."

In a manor as large as Norland, it was almost amazing how many times a person could still run into someone in a day. It seemed that every time Elinor turned a corner, or entered a room, Edward would be there, talking with the butler, charming cookies from the cook, or admiring the library. He seemed to go out of his way to talk to every member of the household, to learn about them, to get to know them. He didn't treat them like they were beneath him: he spoke to them as equals, genuinely curious about their lives. He was respectful to her mother, deferring to her in conversations or decisions, treating her with the proper courtesy and dignity of the lady of the household.

Elinor truly admired that.

In his family, he had told her, when his father had died some years ago, it had been set up that his mother, rather than him, would inherit the estate. It was a rare arrangement to be sure, but none would dare to question his mother.

"It gives me a unique perspective, I suppose," Edward said one day when he had joined Elinor on one of her daily walks. "I never understood the law that said a wife could not inherit the husband's estate, that instead she is entirely dependent on his will and his next of kin. Why shouldn't a woman be seen as having the same worth and value as her husband?"

When Elinor gave a soft sound of agreement, he stopped for a moment to watch her, his Cobalt eyes considering her carefully.

"It must pain you to watch my sister refurbishing Norland after her own... taste."

Elinor shook her head at Edward's words. "No; I mean, it is her house now, so it is only right that she would seek to refurbish the house to suit her needs and wishes."

"Yes, well, I wish she would stop trying to refurbish me as well." Edward's voice held a note of anger, and Elinor tilted her head up to watch him. "She sees me as a disappointment; she would like me to be someone important, someone spoken about, a politician or dignitary of some sort."

"Is that not something that you would want, then?" Elinor asked him, genuine curiosity on her face.

"Me? No... no. You see, I would rather go into the church, run a small country parish..." He smiled at the thought before sighing. "But that is not smart enough for my family." Edward got quiet, his brow troubled. "I feel that we must all find our own way to be happy."

"So do I..." Elinor said with a small laugh, "and I quite prefer your definition of happiness."

"Do you?" Edward turned, his deep cobalt eyes capturing Elinor's with their intensity, as if he was looking for something in them, and smiling softly at what he found. "Good. Quiet country parish it is, then." With a small chuckle he began to walk again, and Elinor trailed beside him, lost in thought over what he had said.

It wasn't long before Edward began to join Elinor every day for one of her walks of the grounds, laughing with her at some new antics of Marianne's, sharing tales of their childhood, their visions of the future. He began joining her, Marianne, and Mary for evening readings of poetry and stories, and Elinor found they had similar taste in books. She shyly showed him some of the drawings that she had done, portraits of servants and a charcoal of Norland Manor, and he was in awe of their beauty.

Each day found him standing a little closer, smiling a little brighter at her as they laughed on their walks. One day Edward found a yellow wildflower and carefully picked it for her hair, a compliment to her dress and beauty, he had said, and Elinor had felt her cheeks flush at the compliment. Family dinners were spent with furtive glances between the two: Elinor would look up to see Edward suddenly darting his eyes away, only for him to smile when she did the same.

One afternoon, Elinor lay under one of the oak trees with Marianne, a gentle, happy smile on her face, not seeing the consideration on her sister's.

"Do you love him?" Marianne asked. Elinor started, her face turning towards her sister, but there was no question about whom Marianne was referring.

"I... think very highly of him," Elinor said, very diplomatically, only to be met with the amused expression on Marianne's face. "I like him, Marianne," she finally admitted with a small laugh.

"Do you think he is worthy of you? From what I can see, he has no taste for music or poetry."

"Marianne, there are worse faults than not appreciating your playing," Elinor said, pushing off the ground.

"But his readings, Elinor! He's so calm: there's no passion, no spirit in it."

"He allows the words to speak for themselves, Marianne. He has a different style; is that so bad?"

"Well..." Marianne grinned, "the day you tell me to call him brother-in-law, I will find no fault in him at all."

Elinor stilled, pushing herself up into a fully seated position.

"Marianne... no, there is no question of that. He has family obligations, duties."

"But if he loves you, those will not matter, and he will act upon those feelings."

"Marianne, nothing has been said between us," Elinor said, watching her sister's face. "I have feelings for him, yes, and I do believe that he has feelings for me, but please, do not hope for something that may actually never happen."

"You mean you are ... not engaged?"

"Engaged? What would give you that impression?"

Marianne's lips pursed as she considered her sister. "I thought, for sure, that he had asked you in secret, that there was an agreement between you two."

"No." Elinor said with exasperation, "nothing of the sort."

"Well, it is only a matter of time; in fact, I am sure it will be very soon."

Elinor shook her head at Marianne, her stern expression giving way to a smile as her sister began to giggle. When Marianne saw Edward approaching from the house, her giggles quieted with a knowing look and a waggle of her eyebrows as Elinor blushed and rose to dust off her dress before leaving for her daily walk with Edward.

Later, as they returned from their walk, Edward left for the stables to check on his horse, and Elinor continued on to the manor.

"... enjoying his visit, Fanny." Elinor slowed at her mother's words, stopping altogether when she heard Fanny respond.

"Yes, it does appear so... You must understand, my mother has great expectations for him..." Fanny paused for a moment before continuing, "...both in position and in matrimony. So you see, any young woman that may be attempting to... lure him in... would thus wind up gravely disappointed."

Elinor's eyes closed at the veiled warning. She had no expectations of anything coming from her... friendship... with Edward, but still any hopes or dreams were cut to the quick in an instant.

When Elinor finally composed herself well enough to enter the manor, she found her mother standing with Marianne, huddled over a letter. At the sound of Elinor's footsteps Mary's head rose and she gestured for her to join them.

"What is it Mama?" Elinor sighed.

"It's a letter from my cousin, Middleton. He has offered us a cottage on his estate in Devonshire. What do you think, Elinor?" Mary asked her, handing her the letter.

Elinor scanned it quickly, focusing on the key information: the rent, and the size.

"It is small, but the rent is moderate; we would only need one, maybe two servants. I do believe we should consider it."

"I will write to Middleton immediately and accept."

"Without seeing it, Mama?" Marianne asked.

"Yes." Mary's face was hard as she spoke. "I am determined to leave this house by the end of the week."

Elinor watched her mother hurry down the hall, the letter in hand. She knew that the conversation between her mother and Fanny had something to do with her mother's sudden insistence to leave.

It seemed almost surreal—packing up a lifetime of memories, keeping only the dearest of items—to move so far away. There were memories in every corner of

the house: hiding from their father, giggling with Marianne. The library was the
hardest, and thus the room Elinor and Marianne had left for last. Elinor had just
lowered a painting of Norland from the wall when the door to the library opened
and Edward entered, stopping when he saw Elinor and Marianne.

"Ah... I was...hmmm," he stammered, at a loss for words for the first time since
Elinor had met him.

"Excuse me," Marianne said quickly, shooting her sister a glance, "I must
go help Mama." Elinor's mouth opened to ask her to stay, but with a wink
Marianne was gone, leaving Elinor alone with Edward.

Edward watched Elinor for a moment, emotions swirling in his eyes, but
Elinor was unable to read them.

"Devonshire..." he finally stated, "that's... that's so far away."

"Yes," Elinor breathed, "but it is not too far for true friends to come visit."

"No... no it's not," Edward responded, his hands clasped behind his back, his
expression unreadable. "It... it must be hard to leave Norland."

"Yes..." Elinor said hesitantly, "but in light of the circumstances..."

"Yes, of course... of course..." Edward paused again, and Elinor felt her heart
begin to race even as Fanny's comments floated through her thoughts. "Elinor,
you must know that these past few weeks have been very happy for me."

"For me as well..." Elinor responded, her eyes shining.

"I... I don't think I've ever been happier." Edward's voice showed his
nervousness. When he looked up and met her gaze all Elinor could do was nod as
he smiled. "I'm... I'm very glad that I was able to be here, to be a friend, during
these troubling times and I want you... I want you to know that I..." His gaze
became troubled as his throat caught, "I value your friendship too."

He took a step forward, his mouth opening as if he was going to continue,
only to pause, taking in Elinor's face before meeting her gaze again. Elinor could
then see it in his expression, there was so much that he wanted to say and yet... he
couldn't. He drew his hands out from behind his back to show a small, wrapped

package. His mouth opened again, as if to speak, before snapping closed. He set the package on the desk, tapping it gently. When Elinor looked up, she could see the shimmer of tears, and knew they were in hers as well.

"Excuse me," Edward said brokenly with a small nod as he turned and walked out of the library, leaving Elinor standing behind the desk with a stunned expression on her face.

Elinor took a deep breath as she stepped out of Norland Manor for the last time, descending the steps towards the carriages. A hand reached out to help her, and she looked up to meet Edward's troubled Cobalt eyes before placing her hand in his. His hand held hers for a second too long, earning a stern throat clearing from Fanny, who glared at Elinor. He released her hand reluctantly and Elinor stepped away to ascend into the carriage, the small package from Edward tucked safely in her hands.

John stepped up to close the carriage door with a nod to Mary before stepping back to his wife, who watched with glee.

"You will come and visit us soon, Edward?" Marianne asked, shooting a sly grin at her sister.

"As soon as I can," Edward promised, his gaze never leaving Elinor's. As the carriage started to pull away, she watched him through the window, their eyes never breaking contact until the carriage turned a corner and he disappeared from view.

"Well, my dear?" Mary asked, drawing Elinor's attention back to her mother.

"I... I have no news for you," Elinor said softly, glancing at the package in her lap.

"He will come visit us soon; I know he will," Marianne smiled, resting her hand over Elinor's.

Elinor just nodded to appease her sister, then let her gaze turn out the window, watching as they left Sussex behind. As they traveled, the view changed, from towering woods to sweeping plains and hills, yet Elinor saw none of it, even as she watched. When Mary and Marianne fell asleep she carefully opened the present from Edward to reveal a leather bound book. A small smile curved her lips as she saw it was a book on local flowers and herbs in Devonshire, a gift designed to appeal to her practical heart. She opened the book and saw the signature on the message on the first page:

Your affectionate Friend- E. Ferrars.

Her fingers lightly traced the letters before she settled the book carefully in her purse. Elinor sat back in the seat, letting her head fall back as she closed her eyes as she drifted off to sleep.

The entire journey to Devonshire and their new cottage took six days to complete, and Elinor was grateful when the carriage finally drew to a stop. The crashing waves of the sea drew Elinor's attention as she stepped out of the carriage; their new home sat near the cliffs, and she stopped for a moment, in awe of the view, before her mother called her name and she turned to see the cottage for the first time.

It was small, much smaller than Norland Manor, yet Elinor knew it would do for the three of them and the two servants they had brought with them. She saw the small garden plot next to the house, and sighed with a little relief that they would be able to grow some of their own food to reduce costs.

The cottage was as different from Norland Manor as it could be, with rustic floors and walls free of any wallpaper, the stucco clearly visible. The ceilings were much lower than the vast chambers of Norland, making the cottage seem closed in, yet also welcoming. The sound of a musical note told her that Marianne had found a piano; at least her sister would not be bereft of all of her comforts.

Mary stopped Elinor as she walked past, intent on viewing the kitchen.

"Elinor, can we really live here?" Mary whispered, her eyes full of shock and near horror.

"Of course we can," Elinor said with a smile. "We must."

CHAPTER THREE

Marianne let her fingers trail over the keys of the small piano that stood in the foyer, wincing at the sound. It was obvious the piano had been left unattended for a time for the notes to sour like that. She sighed, thinking of the tuner she had to leave behind at Norland, hoping that she would be able to properly prepare this new piano.

Marianne pulled herself away from the instrument; there would be time to try and prepare it later. After all... what else would she have to do so far from everyone? Her nose crinkled at the marks her touch had left through the dust that coated the piano.

'How long has it been since anyone made this cottage a proper home?' she found herself wondering as she wandered through the rooms, before a new thought struck her...*'how can we make this a proper home?'*

Coming from the splendor that was Norland, the cottage seemed... cozy at best, confining at worst.

"Elinor, can we really live here?" Marianne heard her mother whisper, the soft sound carrying through the small home.

"Of course we can," Elinor responded. "We must."

Marianne had to smile even as tears threatened. In a world that had been turned on its head, the one constant was Elinor, ever-practical Elinor. No matter how bad the situation was, no matter how dire Marianne and their mother thought things were, Elinor would find a way to hold them together, to keep them grounded.

"Hello!!"

A male voice pulled Marianne out of her thoughts as she turned, eyeing the strange man who stood in the doorway. Small black eyes blinked back at her from under a straw hat, his gray mustache drooping under a red nose. His eyes darted around the entry before landing on Mary, and he broke into a wide smile.

"Cousin Mary, it is good to meet you at last!" His voice boomed through the room. A second man scrambled through the door behind him, arms laden with baskets of vegetables and what appeared to be a goose. The first man turned to take one of the baskets, holding it out to Mary, who had no other option but to take it. "Something for your larder to welcome you to Devonshire."

It was the first time that Marianne had seen her mother, ever the perfect hostess, stumble in her reaction. It took Mary several seconds to gather her wits about her and give the man a small curtsey in return.

"We cannot thank you enough for your kindness, Cousin Middleton."

"Oh no no no, none of that!" Middleton drew his hat off, clutching it against his chest. "We are all friends and family; I am delighted that you are here. I am very fond of company you see, and I could not help but see your carriage as it passed the house and immediately wanted to come to welcome you." He turned his head to look at Elinor and Marianne with a nod. "And these must be your girls. How are you, my dears?"

"I... yes." Mary stood, unsure of how to act, as Elinor stepped forward to take the basket out of her mother's arms. With a small sigh of relief Mary turned to her. "This is my eldest, Elinor, and my youngest, Marianne."

Marianne dropped into a small curtsey, her eyes darting to Elinor to see her sister shrug back at her.

"Delightful, simply delightful," Middleton beamed. "My mother-in-law Mrs. Jennings will be thrilled to meet you all, as well. I insist that you all dine with us at Arlington today, and every day, until you find yourself properly settled here."

"Oh, you do not need to troub..." Mary began.

"I insist, I absolutely insist! Family must watch out for family, after all," Middleton interrupted, a twinkle in his eye.

Marianne had to hold back the most unladylike snort at that, and the glare Elinor sent her was proof she hadn't been quite as successful as she had hoped. If John had believed that, they would not be there at that moment, but then again, it was not as if his wife actually saw them as "family," merely a barrier to her rightful place as Lady of Norland.

"...four o'clock, sharp." Marianne caught only the last of their cousin's words before he whirled out of the cottage as quickly as he had entered it.

"I... well... oh." Mary stuttered, her gaze turning to her daughters with a helpless smile. "It appears we are... invited for dinner?"

"But mother, there is so much to do here," Elinor protested, knowing it was in vain.

"I know, my dear, but it would not do to upset our cousin, not after he has done so much to help us."

"I for one am glad to go," Marianne chimed in, shrugging when Elinor turned to her. "It's not as if we are truly prepared for an evening here; we don't even know how to light the fires."

"I can light the fires," Elinor insisted before her expression turned thoughtful, "...maybe."

"It is most generous of Middleton to invite us, and far more than I had ever expected," Mary sighed. "If only John had been as generous."

"But he was not." Elinor wrapped her arm around Mary's waist, resting her head on her mother's shoulder. Mary held out her other arm to Marianne, drawing her close as the three women lost their thoughts to the sudden changes that surrounded them.

Marianne peered out the window of the small, but elegant, carriage that Middleton had sent for them as they approached Arlington. The estate was... well, it could not be called grand in the same way that Norland was, but there was a charm to it, she supposed. The gray stone stood out against the lush greenery, its walls draped with ivy and cream roses. As she lit from the carriage, the soft salt of the sea, so near in Devonshire, teased her senses, and she closed her eyes just to take it in.

Despite the circumstances that had led them there, there was a certain romance to it all: the stormy cliffs, the bright green landscape, and the blue skies so different from the ever-present gray of Norland. All that was missing was the dashing young man to sweep her off her feet, to care for her and her family. While a small part of her had hopes for her sister and the charming Edward, she could not help but dream of her own whirlwind romance.

There had been none that were worth her attention at Norland; the men who had come courting had seemed drab, dull, almost clones of her dear (well, less dear now) brother.

Men that had absolutely bored her. The careful tones, the cultured facade, never a hair out of place, so uptight and proper, looking for an equally proper wife to know her place.

She shivered at the thought.

Marianne had dreams: dreams that were beyond the bounds of what society deemed proper. She would never be a proper, demure wife, doting on her husband, waiting for his attention like a puppy. She wanted what her parents

had known: a true, deep partnership as equals. Few had known that Mary
had helped Henry with his business and investments, proving to be as shrewd
a businesswoman as he was. Her mother had been an instrumental part in
restoring the Dashwood fortune, a fortune John and Fanny now benefited from.

Perhaps this was a chance to start anew, outside the expectations of the
Dashwood name. To meet someone that knew and understood her, rather than
her family connection.

She trailed her mother and sister towards the doors, nodding to the butler that
led them through with a smile. The interior was as charming as the exterior: a
blend of strong wood with soft creams and colors, the obvious hints of a woman's
touch.

"Welcome!" Middleton rushed towards them, his arms open wide. Marianne
giggled; it seemed their cousin had only one volume… booming… when he spoke.
"Welcome to Arlington!"

Middleton offered Mary his elbow, waiting for her to tuck her hand into the
space to escort her through the manor, Elinor and Marianne following behind.
Marianne's eyes lit up as she spotted a piano in a sitting room, the instrument
gleaming, tempting her.

Music was food for the soul; anyone who did not agree was not worth
knowing, in her opinion. Her esteem for their cousin increased as she eyed the
piano.

"I must apologize. My wife is unable to join us; she has taken to bed ill,"
Middleton was explaining as Marianne caught back up with the entourage.
"However, we will be joined by my… Ah, there is my mother-in-law now. I do
believe you nearly kept us waiting, Mrs. Jennings."

Marianne turned to see an older woman emerge from a side door, her gray hair
pulled back into a bun at the nape of her neck. She was a striking figure: small
in stature, but commanding attention nonetheless. Marianne could tell her face

was kind, her eyes sparkling as she took in the guests, with the most curious scar down a cheek.

She was officially the most interesting woman Marianne had ever met.

"Oh, do behave, Middleton." Mrs. Jennings clucked her tongue, though a smile tugged the corner of her lips. She turned her eyes over the women standing before her, and Marianne swore she saw a twinkle as Mrs. Jennings's gaze lingered on her. "Well now, who do we have here?"

"My cousin Mary and her daughters," Middleton beamed before the women could speak. "Elinor and Marianne. Have you ever seen such lovely girls?"

"You are most welcome." Mrs. Jennings reached out to take Mary's hand, drawing her away from Middleton as she moved towards the ornate doors at the end of the room, Middleton following close behind. "Come come, it must be so difficult to settle in! Middleton has told me many things about you, and I am sure only half of them are true."

"Well... I..." Mary shot a glance over her shoulder at her daughters, a plea plain in her expression.

Elinor gave a small sigh as she hurried after the two women, leaving Marianne alone with her thoughts, a reprieve Marianne was grateful for. It wasn't that she did not do well with company; oh, no, Marianne thrived on it, but this... with all the changes, their well-meaning cousin was just a bit... much. Her eyes came back to rest on the piano longingly as she moved slowly through the room, delaying her entrance to the dining hall as long as she could.

"We see what we can do for them Mrs. Jennings, to find them husbands, lovers, that sort of thing."

Marianne started as she came through the doors, her eyes wide as they met Elinor's embarrassed face. There were some things that were just not talked about in mixed company, or those with whom one had so short an acquaintance...

Devonshire was certainly different from Sussex. Marianne steadied her shoulder and moved to the open seat beside Elinor, sliding in as Mrs. Jennings continued the discussion.

"Come now Middleton," Mrs. Jennings scolded, "for all you know, they have left their hearts behind in Sussex."

"Oh, well, Elinor has." The words left Marianne's mouth before she had realized she was speaking, and her cheeks flushed pink as Elinor and Mary both glared at her.

"Well, now we come to it." Mrs. Jennings leaned forward as the servant placed a plate before her. "I thought that I recognized a certain blush on your face: the young flush of..."

"No, really..." Elinor interrupted with a strained laugh, her eyes darting between Marianne and Mary.

"My dear, consider *nothing* settled," Mrs. Jennings smiled as she began to slice her food, "for a certain gentleman is coming to visit us here at Arlington, who may very well make you forget all your fancies. Do you agree, Middleton?"

"Colonel Brandon..." Middleton sat back in his chair, his hand coming to his chin in thought before a smile turned his lips. "Yes.. yes indeed, a long-time military hero, recognized by the crown and given lands for his loyalty and leadership to the Country. Though they say that he had his heart broken once, many many years ago, and he has yet to look at a woman since." He paused... "Well, not in that sort of a way, that is." His eyes flicked between Elinor and Marianne several times before he nodded. "But when he sees the Miss Dashwoods, I do believe that he may change his mind."

"Oh yes, he very well may," Mrs. Jennings agreed over her wine goblet, her eyes once again twinkling.

"A man who stayed faithful to his first love..." Marianne whispered, thinking it over as she smiled. "I like that; it is, of course, as it should be. When I fall in love, I know it will be forever."

"That is very proper, very... romantic," Middleton responded. "Just what a young lady ought to think, I do believe." He lifted his glass as if to toast Marianne, but Marianne could see a glint of humor in his eyes, as if he did not believe her.

"Colonel Brandon is here, Sir."

Middleton's wine nearly sloshed out of the glass as he hastily put it down, turning to nod at the butler. "Bring him in then, bring him in."

Marianne bit back a groan as her head fell forward for a second, only to pull it back up when Elinor's foot hit her ankle.

"But Elinor..." Marianne whispered softly.

"Behave, Marianne," Elinor grit out before turning her attention to the door.

Marianne wrinkled her nose at her sister, but nonetheless turned to the door... Bright amber eyes met hers, and she felt the room slip away for a moment.

Colonel Brandon was definitely not what she had been expecting. A "long-time war hero" was surely an elderly man with silver hair, wizened and twisted with age, not the handsome man who stood in the doorway. True, his hair was silver under his hat, but it glistened in a way that told her it was a natural color; its hue due to nature, not time.

Brandon's face was strong, lean, the amber of his eyes nearly glowing as he held her gaze. He stood tall and proud in the doorway, and she quickly estimated he stood a head taller than her, and could not help the quickening of her heartbeat. After a moment his head shook as if coming out of a daze and he quickly lifted his hat to hand it to the butler, and the slightly pointed tips of his ears were uncovered. Now the "long-time war hero" made sense: the man's ears a testament to his Fae heritage. Marianne had met a few Fae before in Sussex, and knew their lifespans far outlasted humans.

She had never seen a Fae with features such as his, however.... Especially the color of his eyes... Marianne's breath caught as his eyes darted back to hers.

"Brandon, come in come in, we were just speaking of you." Middleton rose, gesturing to the table and the unoccupied seat between Mary and Mrs. Jennings.

"I am sorry; I did not mean to intrude."

His voice was a smooth tenor, polished and proper, much to Marianne's disappointment. Amber eyes shifted to her as she let out a small sigh, and she saw the man stiffen.

"Not a bit of it; you could not have arrived at a better time. Sit, sit, join us," Middleton insisted.

"You have been away far far too long Brandon," Mrs. Jennings scolded, a light tease in her voice.

"I had some... necessary business," Brandon responded, his voice was cool and composed, and yet the sound of it flowed over Marianne, and she quickly drew in a breath.

"Now where are my manners," Middleton said as he turned back to the table. "Mrs. Mary Dashwood, Miss. Dashwood," Brandon nodded to Mary and Elinor in turn as they were introduced, "Miss Marianne Dashwood."

Brandon's eyes met Marianne's again, and for a moment she could have sworn the cool consideration of his eyes had given way to a fire that could take her breath away, but in a moment it was gone, leaving her to believe she had imagined it.

"It is an honor to make your acquaintance." Brandon's gaze lingered on Marianne as he spoke, before turning to Mary with a small nod.

"Well, what do you think, Mrs. Dashwood? He would certainly do as a partner for one of your daughters, wouldn't he?" Mrs. Jennings grinned as Elinor choked beside her and Mary began to stammer.

"Well... I... that is..."

Marianne stole a glance at Brandon, noting the resigned amusement on his face as he watched Mrs. Jennings with fondness. As if he felt her attention, his eyes shifted to capture hers. His lips curled slightly into a faint smirk as Marianne's cheeks heated, shocked at herself... why was she watching his lips... and why couldn't she look away...

As quickly as the smirk formed though, it was gone, his face becoming a mask of cool composure that left Marianne reeling as he took a seat between Mary and Mrs. Jennings. Her face flushed as she ignored Elinor's questioning look, and Marianne turned her sole focus back to her dinner.

Elinor knew something was troubling her sister when Marianne fled to the piano as soon as dinner ended. It had been Marianne's escape for years, losing herself to the music to channel her emotions. The notes soared through the room, the tempo slow, almost haunting, and it hurt Elinor's heart to hear. It was a tune she had heard hundreds of times from Marianne's hand; however, it was usually faster, a song of jubilation, lifting the heart rather than drawing one to tears. She glanced quickly around the room, her gaze meeting her mother's for a moment, before landing on the newest addition to their gathering.

Colonel Brandon was sitting back in his chair, his hand raised to his lips. His eyes were closed, but his ears seemed to stay at attention, occasionally flicking as a strong chord played. His fingers were swaying slightly, as if directing the music. As the song drew to a close, his eyes opened, fixed on Marianne at the piano, his figure still as the others applauded the artist.

"Well done!" Middleton explained, his face bright. "Well done indeed! What do you think, Brandon? I know you greatly enjoy music."

Marianne lifted her gaze from the keys to meet amber, Brandon's eyes glowing in the firelight.

"Remarkable." Was his only response.

Marianne raised an eyebrow as she held back her scoff. She had not been able to keep herself from glancing at him while she played, his eyes shut as if he could not be bothered to give even the courtesy of attention.

Mary crossed to the piano, her hand resting on her daughter's shoulder as Marianne shook off her thoughts, rising to yield the seat to her mother.

Elinor turned with a smile on her lips as her mother began to play, a sound she had not heard since her father had fallen ill. She let the music wash over her as she rose, crossing to a small table laden with pastries.

"Your sister plays with great feeling for one so young." Elinor paused with a biscuit halfway to her mouth, turning to face Brandon.

"Marianne is quite proud of her playing; I would be pleased to tell her of your compliments, but why should you not tell her them yourself." Elinor turned, facing Marianne as she continued. "We were just discussing your performance, Marianne."

"Oh?" Marianne faced Brandon, scanning his face for a hint of his thoughts.

"It was..." Brandon cleared his throat, his eyes darting away from Marianne's, causing her to frown slightly, "remarkable."

"Yes, so you said," Marianne sighed, her head tilting to the side. "I cannot quite tell if that means you approved of it or not."

"I..." Brandon began before pausing. "It was a matter of how I was accustomed to hearing the music. You played the last movement appassionato, I believe, though the composer I think had marked it as allegro for the tempo."

"Oh, so you disapprove of that?" Marianne's voice had a chill to it that had Elinor's eyes widening.

"I did not say that..." Brandon turned now to meet Marianne's chocolate gaze. "Indeed, I found it... quite original I must say."

"Original..." Marianne repeated, a brow raising as if in challenge.

"Quite." Brandon slightly frowned as he straightened, and Marianne was mildly pleased to note she had been right: she barely reached his chin when he stood at full height. "But I have taken enough of your time with your family, I shall take my leave." He motioned for the butler to bring his hat, causing the occupants of the room to turn towards him. "It was a pleasure meeting you,

Mrs. Dashwood," he nodded to Mary, "Miss Dashwood," to Elinor, "and Miss Marianne Dashwood." His nod was deeper, slower, as he paid his respects to the host, his silver hair gleaming down his back as he spun and strode from the room.

"Colonel Brandon has been a fine and upstanding..." Middleton's words to Mary faded into the background as Marianne stepped to the window to watch Brandon's figure disappear into the night. "...yes, he would be a fine match for one of your girls." Marianne's brow twitched in irritation.

"Marianne." Elinor pulled her sister out of her thoughts with a hand on her elbow. "Come, it is time we take our leave as well."

Marianne curtsied to Middleton and Mrs. Jennings, going through the motions of proper etiquette, her mind working over the puzzle of Brandon. She was uncharacteristically silent during the carriage ride back to the cottage, a soft line between her brow alerting her mother and sister as to the cause. She held her tongue until she reached the room she shared with Elinor, the chill in the air finally loosening her from her thoughts.

"Will they be like this every night?" The words burst out of Marianne as she carefully removed and laid out the dress she had worn, shivering in the night air.

"Marianne, do not be unkind," Elinor chided as she took the warmest sleeping shifts she could find, passing one to Marianne before drawing hers on. "Middleton is very kind, and both he and Mrs. Jennings seem to be delighted to have company."

"But Elinor, their teasing? It was relentless and almost...vulgar...at times."

"Marianne," Elinor's tone was exasperated, "yes, of course I was embarrassed, but they meant no harm. We are not in Sussex anymore; we cannot compare everything to those we knew before."

"But Elinor, they have no appreciation for music; none of them truly listened to it or really cared for it."

"Colonel Brandon seemed to care for it; he was listening with great attention as you played."

"Only because he found fault with it," Marianne groused, her cheeks flaming at the memory.

"He may have a more... cultured and refined ear than those you are used to playing for, Marianne. I can imagine sound would be of great importance to a Fae such as him. They have more delicate hearing I have heard"

Marianne thought that over for a moment. Elinor did make a good point: his hearing might be more sensitive than others, but that did not excuse his comments or his attitude.

"No, Elinor; I do believe he is the type of man who would find fault with everyone and everything."

"You do not even know him, Marianne. How can you say something like that?"

"I don't have to know him, Elinor." Marianne sighed as she pulled the blanket close to her to ward off the chill in the room. "I have met many many men just like him: the prim and proper lord, never a hair out of place, never showing any emotion. Bland, boring, despite how interesting he appears. He is no different from the men who came to court us at Norland, and you know how dull I found them all."

"Middleton and Mrs. Jennings seem fond of him."

Marianne laughed. "That isn't necessarily an endorsement. I am not sure they would be the most reliable to judge a character."

"I for one thought he seemed quite nice," Elinor said as she lay down, pausing to blow out the candle. "I think there is more to him than meets the eye."

"There never is, though," Marianne grumbled. As her eyes closed, her mind turned back to one moment, a second where Brandon's amber eyes had blazed hot like the sun, scorching her, before cooling, hiding behind a veil of propriety. "No," she repeated sadly, "there never is."

CHAPTER FOUR

I t took far too long in Marianne's mind to make the cottage truly feel like home. Once their manservant Jonathan had arrived with the last of their belongings from Norland, it had taken them three days to unpack everything and to try and find a location to store or place them.

It had become abundantly clear that neither Marianne nor Mary had truly been prepared for just how much smaller the cottage was from Norland, the bedrooms bursting at the seams to hold the cloth and clothes that Marianne and Mary had deemed irreplaceable in their move. Elinor had merely shaken her head at them, then helped them fold and store the extra clothing.

After securing the bedrooms and packing them all properly, they had turned their attention to the main floor of the cottage, working with Jonathan and his wife Martha to clean every space. When Mary had despaired that the curtains did not fit the new windows, Elinor once again stepped to the rescue, altering the curtains to fit with needle and thread as Mary and Marianne looked on with fascination.

"Elinor, dear, would you help me?" Mary held out the edge of a curtain to her eldest before placing the thin rod that would hold it up over the window. Marianne grabbed a wet rag and moved to the piano, carefully wiping down the instrument as Elinor and Mary placed the curtain.

Elinor took a moment to breathe, looking out the window at the view of the ocean. She was beginning to love the cliffs, the sound of the water hitting the stone, so unlike the quiet of Norland. There were few trees around the property, giving a clear view of the road leading to Arlington...

And the rider that was now making their way along the path.

"Mama," Elinor gasped, turning with wide eyes, "Colonel Brandon."

Mary looked over with a start before turning to Marianne. In a moment all three were moving in a panic, grabbing the rags they had used for cleaning as Jonathan took the bucket of water out the back. Marianne pulled the apron she had been wearing off, looking frantically at the pale blue dress she wore, brushing dust off the skirt and sleeves as she threw the apron into a trunk and grabbed the pillows it contained, hastily throwing them onto the sitting couch they had just arranged earlier that day.

Mary scanned her daughters, tapping near her forehead as she looked at Marianne. Marianne hastily tucked a wayward curl behind her ear as Mary hissed at Elinor, who frantically pulled the apron she still wore off, bundling it into her hand as her eyes darted around for a place to put it. Marianne reached out a hand as Elinor tossed the fabric towards her, before she turned to hide it in the blanket draped over the piano stool.

"Colonel Brandon, Ma'am," Jonathan announced.

Marianne quickly straightened, turning to hide the blanket from view as Brandon stepped through the door, a thin book in one hand and a bouquet of flowers in the other. Marianne dropped to a curtsy as he bowed to them, but her eyes never left his figure.

There was no denying he was the most beautiful man she had ever met. He looked even better in daylight than he had in the romantic flickering of the fire, his silver hair shining in a long tail down his back, his red coat vibrant against the cool pastels of the cottage walls.

"I... I had the opportunity to go by my estate Hartland this morning," Brandon stated, his amber eyes darting to Marianne and then back to Mary. "I took the liberty of bringing you some of the flowers from its garden, Mrs. Dashwood."

Mary's cheeks turned pink as she took the flowers, a mixture of pink and cream-colored peonies. Marianne smiled—she couldn't help it—the fact that he had brought flowers for her mother went a long way to improve her opinion of him. Elinor shot her a glance, the look in her eye clearly going 'SEE?', and Marianne responded with a mock glare.

"Thank you; they are lovely," Mary gushed as she held the flowers close, gently breathing in the light fragrance of the peonies.

"And, I brought some music that I thought may be of some interest to Miss Marianne."

Marianne's jaw dropped at the statement... no... no one had ever thought to bring her music before. She had made do with the sheets her father had owned and those brought in by her instructors, but she had not had anything new in *ages.*

Brandon stepped forward, his ears almost quivering as he moved closer, the music held carefully in his hand. Marianne took a moment to admire the delicacy of his hold. She had not seen the claws on each hand when they had met before, and if he were like some of the other Fae she had met, the music would have been full of holes, but the book in his hand was pristine.

Brandon held the music out to her, and after a moment's hesitation that caused his ears to lower, she reached out to take it. Her finger brushed against his and she saw him freeze, his ears dropping to his head, disappearing into his hair as he hastily pulled away, his posture now stiff. An unexpected... and unwelcome... pang went through her at his motion. Granted, it was partially her own fault for being so bold, but she had not been able to control the need to touch him, just to see. With a sigh of disappointment, she turned her attention to the music she now held, her eyes flying over the notes and complexity of the music.

"I think you overestimate my abilities, Sir," she whispered as she scanned the sheets.

"No, I think not." Marianne's head flew up to see a faint smile on his lips that soon faded. "You do have an instrument here, do you not?"

"Well, yes... of sorts," Marianne admitted, stepping to the side to reveal the small piano she had stood before.

Brandon considered the instrument for a moment, seemingly lost in thought. "I have a fine piano forte at Hartland that deserves to be played more often than it is at the moment. You are more than welcome to come and try it one day."

"I... ah... Thank you." Marianne's voice softened as she spoke, unsure how to take his offer. His eyes shifted to meet Marianne's, and she felt a strange fluttering in her stomach. She looked to Elinor, who recognized the near panic in her sister's eyes.

"Would you like to sit down, Colonel, and join us for some refreshments?" Elinor interjected, drawing Brandon's focus to her, breaking the spell that seemed to hold him as he had watched Marianne.

"No, thank you; I must be going and shouldn't intrude on you any longer. I am sure I will be seeing you all fairly soon at Arlington. I bid you all a good day." His eyes turned back to Marianne to linger before withdrawing from the room.

Mary turned to her daughters as she held the flowers fully to her nose to take a deep breath, her eyes twinkling over the bouquet. Elinor bit back a grin as she winked at Marianne, a giggle breaking through despite her attempt to stay silent.

Marianne fought back nerves as she looked at the complexity of the music. She thought... she had thought he had not been paying attention, that he had found her playing lacking, but this... she looked through the three movements of Beethoven's Moonlight Sonata. The first movement she had heard before, and knew she would be able to follow it, but the second and third movement, with the speed and complexity of the notes...

Yet, somehow, he thought that she was capable of playing this. She slid towards the piano, arranging the music before her as she lifted the cover from the keys. She shot a look over her shoulder, the consideration on her mother's face and the humor on Elinor's had her turning back to the piano. She took a deep breath and placed her hands on the keys, letting the beauty of the composition surround her as she began to slowly follow the music, wincing as she heard the sharp sound of a wrong key, stopping and starting again.

She started to bring the music with her to Arlington, practicing on the first movement with Middleton and Mrs. Jennings each night after dinner, tackling the more difficult movements at the cottage; it would be a bit before she was comfortable attempting those around anyone but family. The music was so beautiful, capturing her complete attention, just as it did every night. She started, her playing faltering for a moment when a hand reached out to turn the page, and Marianne looked up to meet Brandon's amber eyes. She smiled at him as he returned the gesture, his eyes uncharacteristically soft as he watched her.

Somehow, his being near gave her more confidence, her hands more sure on the keys as she played. Had she thought his eyes were cold and uncaring? There was such depth and emotion in his eyes if one knew where to look, that was revealed to her with that one glance. His hand rose, moving as if he were to touch her shoulder, only to pause, his hand a breath away from her skin. Out of the corner of her eye, she saw his hand close and drop away as he took a step back. She glanced up at him, sighing internally as his eyes shuttered, the cool mask back in place.

Her hand faltered for a moment on the keys before recovering, Brandon's eyes lowering to meet hers as they did before flicking back to the music. As she came to the end of the movement, she gave a subtle nod and Brandon turned the music back to the first page, stepping back as she began again.

Elinor watched the exchange with mixed emotions, unsure of what lay between her sister and the silver haired man who stood at her side.

"Marianne has certainly made a conquest with Brandon." Mrs. Jennings's words startled Elinor out of her musings. "I had nearly given up on him, worried that he would never move on from his past." Mrs. Jennings saw Mary's shocked expression, mistaking it for concern. "Oh, do not worry, Mrs. Dashwood. It is a fine, fine match; he is a man with such a good heart, he just needed someone to unlock it."

"I... well," Mary swallowed before continuing, "I believe that 18 may be a little young to be married, don't you think?"

"Nonsense," Mrs. Jennings smiled at the oblivious duo. "I was married at 17 myself. What do you say, Miss Elinor? I do hope you did not have any designs or intentions for the Colonel for yourself, he appears quite besotted with your sister."

"Has he spoken to you of his feelings for my sister then?" Elinor asked, her face puzzled.

"Brandon is not a man of many words, but look at him: it is written clearly across his face. Oh, he is a fine catch for any girl, I can only imagine it will be a matter of time before he comes to speak with you, Mrs. Dashwood."

Elinor chewed on her cheek as she listened, her concern growing. While Marianne was friendly towards Brandon, Elinor didn't know if there was any more than that. When Marianne shot a glare over her shoulder at the man, Elinor's unease grew.

CHAPTER FIVE

"**I**s that... is that really what everyone thinks?" Marianne stared at Elinor in shock. "Elinor, please tell me they aren... that people haven't... Do they *really* think that?"

Elinor's nod was slow as she watched the emotions that rippled across Marianne's face.

"Yes; apparently they expect him to visit Mother any day now."

"But, Elinor..."

"I thought you liked Colonel Brandon, Marianne."

"I..." Marianne paused, panic starting to rise in her chest. The problem was... she did like him. No other man or Fae had ever thought to bring her music, to challenge her to improve the way that he had. "Yes," she admitted softly. When Elinor smiled in reply, Marianne's eyes went wide as she looked between her sister and mother. "But that's because he's really the only one with whom I can have a conversation that goes beyond idle gossip... that doesn't mean... I never thought..." The panic threatened to consume her as her thoughts spun. "Elinor, he's too... too... proper."

"Too proper?" Mary laid her embroidery down to consider her youngest. "He is a fine upstanding citizen, a good example in the community, and, I must say, quite easy on the eyes."

"Mama…"

"Besides, you were raised in a proper household; I never saw your father or I as being less for it."

"You know that is not what I meant," Marianne sighed as she dropped onto the settee, ignoring her mother's glare. "It's just… He is everything you hear of how Fae act, cold, aloof… he never does anything out of place: he's always the perfect picture of what is proper, of what a perfect lord should be."

"You say that as if it is a bad thing." Elinor's eyes met Marianne's over the lip of her cup as she took a sip of her tea.

"It IS," Marianne insisted as her head dropped to the back of the settee. "He's—oh, how do I say this—there's this, he's…"

"Too proper?" Mary responded with a small grin.

"YES!" Marianne cried, then groaned when she saw her mother's look. "You don't understand. I can't be proper; I can't be hidden away: a good and silent wife. I have no idea what it would be like to be with a Fae who would demand perfection all the time. I want what you had, Mama: a husband who supports me, who appreciates me. I would wither and die if I had nothing more to do than to plan a party or oversee the staff, or to maintain a household, I would die of boredom."

"But how do you know that is what the Colonel would want?" Mary asked. "Fae are different from humans, after all; things could be very different with him."

Marianne paused. Her mother was right; she *didn't* know if that was what Brandon would want or expect, but how could it be otherwise? There were moments when his eyes would flash, the heat in them nearly taking her breath away, only for it to vanish as if it had never been.

She clasped her hands before her as she thought, unconsciously sliding her fingertips against the one place he had touched on her hand. Her cheeks warmed at the thought, then cooled as she thought of his expression, his words, when they had first met. If there happened to be more to the man than she saw, he was excellent at hiding it, and from her experience, no one was that good of a performer. No, this was a man who had embraced the rules of society and all the limitations that came with it. He was beautiful, she could not deny that, but that alone was not enough for her.

"No one is forcing him upon you, Marianne." Elinor interrupted Marianne's thoughts, and she brought her eyes to her sister's.

"You know that I will not be able to speak with him outside of company again, don't you?" Marianne sighed. "I can do nothing to encourage him, or the gossip mongers that surround us."

Elinor's eyebrow rose at the flush on Marianne's cheeks, but kept silent as her sister stewed.

"Pardon me, Ma'ams." A cough at the door had Mary turning to see Jonathan wiping his hands on his apron. "Colonel Brandon is riding down the way."

"Ahh, thank you Jonathan," Mary responded, her eyes darting to see Marianne's face pale.

"Well, I think it's a perfect time for a walk!" Marianne exclaimed as she jumped to her feet. She flew to the back door, grabbing a shawl to wrap around her shoulders.

"Marianne, really." Mary's voice was exasperated, but Marianne only turned back with a determined look in her eye.

"I told you, Mama." The knock from the front door made her eyes go wide before she fled out the back, the door slamming behind her.

Elinor rose from her seat with a small sigh before schooling her face into a polite smile as Colonel Brandon stepped through the door, his hat in his hand nearly covering the books of music he held, his ears almost flattened to his head. His eyes darted to the rear door and back, and Elinor swore she saw a hint of pain before it was quickly hidden in his golden orbs.

"Ah, Colonel Brandon, what a pleasant surprise." Mary stepped forward to give a little curtsey, Elinor following suit. "Will you join us for tea?"

Elinor was unsure of how much time had passed; however, it was one of the most awkward teas she had ever attended, and that included any where Fanny had been in attendance. Her mother tried to make small talk to keep the conversation going, but at some point, it seemed to do little to ease the tension. Brandon's eyes kept turning to the back door as an ear twitched, no doubt searching out sounds she would never be able to hear, any indication that Marianne was on her way back. When the first drops of water hit the window she saw the slight slump of his shoulders, and with a swift inhale she realized what it meant... he wouldn't be able to hear or smell Marianne with the rain.

Six cups of tea later Brandon finally stood, his gaze resigned.

"My compliments to Miss Marianne..." he began, only for Mary to interrupt.

"Marianne will be sorry to have missed you; I'm sure she would want to thank you for the music. it is most kind of you, and I know she has greatly enjoyed learning the pieces."

"Think nothing of it." Brandon's voice was tight and controlled in Elinor's ears.

"Why don't you wait?" Elinor asked, her cheeks warming as Brandon lifted his eyes to hers. "At least until the rain has stopped?"

"Thank you but no, I fear I may have..." His gaze darted to the rear door and back, "overstayed my welcome as it is. I wish you both a good day."

The sound of thunder roared in as he stepped out the door, his clothing instantly soaked from the downpour. Elinor turned with wide, worried eyes to her mother, who shared her concern.

Marianne had yet to return.

CHAPTER SIX

Marianne shivered as she walked, her gown and shawl long since drenched, but pride kept her out along the path. She knew she should have turned around and returned home, but the odd chance that Brandon was still there kept her feet moving.

It wasn't that she didn't want to spend time with him; she enjoyed his presence and talking to him, but that wasn't enough, not for her. There was a subtle warmth when she looked at Brandon, with his long silver hair and golden eyes, but there was none of the fire or instant longing that the poets spoke of.

Marianne sighed as she drew closer to the cliffs. There had to be more to life than being a silent ornament, keeping house, raising children. All the roles that proper society would force her to accept, but she knew she needed more, so much more.

As she walked, her thoughts kept turning back to Colonel Brandon. She couldn't figure out which was the mask: was it the hints of fire, of temper that she saw when they verbally sparred, or the cool indifference that seemed to dominate his being. If he had even shown a hint of being unkempt, his hair mussed, a coat slightly out of place, a scuff on his shoe, even a word spoken out of turn, she wouldn't dismiss him so quickly. But in the weeks she had known him, he had never displayed anything but that cool civility. Even as Middleton and

Mrs. Jennings spoke of him, it was all about how *proper* he was: the *epitome of a gentleman.*

And then there was his first love, whom no one seemed to talk of. He had been true to her for years: no one was quite sure how long. To have found a love that was so enduring, so encompassing, anyone else would surely fall short of such a paragon, and Marianne was not one to accept being second or a replacement for any other woman. When she married, she would be first in her husband's heart, until they had children. Only then would she accept not being first in his heart.

But there was something to be said about being the one to awaken his ability to love again. She had heard the whispers—people saying she was the one to heal his wounds, to help him open up, to let someone else in. What would it be like to be the one to piece his heart back together, to make it her own...

She shook her head, a wry laugh breaking through her lips, the sound captured by the wind. Why was she thinking of him? She had made up her mind: she did not want to do anything to encourage him, to draw him closer... hadn't she? But at the same time, the thought of not seeing his golden eyes, of not feeling his warmth near her, she...

The ground giving way under her foot yanked Marianne from her musings as she felt herself begin to fall. Her scream was nearly covered by a resounding clap of thunder as the ledge she was standing on crumbled, the soil saturated with water. She reached out to try and grab on to anything she could to stop her momentum, to keep her from tumbling over the edge of the cliff. She screamed again as the earth continued to collapse around her, the sound choked as she landed on her ankle on a blessedly stable ledge and pain shot through her leg, driving her to her knees. She eyed the edge above her helplessly; even if she could stand, she would be unable to reach it. Her eyes filled with tears as her head dropped forward.

Stupid stupid stupid. Marianne knew she had no one to blame for this but herself... she didn't really need to avoid Brandon; she had just gotten nervous, panicked as she felt the weight of others' expectations closing in around her. And now who knew how long it would take for Elinor or her mother to realize she was still out, and then to find her and...

"Are you hurt?" Marianne's eyes went wide at the sound of the smooth baritone above her. She shifted, wincing at the pain in her ankle as she tried to look up to see who had found her.

"Don't move. Stay there; I will come to you." A moment later, a male figure landed before her, black hair streaming behind him as he knelt beside her. "Where are you injured?"

"My..." Marianne's gaze lifted to the richest crimson eyes she had ever seen. "My ankle," she whispered.

The man turned his gaze to her leg, his hand reaching out before hesitating.

"May I? Please, I know a little about these things." His head turned to Marianne with a reassuring smile, and she caught the hint of fangs. Mutely she nodded, her breathing shallow as he wrapped a single hand around her ankle, the touch almost scorching against her soaked stocking. "It isn't broken, thankfully, but it is a bad sprain. You shouldn't be walking on it. May I have the honor of escorting you home?"

Marianne nodded again, her eyes locked on his figure as he knelt beside her again, one hand resting on her back, the other stealing behind her knees. Her breath caught as he lifted her as though she were a feather and leapt, easily clearing the ledge and landing again on solid ground.

"Where can I take you?" The crimson eyes were even brighter up close, and Marianne found herself speechless for a moment, trapped in their depths.

"I... The cottage of Arlington..." she finally murmured, the words trailing off as the man shifted her closer and the warmth of his body chased away the chill from the rain.

"I'll have you there in a moment, miss," he promised before turning to dash through the rain, running faster than any man should move. Her eyes drifted up to the sharp points of the ears at the side of his head, and he grinned again, his fangs sparkling against all odds in the dim light.

Elinor stole a glance at the lone clock they had in the cottage before turning her gaze back to the storm that raged outside the window. Marianne had been gone for far too long, and Elinor's unease was growing. If it had been Norland Park she would not have hesitated to go after her sister, knowing the younger girl's favorite spots, but the cottage was still new—there was no telling where Marianne could have gone. She rose, pacing yet again to the window, only to pause as movement caught her eye through the rain. She could just make out the fluttering of a man's coat, but more importantly, a light shade of pink, as lightning lit the sky.

The same pink Marianne had been wearing...

"Mama, quickly, I think Marianne has been hurt!" Elinor cried, turning to her mother with wide eyes. Jonathan hurried to the door at Mary's glance, opening it just before a dark-haired man reached the door, Marianne cradled against him, her arms wrapped around his neck.

"Please, I beg you: do not be alarmed." The man strode through the room to lay Marianne on the settee as he spoke, stopping to kneel beside her, the movements gentler than Elinor expected from the speed with which he moved. "Her injuries are only minor. At most a sprained ankle and some bruising, nothing more."

"Are... are you sure? Should we fetch the doctor?" Mary waved towards Jonathan as the servant reached for his slicker, intent on carrying out his mistress' orders.

"That should not be necessary." The man kept his place at Marianne's side, his crimson eyes scanning her carefully, and Marianne found herself lost in them, almost missing his gentle sniff. "I do not smell any blood, and the swelling does not indicate a fracture. A few days' rest and she should be back on her feet." He pushed himself upright with a grace that Elinor could only envy. "I apologize for the suddenness of my appearance. I was walking through the area and saw her fall, and I did not see anyone nearby to aid her."

"No, that is most helpful... most helpful, err..." Mary's gaze met the man's as he turned to bow to her.

"Willoughby, Ma'am, Willoughby of Allendale."

"Lord Willoughby." Mary dipped her head slightly, her eyes darting back to her daughter. "Please, sit, could we offer you some tea, to... to warm you? It is the least we could do."

"No, thank you. I have imposed on your hospitality enough, and I must be getting back to my clan. I would request the honor of stopping by tomorrow to see how your daughter..." He paused for a moment, his crimson eyes sparkling, "your daughter..."

"Ah, my youngest daughter, Marianne Dashwood," Mary supplied quickly, a slight flush on her cheeks.

"Marianne." Willoughby's voice lingered over the syllables as his gaze turned back to Marianne, a small smile on his lips causing the faint hint of his fangs to gleam in the light.

"By your leave, then, until tomorrow." He bowed first to Mary, then to Elinor, and with a grin, tilted his head towards Marianne. Between one breath and the next, he was gone, the slight ruffle of the curtains the only sign of his departure.

"Well..." Mary exclaimed, her hand coming to her chest as she turned back to her daughters.

"Oh, Mama, you should have seen it," Marianne gushed, her eyes shining. "He cradled me in his arms as though I weighed nothing, and just... leapt into the air as if he were flying."

"I noticed your arm was wrapped nice and tightly around his neck, dear sister," Elinor chided, her eyes slightly disapproving.

"What does propriety matter in times of need, Elinor, if I held on tightly it was merely to secure myself? Oh, the speed at which he moved! It was like nothing I have ever seen."

"Mmmm, yes, I am sure you were certain to fall with how closely he held you." Elinor's voice had turned back to amusement at the pout on her sister's face, chuckling as Marianne fought to hold back a childish gesture.

"Well, it is most fortunate for you that he was there, Marianne." Mary's eyebrow raised as she perched on the settee arm near her daughter. "I have to say he made quite the dashing figure as he carried you into the house."

"Oh, and his eyes, Mama! Did you see his eyes?" When Mary nodded, Marianne sighed. "He had such fine eyes. I have never seen crimson eyes before, he must be a Fae, but they were so striking." She let her thoughts drift as she leaned her head back.

"Willoughby, Willoughby of Allendale" Marianne whispered, letting her own eyes close as her mother brushed her hand down Marianne's hair. "It is a very fine name." She saw crimson eyes in a tan face grinning down at her in her thoughts. In her mind she reached out to touch the man's cheek, smiling as his lids closed at the touch, only to open, his golden orbs almost burning her with their intensity...

A slight frown pursed her lips as her lids snapped open.

Gold... but Willoughby's eyes were crimson

CHAPTER SEVEN

"*L*ove *and harmony combine,* □
And round our souls entwine
While thy branches mix with mine,□
And our roots together join."

Marianne smiled softly as the words spun around the room, the rich male baritone bringing a new experience to words she had read a thousand times.

"*Joys upon our branches sit,*□
Chirping loud and singing sweet;
Like gentle streams beneath our feet
Innocence and virtue meet."

Willoughby's voice trailed off at the end of the stanza, a slight nod encouraging Marianne to continue. She thought for a moment, her eyes wistful as she smiled, continuing from memory.

"*Thou the golden fruit dost bear,*□
I am clad in flowers fair;
Thy sweet boughs perfume the air,□
And the turtle buildeth there.
There she sits and feeds her young,□
Sweet I hear her mournful song;

And thy lovely leaves among,□
There is love, I hear his tongue.”

Willoughby's voice took up the poem, and Marianne let her eyes close as she listened.

“There his charming nest doth lay,□
There he sleeps the night away;
There he sports along the day,□
And doth among our branches play.”

Willoughby finished the stanza, the book of poetry he held now folded in his lap, his gaze fixed on Marianne.

A cough that sounded suspiciously close to a scoff sounded from the corner, causing Marianne to glare at Elinor before turning her attention back to Willoughby.

“I have not met many others that are familiar with Willoughby Blake.” Willoughby's brow lifted as he closed the pages. “Especially with these works, I am sure it must have been published before you were born.”

“Our father.” Elinor supplied, drawing Willoughby's gaze to her as she continued her embroidery. “He was an avid collector of poetry.”

“It brings back memories to hear you reading,” Mary sighed as her eyes turned misty.

“Forgive me, I did not mean offense.” Willoughby was quick to stand, only to pause as Mary waived a hand, urging him to sit.

“No offense my good sir, they are pleasant memories, I thank you for that.”

“You speak with such emotion in the words,” Marianne sighed, shifting her shawl closer around her as she spoke. “Never have I heard Love and Harmony delivered in quite that way.”

“If you do not feel the passion of the words, what is the purpose of speaking them?” Willoughby challenged, the sparkle back in his eyes. “To speak such poetry with no inflection... one must be quite cold and unfeeling indeed.”

"That is exactly how I feel." Marianne whispered, her gaze lingering on the gleam in his eyes. "The words are so moving, how can you not…"

"Share it with the world." Willoughby said as he leaned in, his head a touch closer than propriety allowed, Elinor noted with a frown.

"Marianne…" Elinor began, only to go silent as her sister looked up.

"I do have to find it remarkable that you were the one to save me, Lord Willoughby ." Marianne sighed; her cheeks flushed a light pink under Willoughby's gaze.

"Hmmm, yes," Elinor mumbled, "the horror of it being someone who was not familiar with Blake."

"Elinor…" Marianne hissed, her cheeks deepening to red as Willoughby held back a chuckle.

"It's perfectly alright Miss Marianne," Willoughby assured with a wink, "your sister is just being protective of you, a commendable trait. Loyalty to one's family is a valued trait among my clan."

"Do you care for dancing, Lord Willoughby?" Mary's eyes sparkled as Willoughby turned to her. "My daughter is quite fond of dancing."

"Indeed, I am," Willoughby grinned, "and I hope to have the opportunity to dance with each of you before long," his gaze turned back to Marianne, "when Miss. Marianne has recovered, that is."

Marianne's responding smile was hesitant and shy. To have one such as this Lord showing her such open admiration and attention, it was a far cry from… Her head tilted to the side as Willoughby's eyes turned cold a moment before they flashed to the window, and Marianne swore his lips curled into a snarl, the first negative expression she had seen on his face.

Marianne's musings faded at the sound of a knock on the door, her brows furrowed in confusion. Who was…

"Colonel Brandon, Ma'ams."

Marianne's pulse skipped a beat at the three simple words, her cheeks flushing at the reaction. Surely, she told herself, it was only the concern for the rumors that Elinor had shared, oh had she been contemplating them only the day before? Marianne barely registered Willoughby's sharp glance at her before he stood to move from her side as she began to smooth imaginary wrinkles out of her skirt. Her head lifted as Brandon rushed into the room, his breathing ragged as if he had run a large distance. His golden eyes met hers as she watched the sharp fear in them fade to concern. The sheer feeling that one glance had held left her breathless.

"I... I just heard of your accident." Brandon's claws slightly pierced the hat he held in his hand, as Marianne's eyes drank him in. It was the first time she had heard him almost at a loss for words, and the first time she had seen him shaken... was it... was it for her? No, it couldn't be... could it? "I trust... I do trust you are not seriously injured?"

"No, no I am not." Her voice sounded breathless, even to her own ears as golden concern gave way to relief, and the tension left Brandon's shoulders.

"No, I can see that you are not. I thank God for that." Brandon started to step forward, one hand leaving the brim of the hat as he moved towards Marianne.

"Colonel Brandon," Marianne started as her mother spoke, suddenly realizing the woman stood before her, "do you know Lord Willoughby?"

As Mary stepped to the side, all softness and concern left Brandon's face, his countenance hardening as he strained, his shoulders squaring off as he drew himself to his full height.   The sudden change left Elinor curious...what had happened between the two men?

"Yes... How do you do, Sir?" Brandon's voice was terse, a thin hint of ice in the tone.

"Very well, thank you... Brandon."

Marianne's eyes darted from Brandon to Willoughby at the curt and somewhat disrespectful response. There was no denying the tension between the two men as they stared each other down, and the thinly veiled disdain on Willoughby's face surprised her. When her gaze turned back to Brandon she found his eyes on her, the golden globes dulled slightly as if hurt. His eyes lowered slightly, and after a moment his lips curled sadly as he gripped his hat tightly with both hands.

"I am... glad to see you are well. I will intrude no longer," Brandon's voice had chilled, his voice almost flat, and Marianne could not hold back a shiver at the sound. She could not say why it affected her so, but hearing him speak that way seemed unnatural... and it hurt. More than it should, it hurt as he turned with one last glance to her and disappeared as quickly as he had entered.

"How extraordinary..." Mary exclaimed, turning to Elinor with wide eyes.

"He is an extraordinary man, such as it is." Marianne heard Willoughby respond, a hint of mockery in his voice making her frown. Her eyes trailed out the window to watch as Brandon strode away. He paused for a moment and she saw his arms tense before falling to his sides, each holding a piece of his once whole hat clutched in his fist before he disappeared from her sight...

A part of her thought she should be horrified by his destruction of the hat, but that hint of temper, of passion had her...

Willoughby's laughter, a sound that had so charmed Marianne when he had first arrived that morning, rang through the room but she barely moved. Her unfocused gaze stayed on the window as Willoughby fell into an easy conversation with her family. A hand brushed her shoulder and pulled her out of her thoughts as Marianne lifted her head to meet Elinor's concerned gaze. Marianne's hand raised to touch her sister's as she leaned back against the couch, letting herself smile as Willoughby charmed her mother.

He truly was the epitome of the dashing young hero, the man who had literally swept her off her feet. The romantic in her heart sighed at the thought, for surely this beautiful man with the crimson eyes was destined to be her one love...

Wasn't he?

... if he was, why did his laugh seem somehow hollow?

CHAPTER EIGHT

Elinor watched her sister spin around the room, Marianne's laughter making everyone nearby smile. It did not matter where they were, no one could resist Marianne's charm and joy. Marianne curtsied to her current partner as the music trailed off, smiling at the dazed man for a moment before her hand was claimed by Willoughby. Elinor's smile faltered as Willoughby drew Marianne off the dance floor, disappearing into the crowd.

"Your sister has them all in the palm of her hands." Brandon's voice shook Elinor out of her thoughts, her eyes shifting to the man whose own gaze was locked to where her sister had disappeared.

"Yes, it is natural for Marianne," Elinor sighed, "she doesn't even realize how she draws people and their attention."

"I just hope for her sake that the attention is... honorable, shall we say."

Elinor's eyes went wide as she spun to watch his profile.

"Whatever do you mean?"

Brandon turned his focus to Elinor. "Has Lord Willoughby made his intentions with your sister clear?"

"I..." Elinor started, her eyes darting between the last place she had seen Marianne and the silver haired Colonel before her, "I believe he has, but I must admit I have not asked her. Why– why would you ask a question like that?"

"Let's just say, I have her best interests at heart, and I hope he does as well." Brandon's eyes hardened for a moment before they turned back to the dancers. "Your sister is beautiful, there is no doubt, and to some, beauty is a prize to be won but easily discarded once it is gained." His hand clenched, and Elinor noted the faint scent of blood at his action. "I only ask that you help her to be careful, reputations can be easily lost by the most innocent of an action."

"I–" Elinor's words were cut off as Marianne's laughter peeled through the room a second before she emerged, Lord Willoughby close behind her. Elinor's sharp gaze caught the slight musing of Marianne's hair, and the smirk that Willoughby held as he watched her move through the crowds. "I thank you, Colonel. I will speak with her, though I am sure he has made clear his intentions towards her, and I hope, no pray, they are entirely honorable."

As Elinor watched, Marianne's gaze turned towards her... no, not her, the man beside her. As Brandon shifted his head towards Marianne, she froze, and Elinor saw the slight frown on Willoughby's face as he shot a glance towards Brandon before trying, unsuccessfully, to get Marianne's attention until he wrapped an arm around her waist and moved her, startling Marianne out of her daze.

"Yes, I will talk to her." Elinor murmured to herself, her thoughts on the ball and the gathering darkening as she saw the glances towards Marianne and Willoughby, the giggles of the ladies, the disdain in the eyes of the gentlemen.

"May I get you a punch?" Marianne fought back a groan of irritation at Willoughby's question.

He was trying to be helpful, she knew, but for some reason, his doting irritated her. There was no doubt that he was acting the perfect courtier, the rapt attention, the soft caresses of her gloved hand, the slight tightening of his hand around her waist. It was everything she had thought she wanted, everything that books and poetry led her to believe were the makings of love and yet...

He was almost suffocating her.

"Thank you, Lord Willoughby, I am quite parched." She responded, her forced smile turning more genuine at the look of happiness in his eyes at her response. There was something endearing about him, something she felt she could grow to appreciate, maybe love, if given the time to...

"May I have this dance, if it is not already claimed?"

The voice had Marianne fighting to hold back a shiver as she turned her eyes to meet golden. A slight nod was her only response as Brandon offered her his hand, waiting for her to place it in his before leading her to the dance floor. As she stepped into line beside the other ladies her attention was focused solely on the man who stood in front of her.

How different they were, the two gentlemen, one the flash of crimson fire, the other a cool silvery ice. One who made her laugh with his wit and charm, the other who made her... she couldn't even say what Brandon made her feel or do, other than, in a strange way, wanting to see him smile, but not just any smile, a smile at *her*. His hand caught hers in the opening steps of the dance, and she felt the heat of his hand clearly, as though there was no glove between them. Her breath caught as he drew her close, his hand spanning her waist as they moved across the floor, the other dancers completely forgotten as she lost herself in his eyes.

What was it about him that drew her so? As she saw it, logic would say she should feel this way with Willoughby, not Brandon, and yet... She stepped away to follow the intricate steps of the dance, her eyes trying to follow Brandon as he moved with his new partner, her breath only resuming when his hand took hers again.

No, Lord Willoughby did not make her feel this breathless, the fluttering's in her stomach. There was such heat in the golden gaze, so at odds with Brandon's stern and stoic countenance, she wanted to see the ice melt, to feel the passion hidden in his eyes, to see him lose...

Brandon's eyes darkening with irritation was her only warning after the dance came to an end before another hand was at her waist, drawing her back into the crowd, the faint sound of Brandon's growl lingering in her ears.

"Marianne, you must meet some of the members of my clan who are here," Willoughby's voice was tense as he spun her, breaking the contact with Brandon. "I have been telling them about you, and Geoffry and Henry wanted to meet the woman I have not stopped talking about."

Marianne paused for only a moment before a smile curved her lips, her attention turning to focus on the Fae beside her.

"Then let me meet them." She agreed, even though her heart was not anywhere near as eager as her tone made her appear.

"He has a very curious clan dynamic," Marianne sighed as she fell backwards against the feather mattress, "it seems while Willoughby is the lord, the clan is actually ruled by consensus." She frowned slightly as she stared at the ceiling. "I confess, I do not understand the Fae way, though I suppose you could say it is more fair than the system that we follow. At least they take care of each other, rather than casting out unwanted siblings."

"Marianne, that is not what happened to us." Elinor shook her head as she folded her dress from the ball, carefully storing it in a chest. "John did not cast us out."

"You cannot say that Fanny did not though." Elinor's silence was all the response Marianne required. "There is some comfort though in knowing that if one should lose their husband, they and their children would still be welcomed and taken care of by others."

"Yes, I am sure that must be some comfort indeed." Marianne turned her head at the sharp tone of her sister's voice.

"You disagree?" At Elinor's droll look Marianne dropped her head back to the mattress, "no, not disagree, you disapprove. But do you disapprove of their lifestyle, or of my choices?"

"Marianne..."

"Ah, my choices then," Marianne let out a wry laugh.

"To so openly favor Lord Willoughby the way you do, I would think tha..."

"And what would you have me do then Elinor, sit in the corner of the room, separate and apart from the activities?"

"No, no one would expect that of you, Marianne, but people are talking, the only person you danced with at the ball besides Lord Willoughby was the Colonel." Marianne's eyes closed at Elinor's words as she tried to hold back the heat of her cheeks, thankful for the few candles they had in the room that may keep Elinor from seeing them.

"Pray, tell me who else was there to dance with? Cousin Middleton?" Marianne shot back, irritation plain in her voice. Whether the irritation was directed at Elinor or at herself, she wasn't quite sure. "They were the only two gentlemen of suitable age to dance with."

"Marianne..."

"Why have we not heard from Edward?" Marianne interjected, noting how her sister's step faltered as she made her way to her bed.

"I... I suppose he must have other obligations that keep him from writing or coming to visit." Elinor sighed, her hand brushing the book he had given her at its place on her nightstand. Her hand began to tremble as another thought occurred to her, she pulled it back against her as she dropped against her own bed. "Either that or he prefers to be and remain elsewhere."

"Why are you so calm about it?" Marianne pushed herself up to watch Elinor.

"What good would it do me to dwell on it or to be upset?" Elinor replied. "We are here, he is... somewhere. Would you prefer that I was despondent, unable to go on without a word from him? I remind you, there were no promises spoken, I do not have the time to hope and dream about something that may never happen."

Marianne slipped out of her bed to dash to Elinor's, crawling in to rest her head on Elinor's shoulder. "Then I will hope for you."

Elinor sighed as she tilted her head against Marianne's as Marianne's arm wrapped around her waist. The sisters lay there for a moment, each lost in their own thoughts, as the candlelight flickered in the breeze from the windows.

CHAPTER NINE

Elinor stood on the cliffs by the cottage, her thoughts as tumultuous as the sea itself. Her thumb stroked the covering of the book of flowers and herbs Edward had given her absentmindedly, the feel of the soft leather soothing her. She didn't know why he stayed away, he had promised to come and visit them, but it had been several months with no word.

She sighed. Perhaps it really was as she had said to Marianne that night so many months ago, that he preferred to stay elsewhere. She had little doubt that she had fallen for the beautiful young man with his Cobalt eyes swirling with dreams, but there was no true indication that her feelings were returned. Yes, they had engaged in deep conversations, sharing their own hopes and thoughts of the future, and also yes, she had felt herself longing to know what his lips would feel like against hers, but it was also possible that she had imagined the affection in his gaze when he looked at her.

She raised the book to her chest as she breathed in. Then there was the look in his eyes in the library before he had shuttered it away, that one look had filled a number of her dreams over the months at Devonshire. She could swear she had seen affection, longing, and dare she even dream it, love, but he spoke no words, made no promises towards her.

Oh, Elinor knew that her mother had hoped, and yes, she herself had hoped, but there was little good that came from waiting and pinning all your thoughts on something that may never happen. No, it was better to take life as it came, to move forward and make the best of the situation one was handed, rather than wasting away waiting for another to help you. She knew that her mother and sister were not able to do that on their own, both driven by flights of fancy and emotion rather than sense.

At least it seemed that her sister's future was to be secure, with the attention that Lord Willoughby was paying her. Over the past two months he had become almost a constant figure at their cottage, bringing flowers, a smile, or a basket of vegetables for the table. One could hardly doubt where *his* attention lay, though Elinor could not say the same for her sister.

While Willoughby was dashing, Elinor had seen Marianne's eyes follow the figure of Colonel Brandon when she felt no one would see her. Elinor knew the hours of practice that Marianne had endured to learn the music that Brandon had given her, the melody now a familiar one in the house, even Willoughby had brought her sheet music as well once he had heard of Brandon's gift, sheet music that had only been looked at once before it was replaced by the first from Brandon.

Either would make a fine match for her sister, though Elinor had to say she was more partial to Brandon than Willoughby. Willoughby was very much like Marianne, chasing pleasure and foolish thoughts, while Brandon was more settled, more focused. Marianne would need someone to help her stay grounded, lest she disappear into her dreams.

The whinny of not one but two horses caught her attention and she turned back to the cottage, her eyes straining to see who the horses belonged to. It was not unusual for one horse to be tied to the fence outside their cottage, but it was rare for there to be two. As she drew closer she recognized the dark brown stallion that Willoughby usually rode, but she did not know the sleek black mare beside him.

"...ank you, so much, Lord Willoughby–"

"Just Willoughby, please." Elinor's eyebrows raised as she walked towards the cottage, trying hard to appear as if she wasn't listening.

"Willoughby then," Marianne sighed, her gaze going over the beautiful mare. It truly was a beautiful gift, and yet- "As I was saying, thank you, so much, but I could not possibly accept her."

"Nonsense," Willoughby smiled as he leaned closer to Marianne, "Maybel is a wonderful mare, and you will be the picture of perfection on her."

Marianne did have to admit, she could absolutely see it. The gleaming black coat of the mare was almost a match to her own hair. If she wore her red muslin dress, oh it would be so striking to ride the cliffs, feel the air on her face without having to worry about propriety or manners. There would be no one to care or chastise her if she were to shout her joy, her happiness at being free of the confines of being a woman of her era, where she could just imagine that she...

No matter how tempting it was, though, to the vain part of her, the little voice that sounded suspiciously more like Elinor each day was reminding her there was nowhere for them to keep or maintain a horse, let alone enough money for the care that it would need.

She ran her hand down the neck of- Lucy as it that Willoughby had said- letting herself enjoy the moment. It was a thoughtful gift, and if they were still at Norland Park she would have absolutely jumped for joy, but their situation was much different now, something she was only just now starting to acknowledge and accept.

"I thank you, my lord, for this wonderful gift," she sighed, pausing to breathe in the comforting scent of the mare, "but I truly canno–"

"Oh how foolish of me," Willoughby interrupted, "of course you cannot ride her without the proper tack." He snapped his fingers as Marianne bit back her irritation at having her sentence interrupted, yet again, and two Fae Fae she had never met came scurrying down the path, carrying a side saddle and blanket between them and placed them at Marianne's feet. "There, now you have everything you need, and I shall look forward to our rides together."

"Willoughby, please, I–"

"I must be off, but I will return in two days. I have business with the clan tomorrow, but we can take our ride then." Willoughby winked as he bowed to Marianne, taking her hand to place a kiss on the back. Marianne heard Elinor's quick inhale as she looked up at her sister, her face beginning to heat at the liberty that Willoughby had taken without permission, but before she could say anything the Fae and his kin were gone, the sound of hooves galloping away loud in the silence.

"It t'is– a beautiful horse?" Elinor murmured as she stepped closer to her sister.

"It is, but Elinor, where would we be able to keep it?" Marianne sighed again as she watched Willoughby ride away, his two lackeys on foot, keeping pace with their leader. "I doubt we have much funds to spare to be able to feed her, or keep her exercised."

"No," Elinor agreed as she reached out to stroke the horse, "right now we are barely able to afford sugar and meat and tea, while the rent here is reasonable, we do not have much funds to be able to spare."

"Argh," Marianne groaned as she let her head fall to the horse's neck. "There are times I miss Norland Park."

"I know you do Marianne, we all do." Elinor whispered as she wrapped her arm around her sister's shoulders.

"As embarrassing as it would have been to decline his gift, I wish he had just let me speak, to tell him." Marianne's voice was resigned as she stood. "He has been doing that lately, not letting me get a word in edgewise unless he likes the topic of the conversation. And this, as wonderful a gift as she is, it is so impractical, so impossible for us right now."

"He means well," Marianne shot her sister a look at the words before letting out another sigh.

"I know, I just wish he would think sometimes before he does things. Look Elinor," Marianne groaned, "he gave me a side saddle. A SIDE SADDLE. Yes, I know that is what a proper lady should be riding, but when have I ever been proper and used a side saddle?"

"Oh, is the dashing, romantic rake not all that you had thought he would be?" Elinor smiled as she watched Marianne pout at the words.

"WHY ARE WE SO POOR." Marianne moaned. "It is not fair that John and that horrible Fanny got everything, and we are here, trying to survive as best we can."

"We are managing," Elinor told her, her eyes drawn to the path to the cottage as she caught movement. "And we have more visitors now than we ever did at Norland."

Marianne's head turned to the path to see a gray horse, a stallion she knew now from the number of times it had been at their cottage. The sun was almost behind the horse and rider, and the image of it almost took her breath away. The deep gray coat that only made the rider's hair look more silver, the grace in which Colonel Brandon sat on the saddle, his body shifting with the ease of one long used to riding.

'If only he were not so proper' Marianne found herself thinking as her heart began the fluttering that seemed to only occur when Brandon was near.

"Good day to you Miss Dashwood, Miss Dashwood." Brandon smiled as he drew his horse to a stop, a bouquet of flowers in his hand.

"Colonel," both ladies murmured as they gave him a slight curtsey.

"None of that, we are all friends here are we not?" Brandon sighed as he dismounted, leading his horse to tie it to the fence. His golden eyes met Marianne's, and she felt her cheeks heating at the momentary connection before her attention was drawn to the floor.

"What lovely flowers, Colonel." Elinor smiled as she saw him start, his attention turning to her quickly.

"They– ah– are for your mother," his cheeks now held a distinct pink hue to them as his gaze darted back to her sister. "I was not able to bring any vegetables or game this time, but it is always proper to pay respects to the lady of the house."

Marianne found herself smiling at his words, even as she refused to lift her gaze. That was another difference between the Colonel and Willoughby, Brandon never came without some gift for their mother or their household, while Willoughby seemed to bring gifts that only Marianne could use.

"I will take them to her," Elinor's hip nudged her sister as she stepped forward, taking the flowers in her hand. When Marianne's head still hadn't lifted, Elinor made sure to elbow her as she stepped past, grinning at the glare Marianne shot her.

"Thank you, Colonel, it is most appreciated." Marianne said, her head finally lifting to meet Brandon's gaze.

"It is nothing, I am only sorry I was not able to bring more today, business had called me away for a few days." Brandon's brow furrowed as he looked to the woods nearby. "I can bring some tomorrow if–"

"Oh no, Colonel," Marianne quickly interrupted, drawing his focus back to her. "It was not to criticize, I was truly saying it is appreciated." Her lips curled into a smile, her breath catching as his gaze darted to them then back to her eyes. "You are most attentive to our family, I know my mother appreciates the respect and assistance you give, as we all do."

"Yes- well-" Marianne's brows rose when Brandon's cheeks began to flush pink at her words, his attention now on the hat he held in his hands rather than on her. Could it be that her words had flustered him? Brandon cleared his throat, and Marianne had to fight back a giggle at his actions. "This is a lovely mare," Brandon continued, quickly turning his attention to the gleaming black horse."

"She is," Marianne sighed, once again wishing that she could keep Maybel, "a gift, but unfortunately one that we cannot keep."

"Why not?" Brandon asked, his focus still on the mare, inspecting her closely to make sure the horse would be safe for Marianne to ride.

"Where would we keep her?" Marianne's response had him looking at her, the resignation in her eyes. "We have no stable here, no stable hands or grooms to help care for her, and it would not be fair to have her held outside, tethered to the fence no matter the weather. No, it is better for her to find another home, someone who could care for her as she deserves." Marianne's hand stroked the neck of the horse, who let out a soft whinny and butted her head against Marianne, causing the woman to laugh.

Brandon stepped away as Marianne came close to the horse, her hands rubbing its back and down its flank. It was easy to see the appreciation that she had for the mare, and easier to see that she knew her way around horses.

"What about stabling her at Hartland?"

"What?" Marianne breathed as she turned to Brandon.

"I was— I mean– We have room in the stables at Hartland, and it is no more than a 30 minute walk from here. I have a groom and stable hand that can help care for her, and you are more than welcome to come to visit her as you like. And when you..." his voice faltered for a moment and a flash of pain crossed his face, "when you leave to form your own household, if they have a stable she would be ready for you to take her with you."

"Are– are you sure? She wouldn't be any trouble?" Marianne's eyes were wide. She had never been to Hartland, but thought of going there frequently to visit Alexa– no Maybel– appealed to her.

"Yes," Brandon's ears had perked straight up, quivering as he thought, "she would be welcome at my estate, and she would be no trouble at all."

"Colonel, I tha–"

"Colonel Brandon, what a pleasant surprise!" Mary's interruption had Marianne spinning to see her mother and sister approaching. "We have missed you these past few days."

"Yes, unavoidable business I am afraid." Brandon coughed, "I apologize for my absence."

"Not at all my dear boy," Mary beamed as she gave a small curtsey, "you do not need to apologize."

"Oh Mama, the Colonel has just offered to stable Maybel for us." Elinor's brow raised at Marianne's use of 'us' rather than 'me.'

"Did he?" Mary's eyes gave away her amusement as her daughter fought the urge to blush, yet again, at her words. "That is most generous indeed, we are indebted to you sir yet again."

"There are no debts, Mrs. Dashwood, it would be my pleasure."

"Your pleasure." Marianne groaned at her mother's smile... she knew that smile, and nothing good ever came from it. "Still, you do us a great service, Sir."

"I– ah– think nothing of it." Elinor smirked at Brandon's look of panic, yes, their mother was truly a force of nature, and she clearly had Brandon in her sights for her youngest daughter, not the Lord Willoughby.

"Well, then it may be best to take Maybel to the stables, it will be late soon and you do not want her to be out in the cold all night, would you Marianne?"

"I–"

"You can take Martha with you as chaperone, I am sure that Colonel Brandon would be sure to send you both home safely." With a nod and a wink to her daughter Mary turned, grabbed Elinor's hand to drag her sputtering daughter away, her voice ringing out for Martha to join them outside.

"Please forgive my mother," Marianne was trying not to die from embarrassment, could her mother be any more blatant.

"There is nothing to forgive." Brandon's voice held a tone of amusement that Marianne had not heard before, "Your mother is a true force of nature."

"She is at that," Marianne smiled, glad he had not been put off by her mothers antics.

"Once Maybel is settled into the stable, perhaps we could see about getting her fitted for a proper tack?" Brandon knelt beside the quilt and saddle that had been left on the ground. "I do not believe anyone actually enjoys riding sidesaddles."

"No, I do not believe they do," Marianne laughed, relieved that he understood her concern, "it is more for show, to look dainty as one rides through town."

"I do not think you would need any assistance to look dainty, however you chose to ride."

Martha's running up from the house spared Marianne from having to come up with a response, not that she would have been able to either way. His gentle complement had affected her more than the poetry that Willoughby showered upon her, and she could not find her words to respond.

CHAPTER TEN

The walk to Hartland had passed quickly, and Marianne had found herself laughing at the stories Brandon had to tell, learning from him as he pointed out local flora and landmarks. Martha had walked a few paces behind them, a slight smile on her face as she watched the pair with their color coordinated horses. She agreed with Mary, they were a fine match, if they could sway Marianne's attention from Lord Willoughby.

"Oh it is beautiful!" Marianne gasped as she stepped to the top of a hill and saw Hartland for the first time.

The building rivaled Norland Park for its size, but it also gave an appearance of being homey, despite its grandeur. The house itself stood at two floors, its white brick facade covered with windows that would bring in the natural light to the rooms. There were two gardens that she could see, one the more traditional formal garden with its intricate designs and landscaping, formal white roses stacked in perfect rows, and the second to the side a riot of flowers, climbing roses with clematis, butterfly bushes and hydrangea, along with a sea of wildflowers that just called her to walk among them.

The grounds were a bustle of energy with staff and grounds workers, all of whom stopped to wave at Brandon as they made their way closer. More than one stopped to come to shake his hand, welcoming him home, nodding to Marianne and Martha. One gardener stepped close and whispered something to Brandon, causing him to throw his head back with a bark of laughter.

It was the happiest and most relaxed that she had seen him, the veil of ice seeming to melt as he smiled back and said something low that caused the gardener to chuckle and slap his back before returning to his task. The smile stayed on Brandon's face as he turned to her, nodding his head in the direction of the stables.

Had she thought he was handsome before? The smile changed his whole face, and she knew it was the type of smile she had longed to see on him for the months she had known him. It was not the polite smile of society, but one of comfort and happiness, and she knew she wanted to see that smile more often. Her step faltered as she followed him, the mare beside her shying as she stumbled and Brandon turned quickly, leaving his own stallion to dart to catch her before she fell.

"Tha– thank you." Marianne whispered, afraid to speak any louder and break the spell that had come over him the moment they had reached his property.

"It is nothing," he whispered back, his eyes so close to hers, closer than propriety should allow, the feeling of his breath against her cheeks sending shivers down her back.

"Ahem..." Martha cleared her throat and Brandon sprang back quickly, the look that Marianne now knew to be a mask coming back over his face, although his cheeks were tinged with pink.

"This way," Brandon's voice was deeper than normal as he turned and stepped forward, putting some distance between himself and Marianne. Marianne followed meekly, her heart racing from the close contact.

On one hand, she was grateful for Martha's interruption, but on the other...

No, she would not let herself think that– or could she?

She watched silently as Brandon took the reins from her to lead both horses to the stable, being met by a small red haired Fae who grinned at Maybel. Marianne could not hear what was being said, but the boy's head bobbed vigorously as he practically danced in place at the new charge.

"Samuel will take care of her," Brandon smiled as he watched the stableboy, Samuel, lead Maybel into the pasture. "He was thrilled to have a new horse to care for. She will be ready for you whenever you choose to come visit her. Samuel knows all the trails on the estate, and would be more than happy to show them to you."

"I appear to be thanking you a lot today, Colonel." Marianne's voice was soft, and Brandon's ears flicked towards her, as if seeking to catch every sound.

Brandon's face warmed as he turned to her. "There is no need, it is my pleasure to help where I can. As I have said before, feel free to come and visit her, and the invitation is there if you want to come to play the piano in the foyer, you are more than welcome, it has gone unused for too long." He stepped closer to her and offered his arm, "Would you care to see the grounds before I have the carriage send you home?"

Marianne only had to think for a moment, getting to walk in that beautiful cottage garden that she had seen? "I would love to!"

To her disappointment though, Brandon led her to the formal gardens, Martha a few steps behind them. She half listened to Brandon discussing the gardens, going through a speech as though it were memorized, but she heard no tone of pride in the garden, as if it were just an expected part of his lands.

"They are quite fine, Colonel." Marianne said at the appropriate time, trying to hold back her own thoughts.

Brandon let out a breath. "They are prim and proper aren't they?" He chuckled, his hair dancing behind him as he shook his head. "It is the one thing in the estate that I haven't had much luck changing in the hundred years I have been here, I am told it is to be expected at all great manors to have a formal garden like this but, it isn't one for really enjoying."

"No, not it is not," Marianne bit back her own chuckle at his words.

"I've asked them to raze the entire thing to the ground and do a more informal garden, but no matter how many times I have asked, no matter who the gardener is they refuse to."

"Because it is expected, Colonel." Marianne grinned as she turned her head to look up at him. "All of your guests will expect to see the formal garden, it would be quite scandalous to not have one."

"Bah." Brandon grunted, and Marianne had to laugh at the sound, so unlike the image she had of him in her head.

"If you could change any portion of it, what would you change?" His question stunned her, stopping her laughter cold. "I mean it, if there was one thing you could change, even though I have to keep the garden formal, what would it be?"

"I…" Marianne thought for a moment, her eyes sweeping through the garden before landing on the harsh rows of the roses. "I would start with those." She gestured, her head tilting as she thought. "While they are beautiful, they seem cold, impersonal in their straight lines. You could change the feel of the garden by putting another flower, say a hydrangea, or something soft like that, in their place. They would still add some color, and stay within the formal garden structure, but it would make it less– rigid in a way."

"Hydrangea…" Brandon's right ear flicked away a fly as he considered the area, the motion drawing Marianne's attention. "I think you may be right."

"It's just a suggestion, Colonel." Marianne murmured, trying not to feel pleasure that he was actually considering her thoughts.

"And a good one, I will talk to my gardeners about it right away." He turned to her, his face sincere, all ice gone from his eyes as he spoke. "Thank you, really."

"Anyone could have made the same suggestion." Marianne felt her cheeks warming under his gaze.

"Yes, but none have. And it is not something I would have thought of on my own."

"It is just flowers in a garden, Colonel, I'm sure you have many more things to worry about."

"That is true," Brandon nodded, his head tilting as he considered her for a moment, "there are some things that I have trouble with though, would you be interested in hearing about them and giving your opinion?"

Was he– did he really– would he actually want her opinion? Marianne's heart began to race, the straightening of Brandon's ears telling her he caught her reaction. "I would–"

"Miss Marianne, I do apologize, but it is getting quite late." Martha's quiet voice drew Marianne from her musings to see the apologetic expression on the maid's face. "The sun has nearly set my lady."

Marianne's eyes widened as she became aware of the colors of the sky, the blues and pinks deepening into purple as the sun dropped from view.

"Ah, I lost track of time." Brandon pulled his arm from Marianne's as he bowed to her and to Martha. "Forgive me, let me get the carriage ready to have it take you home."

"I am sorry Marianne," Martha whispered as Brandon strode back towards the stables, "I did not want to interrupt but it is getting late."

"You are fine Martha, thank you," Marianne responded, her eyes still watching Brandon's figure as he crossed the grounds.

The carriage ride back was quiet, Marianne lost in her thoughts and Martha watching out the window at the scenery that passed.

This was a new side to Brandon that she had never seen before, but one that she desperately wanted to see more often. This Brandon, the laughing, smiling, caring Brandon was dangerous to her heart, that she knew.

It wasn't until she lay in bed, listening to Elinor's soft snoring that it suddenly dawned on her that she had not thought of Lord Willoughby the entire time she had been at Hartland.

CHAPTER ELEVEN

To Marianne's chagrin, it was another two weeks before she was able to return to Hartland, but this time she was not alone. Colonel Brandon had invited her family to his estate for a picnic, a chance to enjoy the fresh summer air and to visit his home and grounds. Middleton and Mrs. Jennings had also been invited, to Marianne's slight irritation, but now that they were no longer trying to match her up with the closest eligible bachelor, they were not quite so intolerable. No, now she found their antics amusing, the ease that Middleton would tease Mrs. Jennings, her sharp retorts back, all had Marianne laughing as she had spent time with them.

The sound of a second carriage behind them almost had her groaning. Lord Willoughby had been visiting when the invitation from Brandon had come, and he had insisted that he come along as well.

"The invitation is for your family, yes?" he had said when Marianne had tried to end his visit, "Then I must be invited to, as I am nearly a member of your family."

The words had made Marianne's stomach turn, and she was sure she could not hide her slight frown, but it seemed he thankfully did not see it. When Willoughby had asked her to join him in his carriage for the trip to Hartland, she had graciously (but also quickly) declined, for she knew her mother and sister would have questions about the estate, as she had been there once before. Instead, he had agreed to have Mrs. Jennings and Middleton ride with him, rather than taking a third carriage.

Whether he accepted her excuse or not, it had taken the entire trip to Hartland for Marianne to gather her thoughts. Willoughby had been visibly perturbed that Maybel was stabled at Hartland, and a large part of why she had not been able to return to visit Alexan– err her mare. Willoughby had come to visit every day, always first thing in the morning, flowers for Marianne in his hands, roses in full bloom, lilies in various colors, all carefully cultivated and cut for their beauty. Often he brought gifts of poetry books, sheet music, gifts that had her mother and sister's eyebrows raising with how often they were brought. It was most difficult to end his visits, where normal convention would have a caller staying for an hour, two at most, the sun was nearly setting each day when he left, leaving no time to visit her mare at Hartland.

Marianne couldn't say that Willoughby wasn't attentive; she had merely to speak about something she had seen or reminisce on a favored sweet and the next day it would be handed to her with a smile and crimson eyes twinkling. He was attentive, often trying to finish her sentences before she had fully formed the thought for herself.

It was exhilarating.

It was also a little... smothering.

While she appreciated his attention, there was something–

"He is persistent, is he not?" Elinor chuckled as Marianne's head dropped.

"Yes," Marianne sighed, "he is."

"Your interactions with him have changed, my dear." Mary mused, watching Marianne's face. "I thought you found him dashing."

"He is, Mama," Marianne's head fell back against the carriage, "I just– I would like to get a word in with him, to have a full conversation that has more to do with beauty or chasing pleasure of some sort or some new fancy of his. I want to know about his clan, about what his life is like. If his intentions are what they seem to be, shouldn't I know these things?"

"Not all men are seeking someone to share things with Marianne." Mary chastised. "Some men are seeking a wife to plan events and to look pretty on their arm."

"But Mama, that is not what I want, I want to be an equal, I want to share my thoughts, my opinions on more than just what dishes to serve, or how to seat a room."

"Oh Marianne, you would be surprised how much thought and strategy goes into a seating chart for a dinner." Mary chuckled with a small shake of her head. "It can be its own form of warfare, and requires a lot of planning to get it just right. What you see as simple women's work can be just as strategic as the decisions the Lord of a manor makes when it comes to alliances and business."

That was – not something Marianne had thought about, there was nothing like that in any of her books or poems. Perhaps her expectations of an equal partnership were– too unrealistic, and it wasn't a feeling that set well with her.

"I suppose…" Marianne's voice trailed off as their carriage turned and Hartland came into view.

The sight took her breath as quickly as it had the first time she had seen it, and the murmurs from the others in the carriage told her that they found it as impressive as she did. Her eyes took in the manor, sweeping to the formal gardens and…

The swirls of blue and pink Hydrangea mixed in with the formal hedges made her gasp. She had not thought Brandon would have taken her advice, instead thinking he had been humoring her but here was the proof that not only had he heard her– he had listened to her.

And he had taken her suggestion and...

"Oh how lovely," Elinor sighed, "I adore the garden, the hydrangeas are so beautiful."

Marianne could only nod, for once at a loss for words.

Brandon stood at the door to the manor, his eyes trained on Marianne as the carriages drew to a halt. His gentle smile fell as he glanced at the barouche that trailed behind them and the Fae glaring at him from inside, before sliding back to Marianne and nodding to his footmen to approach Willoughby's carriage as Brandon stepped forward, his hand extended to Marianne's carriage to help her disembark.

A moment before her gloved hand met his, another's hand captured hers. Willoughby's hair still blew in the wind from his dash from the carriage to her side as he stepped close, his shoulder pushing Brandon away from Marianne with a glint of challenge in his crimson orbs. A soft growl rolled through the air, and Marianne's eyes darted to Brandon in shock, realizing that he was making the sound. Golden eyes met hers for a moment before the sound ceased, Brandon's face stealing into its familiar but now so foreign to her somberness. The only outward sign of his disapproval and – dare she even think it– jealousy was the glint in his amber eyes.

"Allow me, Lady Marianne." Willoughby's words held more familiarity than Marianne was used to, even with as much time as he spent at their cottage. His thumb slid across the back of her hand, startling her as she stepped down and lost her step, only to be caught against Willoughby by an arm around her waist.

The warmth of his chest under her hand made Marianne's mind momentarily go blank as she looked up, her eyes entrapped by the light reflected in his crimson eyes. Her hand involuntarily flexed, her fingers caressing against his shirt– the growing growl from beside her received only a cursory thought.

"Marianne are you alright?" Elinor cried as she descended from the carriage, her words pulling Marianne out of her daze as Elinor drew her away from Willoughby.

Marianne felt her cheeks heat at the smirk that formed on his lips before lowering her eyes completely, refusing to glance at Brandon as she nodded in response.

"I– I'm fine," she whispered, leaning into Elinor's side. She kept her gaze fixed on the ground, her thoughts torn between the pleasure of knowing Brandon had listened to her and followed her recommendation, and the feel of Willoughby's firm chest under her hand. She let herself be swept away, led by her sister and mother, for once finding herself without anything to say, as they chatted with Mrs. Jennings and Middleton, their soft sighs and exclamations barely registering.

"Well, now we just need to decide who is riding with whom then." Mrs. Jennings chuckled as she slid beside Marianne, her eyes sparkling with mischief.

"I'm sorry, what?" Marianne gasped as her head snapped up, realizing that more time had passed than she had thought while lost in her musings. A series of three open carriages sat before them, each laden with a picnic basket.

"Well, my dear, we have four women, and three dashing men, we must decide who will be riding with whom to the picnic site." Mrs. Jennings smiled, "I do wonder which one you will choose."

"I–" Marianne floundered, her mind racing with thoughts. On one hand, Willoughby was the logical choice, as he was showing himself to be a serious contender for her hand, dashing and warm... on the other hand, part of her longed to ride with Brandon. Yes, he was all stern and severe, everything she said she didn't want, yet if she were to go with him, perhaps she would see more of him, and possibly the side she had only glimpsed before whe...

"COLONEL BRANDON!" A shout sounded over the thunder of horses hooves as a gentleman in a red coat astride a black horse galloped up to the group. "I bring an urgent message from Her Majesty, the Queen."

Brandon's back straightened and his hands clenched into fists as he marched to the quivering horse, seizing the missive from the young man's hand. Marianne watched his face harden; if she had ever thought he looked serious before, his features now seemed to be carved of ice. His eyes lifted once to look at the young rider's red face and harsh breathing before darting to hers. Their golden color glowed in the sun, a look of anger, hunger, and *regret* as he crushed the letter in his fist.

"I must go," he growled before letting out a sharp whistle, "there is no time to waste."

"But surely you can stay for the picnic Colonel," Middleton started, "it must not be quite as urgent as you make it seem."

"I wish it were not, Sir, but it cannot wait." The clamor of hooves sounded from the stable as Samuel raced from its doors, Brandon's gray stallion trotting at his side, fully dressed. "Duty calls me away, and I must answer. I must ask for your forgiveness, please do not hesitate to use the grounds of Hartland while I am away."

He tipped his hat to Middleton, slightly less to Willoughby, before nodding to each of the women, his eyes meeting Marianne's last to linger for a moment longer than propriety allowed, and Marianne found herself feeling oddly hollow when he turned to leap onto the back of his horse.

"I bid you all adieu, and again, I am sorry that our day has been cut short." With a kick of his heels the stallion burst into a gallop, the young man who had brought the missive following closely behind.

"Well, I wonder what that was about," Mary exclaimed, her hand coming to her chest as she watched the pair fading in the distance.

"I believe I may know," Mrs. Jennings nodded, "he only would ride like that if it was a notice from the palace."

"Ah yes, ever the good little soldier, isn't he?" Willoughby's tone made Marianne frown, while the words were kind, it seemed almost... mocking in a way.

"Lord Willoughby, I am sure that it must have been important," Mrs. Jennings interjected, her eye and set of her mouth showing her displeasure at the man.

"Yes, but it is always important when it comes from the crown, is it not?" Willoughby's jaw set as he continued to watch the way the riders had gone. "A summons from Good Queen Charlotte, for we all know that the King is in no condition to summon anyone, and away he rides off to answer the call."

"He is the Crown's man," Middleton started, "and that mea..."

"Yes, the Crown's man." Willoughby finally turned his head back towards the group, before settling on Marianne. "Always at their beck and call. It is better to be your own man, beholden to none but yourself and your clan, than having to bother with their petty dramas."

"Well with war against France and Napoleon, it does not seem quite so petty to others." Mrs. Jennings's tone had hardened, a clear indicator that she would hear no more of it.

"To some, to be sure." Willoughby's brow rose with a smirk. "But I do believe that rather than let our day be ruined by the Colonel's absence, we do what he said, and enjoy the grounds. I dare say it will be more pleasant now that he will not be here to scowl away the sun."

"Yes, well," Mary tittered, trying to return the mood that had left the group, "I believe we were discussing who was riding with whom?"

"Oh there is no need Ma'am," Willoughby grinned before swooping a startled Marianne into his arms. "I will be happy to take Marianne in my carriage. My estate borders this one, so I am quite familiar with the grounds and would be happy to show her around."

Before Marianne could get a word out she had been settled into his now moving carriage, her eyes darting back to meet Elinor's with a plea for help, only to watch her sister and mother fade from view.

"You know some would see this as kidnapping, my lord." Marianne sighed as she sat against the cushion.

Willoughby chuckled, "I have someplace I wanted you to see, and I would prefer it be without an audience."

"Oh?" Marianne asked, her curiosity peaked.

"As I said, my estates border Hartland, and I thought..." he slowed the horses to a stop before turning to meet Marianne's gaze, "I thought you might be interested in seeing them, and meeting some others of my clan."

"I..." Marianne found herself struggling for words at what he was saying, and what she thought it meant. It was the first time he had shown any interest in her visiting his home, or meeting anyone other than the two Fae she had met in passing only. If he wanted her to see it, and to meet some of the others, then... maybe it meant that he was in fact serious, and that she was more than just a passing fancy to him. Would he be looking for a partner though, or someone to decorate his arm, and to look pretty at the table...

'What you see as simple women's work can be just as strategic as the decisions the Lord of a manor makes when it comes to alliances and business.'

Her mother's words, spoken only an hour before, darted through her thoughts. Marianne tilted her head as she looked into his crimson eyes. Maybe she had been too harsh on him, putting *her* own thoughts of what her parents' marriage had been without really thinking about what he may want.

She owed him a chance to show her, didn't she?

"I would enjoy that, thank you Lord Willoughby."

CHAPTER TWELVE

Marianne did not know what to expect of the Allendale estate, but nothing would have prepared her for her first glance. The house seemed to loom over a collection of smaller homes, all seemingly carved out of stone, but she knew that had to be an illusion. For the first time, she found herself wondering just how many there were in Willoughby's "clan."

Glowing eyes peaked at her from the shadowed doors and windows as the carriage made its way towards the manor, Marianne would get the glimpse of a tail, a yip from a corner, but otherwise the Fae seemed to stay hidden, as wary of her as she suddenly felt of them.

Willoughby smiled as he leapt from the carriage, offering her his hand with a gallant bow. "Allendale welcomes you, my Lady Marianne."

The artwork in the foyer was beautiful, statues of men who must have been Willoughby's ancestors, paintings of large families, all with striking crimson eyes and elongated ears. As they walked the length of the hall, the number of children in the paintings began to grow smaller, until Marianne stood before a painting of a young Willoughby, sitting alone with whom she could only assume were his parents.

"The hall of ancestors." Willoughby's hand took her elbow as he stepped beside her. "The history of the Allendale clan and its rulers, all the way back to when we settled here in 240 AD."

"That long?" Marianne gasped, turning to look at Willoughby as he spoke.

"Surprised?" At her nod he chuckled. "Yes, we were more nomadic before, constantly traveling, avoiding wars, then my great grandfather chose to set down permanent roots, and began to build the compound. Soon most of our clan of Fae came to join him, and formed a council, from that he was elected as the leader of the clan, a position that was passed to my Grandfather, my Father, and now me."

"But that was almost... 1600 years ago?"

"Yes, my great grandfather was already around 2000 at that point, after a few hundred years he passed the mantle to my grandfather, who ran the compound for around 500 years, my father for 700 years, and I took over from him when he chose to step down 100 years ago."

"But then..."

"Yes, we were here before this area became 'England.' The King and Queen have no say over us or our actions, as we never became part of the Country, and have no part in its wars or squabbles. Let others like the halfling fight for a land that will change hands many times, all to fight for favor, but we take care of our own."

Before Marianne could ask who the 'halfling' was, though she was afraid she had an idea, Willoughby led her down another corridor, the whispers that she heard around her stilled her tongue as she watched Willoughby interact with the Fae, carefully hidden out of her sight.

"Sorry, they are wary of strangers." His face was rueful as he looked down at her. "That's part of why I wanted to bring you since we were so close, so they could see you, and start to become accustomed to you."

"A...accustomed to me?" Marianne's voice was quiet as she drew to a stop, halting Willoughby's movements. Her eyes were wide as she tried to draw her arm free, but a gentle tightening of his hand locked it into place. She could not help the racing of her heart, but at that moment, she was not quite sure *why* it was racing.

His cheeks flushed pink as his free hand rose to his neck. "Ah, yeah, that is a bit presumptuous of me I suppose. But I want them to be comfortable with my woman."

Marianne's soft smile turned downward at the phrase 'my woman,' but Willoughby's attention was already back to leading her through the maze of corridors.

"Here is what I wanted to show you." His grin grew into a wide smile, causing the tips of his fangs to show as he nodded towards a window.

Marianne's breath caught at what lay before her. Hidden behind the walls was almost a full city, bustling with activity. She could not see the end of the compound, it lay far beyond her vision, but she could only imagine it would be vast indeed.

Willoughby's arm shifted from her elbow to steal around her shoulders, drawing her close to his body as he looked proudly at the scene. Marianne stiffened at the movement, but he paid it no mind.

"As I said, we take care of our own. We have little need for others, and are able to do most things here. And if we can't, we find someone who can and bring them here."

"To teach?"

Willoughby chuckled. "Well, they do teach, but no, they are brought here also to provide their service or goods; they are well taken care of until they pass."

"Then why do you go into society?" Marianne couldn't help but ask, her attention turning to the man who held her against him. She swallowed softly, nervous at the proximity to him, but not sure how to politely step away.

"Amusement, some fun." Willoughby shrugged before turning his face to hers. "Sometimes you meet fascinating people, like a young woman who defied the cliffs yet found herself tumbling from their wrath."

"Oh, is that what I did?" Marianne chuckled as she tried to hide her flushing cheeks. A soft hand under her chin caught her face, tilting it back up to meet the Fae lord.

"Faced their wrath and tumbled into my heart."

Marianne's breath caught as Willoughby's face lowered, hesitating for only a moment before touching his lips to hers. Her eyes widened as they slid over his face, closer than anyone had been, save her family, and quickly closed them.

Her eyes stayed closed as Willoughby lifted his head with a pleased growl. Her thoughts were racing, and she took a moment to try and bring them back to some semblance of sanity. She finally let her lids drift open–

And immediately froze as she saw three more elderly Fae glaring at her, their eyes shimmering in the faint light, and she swore she saw a slight frown on all their faces. Willoughby saw her attention shift and turned to face them. He let out a growl that had them nod and then fade from view.

"Come on, I have kept you long enough, I should get you back to your family."

Marianne nodded mutely as she let him lead her back to the carriage. She was silent the entire ride back, her eyes unfocused as she stared at the passing scenery as her thoughts went back to the kiss, her *first* kiss.

Somehow— somehow she had always thought that there should be sparks in a kiss. It shouldn't feel the same as a simple handshake... should it?

"Where could they be?" Elinor fretted as she paced the foyer of Hartland. Mary stood at the window, looking out for any view of her other daughter. "They have been gone for hours!"

"I do not think Lord Willoughby would allow anything to happen to your sister, my dear." Middleton offered with a pat on her shoulder as she passed him.

"But they took no Chaperone, do you understand what this could do to her reputation?" Mary sighed at Elinor's words.

"He has seemed to be an honorable gentleman, Elinor, we must put our faith in that... and hope no one saw her with him unaccompanied."

"Lord Willoughby is, if nothing else, an honorable man," Mrs. Jennings agreed softly. "While this is impulsive and rambunctious, it is not outside the realm of his behavior, but I have never heard of him doing anything untoward with any lady. Well, at least not that she didn't initiate."

Elinor whirled, her eyes wide. "You are not thinking that..."

"Oh no no no, my dear, I was just relaying my understanding of him." Mrs. Jennings's eye went wide as she moved towards Elinor. "I was not implying anything at all of that–"

"Oh thank God, here they come now!" Mary's cry stopped Mrs. Jennings's words as Mary rushed out the door, Elinor close at her heels.

"I apologize for keeping your daughter so long, it was not my intention." Willoughby bowed low to Mary before turning to lift Marianne out of the carriage. Elinor stepped close to her sister, noting her downturned eyes and withdrawn stance. A surge of concern coursed through her as she drew her sister into her arms, and noted Marianne's slight tremble as she sagged into her sister.

"Well now, all is well now that you are back, whole and happy, is it not?" Middleton's laugh sounded forced to Elinor's ear as she rubbed Marianne's back with her hand. "I am not sure about you all, but I am famished; let us enjoy the wonderful lunch that has been prepared."

"Thank you, but I must decline." Willoughby stated, his eyes never leaving Marianne. "There is business at Allendale that needs my attention, and I wish to speak with the council about a... personal matter." His cheeks took a tinge of pink. "I must bid you all a fond farewell for now, and I will, if it pleases you, visit tomorrow morning."

Marianne's eyes finally lifted as he stepped into his carriage, and watched him ride away. Her thoughts continued to spin, her pleasure at seeing Allendale, her... disappointment... with how she had felt with the kiss, and crimson eyes taking on a golden hue. She was confused, nothing had felt like the books had told her she would feel, but was that truly what love felt like, or was love more a contentment with the person you were with.

"Marianne?" Elinor's voice was hesitant, but pulled Marianne out of her thoughts to turn to meet her sister's gaze.

"Yes," Marianne's voice was shaky as she gave a faint smile, "I am also quite hungry."

Elinor's eyes stayed on Marianne during the lunch, despite Middleton and Mrs. Jennings's attempts to lighten the mood. Elinor could not help but notice that Marianne, who normally had a voracious appetite, seemed to do no more than pick at her food, taking no more than three bites the entire time.

CHAPTER THIRTEEN

"Marianne, are you sure you are alright?" Elinor's concerns had only grown at her sister's withdrawn countenance the rest of the day. "Did something happen while you were with Lord Willoughby?"

"No– no nothing happened." Marianne sighed as she lay down on her bed, her eyes focusing on the ceiling.

"Marianne–" Elinor started, then stopped, before moving to sit next to her sister on the bed. "I know you like Lord Willoughby, but I do wish you would be more careful about your behaviors. You have no idea how worried Mother and I were when you were gone with him for several hours."

"I am sorry for that but, he wanted to show me his manor, and I– I wanted him to show me. It was not something that was planned, and truly we lost track of time." Marianne's voice was still low, and she began to draw her bottom lip into her teeth, a habit Elinor knew only happened when she was troubled.

"Marianne, what is it?"

"It's– It's nothing."

"Marianne..."

"It's–," Marianne let out a deep sigh, "have you ever had something that seemed to be on its face what you thought you wanted, but when you have it, you wonder if it was really what you wanted at all?"

"Marianne, what are you..."

"Forgive me Elinor, I am tired." Marianne's eyes finally met Elinor's, and her elder sister could see the exhaustion in them.

"I will let you rest then." Elinor leaned down to kiss her sister's forehead before returning to her own bed and extinguishing the candle between them.

As she listened to Marianne's breathing slide into the pattern of slumber, Elinor found her own thoughts drawn to one she tried not to think about.

She would never admit it to her sister, but in a way she was slightly jealous. Marianne had the open affection of two very suitable, well one more suitable than the other in her opinion, gentlemen, and while Elinor knew there were a number of perfectly acceptable men in the nearby village that always treated her with respect and appreciation, none could budge Edward from her thoughts.

Why hadn't he come to visit them, had she imagined things between them? Had she merely been an amusement for the time he was at Norland Park? No, she would like to think that she was a better judge of character than that, though how someone as kind and thoughtful as Edward could be related to Fanny still baffled her.

Elinor sighed as she turned to her side, sleep continuing to elude her. It had been months since they first came to Devonshire, and there had been no word from Edward, no visit, no letter. It was if he had forgotten them, or more she reasoned that he was so busy as head of his family that he had no time to visit them, but even then, there could have been a letter, a 'I hope you have all settled in properly,' but the post had remained steadfastly void of any word from him. The fact that they had not heard from their half brother in that same period was of no importance, but Edward's silence hurt, even though she had only known him a handful of weeks.

'*There is no point in dreaming about things that will never be,*' Elinor thought as she let her eyes close, trying to force herself to sleep. No, it was better not to think about wishes or hopes, and to focus on the practical and day to day. Someone had to help her family stay strong, and while she loved both her mother and her sister, both were creatures of fancy that needed someone to help ground them.

She felt sleep finally begin to claim her, the lethargy spreading through her limbs as she slid into slumber.

Cobalt eyes and a kind, smiling face were the last thoughts she had before dreams claimed her.

Over the next few weeks Willoughby had made himself a daily presence at their house, asking Marianne to take a walk, bringing a picnic basket for the family, flowers for the table, or a selection of fresh vegetables for their table. Elinor watched as Marianne's smile began to relax, the hesitancy and anxiousness that had vexed her easing. Elinor smiled softly into her sewing as Marianne, sitting on a blanket with the dashing lord, threw her head back with a full laugh, a sound that had not been heard in many a month since their father had fallen ill, before her lips turned into a slight frown.

Poetry was now a constant in their house, whether Willoughby was reciting a new poem for Marianne's enjoyment, or a new book was brought to add to their collection. Marianne had smiled over each and every addition, though Elinor had noted a faraway look in her eyes when the topic of the poem came to love. Occasionally, when Marianne believed no one was looking, Elinor had caught her looking in the direction of Hartland, a thoughtful look on her face, before letting her face turn into a happy smile at a new flower handed to her by the crimson eyed Fae.

While Elinor had concerns about how happy Marianne *truly* was, their mother had no such qualms.

"Why do they not announce their engagement?" Mary murmured as she watched her youngest accept a strawberry from Willoughby. "Their behavior would surely indicate that they are engaged, at least in private, yet they have not made any announcement.

"Perhaps he is waiting for something," Elinor mused, setting her sewing into her lap, "he did say he needed to speak with his council on a personal matter, maybe he is waiting for them?"

"But surely he could announce his intentions, or at least to discuss them with us," Mary insisted.

"I am sure he has a good reason not to, Mother." Elinor smiled at her mother's petulant huff.

"Another strawberry?"

Marianne shook her head at Willoughby's offering; he had appeared only a half hour after they had finished breaking their fast, and she was still full from the morning meal. The last three weeks had been similarly filled, and she was once again finding herself flattered by the constant attention of the Fae lord.

Without Brandon's presence to distract her, she had to admit that she may have been too harsh on the Lord before. What she had once found annoying and smothering was now charming, and almost endearing. The slight wag of his tail, a feature that seemed so at odds with his personality, whenever he saw her made her giggle.

But her heart still didn't flutter whenever he took her hand. Where once that had bothered her, now she found herself wondering if that was something that would come in time.

"The council has called a meeting for tomorrow morning." His words stilled her thoughts as she turned to meet his piercing crimson eyes.

"Oh?"

Willoughby grinned as he stood and offered her his hand, helping her rise as well. "They didn't say what it was about, but I have my hopes." He tucked her hand into the curve of his arm as he escorted her back to her mother and sister at the house.

Marianne's thoughts, which had largely calmed over time, once again began to race. Was he implying what she thought he was implying–

And if he was, was that what she wanted?

"My lady," Willoughby gave Mary a slight bow, "I will be speaking with my clan tomorrow morning, and I was wondering if I would be able to come to call at around 4 tomorrow afternoon," he paused his eyes darting to Marianne and back to her mother, "first for a private meeting with Miss Marianne, and then a meeting with you, if that meets your approval."

Mary's eyebrows raised as a smile slowly curved her lips. "Yes, yes of course."

"I will bid you all leave then, until tomorrow." Willoughby reached out to capture Marianne's hand, raising it to his lips. In her flustered state, Marianne missed the side glances between her mother and sister as her eyes dropped to the floor.

Silence fell between the three women as they watched him stride up the path from the cottage. When he was out of what they felt was hearing distance Mary turned to her daughter.

"Is there something we should be aware of before tomorrow?"

"Mama!" Marianne's cheeks flushed pink at the insinuation. "Not that I know of, I am as in the dark as you are."

"Really, Marianne?" Elinor laughed as her sister's cheeks puffed in indignation.

"I swear to you, he has made no mention of this except for just before we came back to join you both."

"Not even when you were at Allendale together? Alone?" Elinor couldn't help tease.

"I... we were never alone, there was always someone near us except for the carriage ride."

Elinor's eyebrow rose at her sister's words.

"Elinor, that is enough teasing," Mary stood, shaking out her skirt as she spoke, "we must prepare ourselves for the visit tomorrow, Marianne. I believe we should go and choose the perfect gown."

The next day Marianne was dressed carefully in her green muslin gown, her hair carefully arranged with her mother's discerning and exacting eye for the events that she believed were to take place.

Marianne herself was a bundle of nerves as the day progressed, sitting in the chair while her mother fussed over her hair with Martha. She had an inkling of what was going to be asked, and what was expected of her, but while she had enjoyed Willoughby's company for the past few months, was there more, or was it just a fondness that she would have for any acquaintance? It was true that Allendale was only a short horse ride away from the cottage, and she was sure that Willoughby would not have a problem with her family moving with her if it came to that, but also… the sheer size of Allendale's holdings and clan gave her concern. She was not above admitting that, while she had been fascinated by the home, she had felt quite uncomfortable with the attention and the stares that she had received while she had been there. While it may be something that she could overcome with time, she had felt none of the ease or sense of belonging that she had felt at Hartland when she had been on the grounds.

And for some reason, despite how pleasant Willoughby had been to be around and the distraction he provided, she couldn't help but feel oddly… distanced, as if part of her were missing, and she had strangely found herself thinking about Brandon, even while Willoughby escorted her on a walk, or when he would recite a poem.

Her mother and Martha continued to cluck around her, fixing her hair, touching up her makeup, and only Elinor was looking at the play of emotions across Marianne's face, her concern for her sister growing the longer she watched.

When the clock on the wall hit 3:45 Mary hurried Elinor out of the cottage, letting Jonathan and Martha have the afternoon off, to give Marianne privacy for the meeting with Lord Willoughby. Elinor had protested, but Mary had heard nothing of it, grabbing her eldest's arm and escorting her out of the cottage. Elinor turned her head back and watched as Marianne's happy smile dropped into a line of uncertainty. Their eyes met for a moment before Mary tugged Elinor, forcing her to follow along and fall in line behind her.

Despite Elinor's best efforts, her mother would not be swayed back to the cottage, insisting that they both needed the fresh air, but also that Marianne and Willoughby deserved some time alone for what Mary was sure was to be a very positive and productive conversation.

"I am not sure that he would make her happy," Elinor sighed as she followed her mother.

"Happiness is a luxury many women cannot afford."

"But Mama, with you and father as her example, why would Marianne want or settle for anything less?"

Mary stopped and turned to face Elinor. "You know that your father and I did not start off as we became, that developed over the years together, growing and learning how to be with each other. Marianne would do the same with whichever man she ends up with."

"But would Lord Willoughby allow her that chance?" Elinor mused, her voice soft. "What does he know, really know, of Marianne?"

"Elinor, my dear, what does any man know of their new spouse when they marry? Courting is not the time to get to know the other, that is what marriage is for."

"Well, I would think that courting would have something to do with knowing the other."

"Oh Elinor, your father and I did not do you any favors keeping you isolated at Norland Park. That was selfish of us; we did not want to lose you, either of you, to the London Ton, so you never had to deal with the intricacies of being out in society. Courting is only about finding someone you are compatible with, if half of the men came to know the women whose favor they were seeking before the marriage, there would be a lot less weddings each season."

"I suppose Mama, but…"

"What is it, Elinor?"

"Have you not noticed how her eyes seem to dull when he is around?" Elinor's words caused Mary's smile to fall. "How often have we heard her talk about how she found him boring, or that he didn't listen to her? Marianne is not a rose to be carefully cultivated and treasured, she is more a hydrangea, sturdy, resilient, but also changes. She will never be happy being put on a shelf or left to just wear pretty dresses and sit around an estate all day."

"What I know is that there do not seem to be many prospects for either of you near here, and Lord Willoughby is a very suitable man who will make sure Marianne is taken care of for the rest of her life. Given the situation that your brother and that witch he married have put us in, that is a very attractive proposition."

"For you Mama, but is it for Marianne?"

Mary went silent at Elinor's words, the quiet broken by the soft whinny of a horse in the distance.

"Well, perhaps we have left them alone quite long enough." Mary quickly turned back to the cottage, her pace now a good deal faster than the leisurely stroll she had led Elinor on.

Willoughby's horse was still tied to the post outside the cottage when Elinor and Mary approached, but there was no sound from inside. Elinor had a strange feeling as they drew close, and suddenly wished again that she had not let her mother pull her from the cottage.

The scene they found upon entering the cottage was not one either woman had expected. Willoughby stood, his hat in his hands, eyes lowered to the floor, as Marianne stood, one hand on the mantle, the other over her mouth. Elinor's breath caught as her sister's eyes met hers and she saw tears forming in them, but the way Marianne held her body, Elinor knew that it was not tears of happiness.

"I... excuse me," Marianne whispered before rushing from the room.

"Is anything the matter? Is she ill?" Mary demanded, her gaze turning to Willoughby with a glint of suspicion in them.

"I hope not, but I fear... I believe she may be a little upset, and I myself am a little disappointed." His hands clenched the brim of his hat, his claws piercing through the fabric.

"Why, whatever could the matter be, did Marianne refuse you? Surely she didn't." Mary pressed on, only stopping at Elinor's hand on her arm.

"No– I... I am disappointed that I am not able to stay in Devonshire longer. I am being sent on business for my clan to– London, and I must leave at once."

"Oh, well, that is a shame, but I hope your business will not take you long?" Mary asked, her voice dropping in volume as she took in the Fae lord's body language.

"Unfortunately, I have no idea of returning to Devonshire immediately, nor will I be able to until this... business... is concluded, which could take a considerable amount of time. I apologize, but I must take my leave now, as I need to leave immediately."

"I..." Mary started, only to pause as Willoughby crushed his hat in his hand and strode out of the cottage, never once looking back over his shoulder.

"I do not understand," Elinor was perplexed as her eyes met her mothers. "He seemed so happy here yesterday, and was quite affectionate with Marianne. Mama, I am not alone in thinking he was going to... Surely they didn't quarrel"

"No my dear, you were not alone," Mary sighed as she crossed to close the door softly. "It is plain to see something happened, something that may have been beyond his control." Her gaze drifted to the stairs where her youngest had disappeared. "Despite her feelings and apparent concerns, I cannot imagine she would have refused him. No, I wonder if perhaps this… council… he spoke of did not approve of Marianne, at least not yet. It could be he left to put some distance between them, to allow time for the council to come to terms with his affection." Her tired eyes met Elinor's. "Can you think of any other answer?"

"No, Mama," Elinor whispered, pausing only a moment before nodding slightly and rushing up the stairs to comfort Marianne.

Mary felt her eyes begin to well at the muffled voices of her daughters from their room on the floor above, her heart breaking for Marianne – and Elinor as well.

"Oh, if only we were still at Norland Park," Mary sighed as she let her hand come to rest on the wall, shaking her head softly at Jonathan as he entered the room, only to back out quickly at her expression. "This would never have happened if her father were still with us. My poor poor girls."

Mary stood, her head dropping to rest on her hand against the wall. After a few moments her shoulders stiffened as she rose, crossing to the desk in the sitting room. She pulled a blank piece of paper to the sitting area and drew out a quill, carefully filling it with ink before taking a deep breath and beginning to write.

CHAPTER FOURTEEN

Elinor's eyes were sad as she watched Marianne wander through the meadow near their cottage. She had never seen her sister act so... distraught was the best way to describe it, but even then it wasn't quite accurate. The memories of her conversations with Marianne played through her mind.

"Elinor, have you ever felt as though you were in love with an ideal, a dream, only to find it... hollow once you held it?" Marianne's eyes had changed, no longer sparkling with thoughts of her dreams, they seemed deeper, and yet more unsettled.

"I do not understand," Elinor had whispered back as she stroked her sister's hair.

"It's... thinking you knew what you wanted, what seemed sure, and then when it is... gone... you realize it – that the absence– doesn't really bother you as much as you thought it would." Marianne had sighed. "Is it possible to fall in love with the idea of love, rather than a person?"

"I'm sure it is," Elinor soothed, placing a kiss on Marianne's forehead.

"But that doesn't make it hurt any less though, does it?" Marianne's eyes drifted shut as she turned, letting her head drop from Elinor's lap. "I am sorry Elinor, I'm tired. I just want to sleep right now, maybe it will all make more sense in the morning."

That had been five days before, and Marianne seemed no closer to it all making sense than she had right after Willoughby had left.

But Elinor could not honestly say that it was because Marianne missed Willoughby. More often than not, Marianne's gaze would turn towards Hartland, her face moving as if scanning the horizon, looking for a figure she never saw, which would then make her face fall even more.

"Is it possible to fall in love with the idea *of love, rather than a person?"*

Yes, Elinor thought as she wrapped herself in a shawl and made her way to her sister, it was possible. It was part of growing up she supposed, yet somehow she had hoped that Marianne would never face some of the realities of adulthood.

"For I have learned to look on natureNot as in the hour of thoughtless youthBut hearing oftentimes the still sad music of humanity."

Marianne's voice was soft as her eyes met Elinor's, a small, humorless smile on her lips. "It was one of Willoughby's favorite sayings."

"Would it be easier if you tried not to think of him so much?"

Marianne let out a sad laugh. "Would you believe it's the first time he has crossed my mind in days?"

"To be honest, no..." Elinor shook her head, drawing her shawl closer around her as she fell in beside Marianne, matching her pace.

"I suppose I deserve that," Marianne sighed. "I'm sure everyone around us believes that I am now despondent that he is gone, and yet..."

"Yet?"

"Yet he is not the one I seem to be missing." Marianne finished in a whisper, her gaze dropping to the path in front of them.

"Marianne–" Elinor wrapped her arm around Marianne's shoulder, letting her sister rest her head against her own as they came to a stop.

The whiny of a horse had Marianne's head snapping up as she frantically turned back to the cottage, her eyes scanning the landscape before landing on the rider making his way down the path, only for her shoulders to fall when she did not see the ...

"It's Edward!" Marianne gasped, her eyes wide as she spun to Elinor.

Elinor's face went blank for a moment before breathing in a sob, her lips curling into a wide smile. She caught her bottom lip with her teeth as her eyes met Marianne's, whose eyes sparkled at her in return.

"Go!" Marianne urged, and with only a second's hesitation, Elinor turned to hurry back to the cottage... and the man that was jumping down from his horse.

"... of you to come visit us, will you be here long?" Mary gestured for Jonathan to take the horse as she spoke with Edward, her eyes darting to her daughters as they came up the path with a small smile."

"Just for the night, I am afraid," Elinor had to hold back a smile at the sound of his voice, "I do hope that I will be nonetheless welcome, even if it is only for a short time."

"Have you come straight from London then?"

"No, I... I have been in Devonshire for a fortnight." Edward's gaze turned to meet Elinor's even as he answered her mother's question. The look of longing but also... discomfort slowed Elinor's steps as she came closer.

"Oh," Mary gasped as she stepped back, giving Edward and Elinor some space.

"Yes, I was visiting some..." his throat cleared before he visibly swallowed "some old friends– near Plymouth." His tone turned bitter as he drew silent.

"Was it–not a joyful visit?" Elinor asked, her head tilting even as her eyes never left his.

"No," he admitted softly before sighing and deliberately pulling his gaze from hers. "But I have no one but myself to blame for that."

Mary tugged on Marianne's shawl and nodded her head towards the cottage, stepping backward to draw her away from the young couple.

"I am–very happy to see you again, Elinor." Edward's voice was soft as his chin lifted again to face Elinor directly.

"And I you." Elinor smiled in response, her cheeks flushing pink as she let her eyes drift downwards.

"Elinor, I–" Edward started, his hand starting to reach for her before he caught himself and let it drop to his side before forcing a smile as he turned to acknowledge Mary and Marianne. "How does Devonshire suit? Lots of pleasant walks, one would think. How have things been with your Cousin, Middleton was it not? I hope he and his family are pleasant."

"Oh, no, not at all, we could not be more unfortunately situated." Marianne's tongue hit her cheek as Elinor turned to glare at her.

"Marianne..." Elinor hissed before shaking her head and turning back to Edward. "Middleton has been very kind and lovely to us, he is a very friendly host. Most amiable, he invites us to dine with him and his family almost nightly, and ensures we are quite comfortable."

"That is... that is good." Edward gave a small half smile as he watched Elinor turn to chastise her sister for her teasing.

Mary's eyes went sharp as his smile fell, his face taking on the look of one in pain as he watched Elinor and Marianne.

Dinner that evening was a loud, joy filled affair at the small table in the cottage. The simple presence of Edward had changed the emotions, dispelling the sadness that had lingered in the air.

"My dear Edward, what are your mother's intentions for you at present?" Mary laughed as Martha began to clear the plates. "Last we had heard from you she had intended a life of a great lord for you, a great orator, in spite of your wishes."

"No," he chuckled, "I think she has finally accepted that I am *not* destined for public life. My brother Robert is much more suited to that life than I am, he thrives in it whereas I would not."

"How do you plan to distinguish yourself then?" Marianne asked as she rose from the table to bring the last plate to Martha.

"I don't think I will attempt it at all." Edward responded, a small smile on his lips. "It was my family's wish for me to be distinguished, it was never mine."

"Well, you are distinguished to us, Edward." Marianne smiled as she gave her sister a small wink, a bright giggle bursting from her lips as Elinor's cheeks flushed. "Besides, what does wealth or grandeur have to do with happiness? One could be happy just with the one they love alone, could they not?"

"I would think wealth would have a good deal to do with it." Elinor interjected as she began to reset the table to its usual coverings.

"Oh come now, Elinor." Marianne teased as she bumped Elinor's hip, causing Edward to chuckle. "Have we not all been happy here in this cottage, as poor as the gypsies?"

"True, however I think we might've been just a bit happier if we might've had even just a little more money." Elinor sighed softly as she moved around the room, forgetting for a moment the Cobalt eyed man who tracked her every move, a slight frown on his face. "You must admit, Marianne, that it would be better if we had some to spare for tea or butter each week."

"Elinor you have no soul." Marianne chided as she stuck her tongue out at Elinor, before both girls' cheeks flushed at the sound of a deep chuckle, making them aware of their guest.

"Perhaps not, but I do flatter myself that I may have a little sense." Elinor's voice dropped in volume as she lowered herself into a chair, accepting the small glass of water that Jonathan handed her with a slight smile.

"What say you Edward?" Marianne shot Elinor a quick glance before turning her attention to the young man. "Do you believe that money has anything to do with happiness?"

At his pause Marianne gestured to the open seat next to Elinor as Mary stepped in closer to Edward, the pair gently herding him towards the seat. Edward took two steps before stopping, shaking his head slightly before giving Marianne a slight bow and gesturing for her to take the seat.

"I believe that Monday can solve… some problems, of that I am certain." Elinor watched as his face became somber, a look she had never seen him with before, at Norland he had always had a glint in his eye, even when discussing serious matters. Marianne dropped into the chair next to her and Elinor reached out to clutch her hand, unease settling in her stomach as Edward continued. "For other things though, I fear it is completely useless."

Edward slid a chair out from its place at the table and quickly lowered himself into it before clasping his hands together and bringing them to his mouth as he fell silent.

Elinor and Marianne's eyes met before Elinor turned to look at their mother, who watched Edward with a slight frown. All three women noticed how different he appeared, as if he were exhausted, almost… defeated.

"Edward, I apologize but, you seem… unhappy?" Mary's hesitant comment pulled Edward out of his thoughts, his focus moving to the others in the room before pausing on Elinor for a moment too long.

"Do I? Forgive me, I am…" he gave a small humorless laugh "I apologize, I'm prone to dark moods from time to time." His shoulders fell as he continued . "Perhaps it would have been better if I had not come at all but– I did want to see you all." His eyes rose to meet Elinor's again, and she felt her cheeks warm under his gaze.

"We are of course very happy that you have come to visit with us, it is good to see you after so many months." Mary's voice was soothing, but it made Edward swallow as if facing the strongest chastisement, but his eyes did not leave Elinor's.

"I am sorry that it has taken me so long to come to visit you. It was not my intent." Edward responded, his eyes now firmly focused on the floor, not looking up to any of the ladies in the room.

Elinor's mouth opened, but she could not find the words she wanted to say, her mind a flurry of questions that she both wanted to know and yet was afraid of having answered, because something in his manner was unnerving her. When his eyes finally did rise to meet hers she had to swallow her gasp, there was no denying the pain in their depths.

CHAPTER FIFTEEN

The next morning Elinor's mood was as wretched as the weather, the slow steady drone of rain blanketed the countryside. Her thoughts were spinning as she helped Jonathan and Martha set the table for breakfast.

As happy as she was to have Edward visit, the difference between the man who had sat at their table and who had spent his days with her at Norland Park was stark. The Edward she remembered always had a smile on his face or in his eyes, a humor that he could not help but reveal. The Edward from the day before however seemed hollow, a shade of that man, as if the troubles of the world had beaten him down. While he still smiled, it was a shade of how vibrant he had appeared.

Elinor knew it was silly to base her opinion off the short time they had spent together at Norland, however the moments were engrained in her memories, cherished in the night. She was happy, so very happy, that he had come to visit them, and while she knew her family felt the same, she couldn't help but think that Edward had come not to visit *them*, but to see *her*.

Why then did his eyes hold the hint of despair in them?

"It was good to see Edward, was it not?" Mary's voice drew Elinor out of her thoughts with a small smile.

"Yes, Mama, it was."

"I am so glad he came to visit, my letter to him had expressed that it had been much too long indeed since we had seen him last."

"Mama, you didn't." Elinor gasped, then raised her hand to her head as her mother nodded with a sly smile.

"Of course I did, he is family in a way after all, and perhaps, in the future, in a much closer state of kin?"

"Mothherrr..." Elinor sighed as she shook her head. "There was never any talk of that, please, I hope you did not invite him here in the hopes of something more than what already exists between us."

"Well, my dear, you think of the sensible, and I will hope for the sensational." Mary winked as she grabbed a small slice of bread to nibble on.

A steady, almost rhythmic *thunk* from outside startled the occupants of the room, Jonathan and Martha quickly moving to check the source.

"That could not be Marianne could it?" Mary breathed as she looked to Elinor.

"No," Elinor shook her head as she worried her lip, "she was still quite asleep when I came down."

"It's Lord Edward!" Jonathan exclaimed, his head leaning back in the door, his hair plastered to his head from the rain.

"Edward? What is he doing out there in this weather?" Elinor gasped as she grabbed a rain shawl and draped it over her head. She ran out the door, Jonathan's words muffled by the rain as he called after her.

It did not take long for Elinor to see what Edward was doing, but the sight that met her eyes stunned her.

Edward stood in the rain, his head tilted back, his eyes closed to keep out the moisture. While that picture was striking enough, her heart began to race at his appearance. His coat had long since been discarded, and the rain had molded his shirt to his torso, revealing the long, slim lines of his chest to her.

His head tilted forward as he lifted the axe she just now realized he held before bending to grab a cord of wood, placing it on the block before splitting it easily in two. The ripple of muscles along his arms and back had her mouth opening in wonder, in awe of the ease of his movements. She watched him, entranced, as he split cord after cord of wood before he finally lowered the axe.

She could almost hear his sigh as he wiped at his face with his sodden sleeve and turned, freezing when he saw her watching him. His eyes met hers, their Cobalt depths burning hers with their intensity, neither daring to move other than to breathe for fear of losing the connection.

After several moments Edward tore his gaze from hers, forcing himself to turn away as he grabbed another cord and continued to split it into firewood.

"Edward?" Elinor asked hesitantly, the question clear in her voice as she stepped closer.

"I saw the logs," he grunted, swinging the ax down into the cord, "I enjoy this work." He tossed the split wood onto the pile, now substantially larger than it had been. "It lets... lets you work through your feelings."

Elinor's mouth fell open as she watched him, her eyes entranced by the muscles rippling under his shirt for a few moments before he sighed and swung the axe to rest in the block.

"You have so little help here." He whispered, his voice almost hidden in the sound of the rain.

"Edward... even so, we do manage." Elinor responded softly, her eyes meeting his. "It is a much smaller house to maintain and..."

"Yes but... If... If only..." Edward ran his hand through his hair, barely reacting to the water that poured from it. His eyes closed for a moment before he turned to grab the ax again and set up a new block of wood. Elinor saw his Adam's apple bob as he appeared to swallow, as if biting back his words.

"What is it?" She asked hesitantly as she took a step towards him, pausing when he raised a hand.

"It's nothing... nothing that I can speak of." He brought the axe down, its speed harder than he had swung it previously, and Elinor flinched as the wood splintered under the tool.

"I should never have come here." Edward panted, his eyes closing as he leaned over the axe, now deeply embedded into the block.

"We are– no, I am glad that you did." Elinor whispered, unable to stop herself from moving to stand next to the man breathing heavily before her. His face jerked towards hers, his Cobalt eyes capturing hers. She gasped at the pain that she saw reflected in them, her hand moving to cover her mouth as her own eyes filled.

"Edward..."

"I'm sorry." Edward strode past Elinor, pausing for a moment beside her as his jaw set. Elinor saw his hands clench into fists in that moment as he shook his head faintly, water dancing in the air from his hair at the movement. After one brief, *searing* look, one that left Elinor feeling breathless and at the same time exhilarated, he turned and stalked back into the house, never once looking back.

"What has happened to you?" Elinor whispered as she stood, uncaring in the rain, her thoughts consumed with the pain she had seen reflected in his eyes.

By the time she made her way back to the cottage Edward had prepared his horse, or perhaps it had already been prepared before he even had gone to the woodshed, she did not know. She listened to Marianne and her mother try to talk Edward into staying, at least until the rain let up, but she knew he would not.

Edward slid his jacket over his wet shirt as his gaze met Elinor's, his eyes never leaving hers as the others spoke around him. He tore his face away from her to mount his horse, only to meet hers again as soon as he was astride. He swallowed, and Elinor once again saw the flash of pain in his face, yet the only word he said was...

"Goodbye."

Elinor felt ice forming in her stomach as fear began to creep in, fear that maybe... just maybe... this goodbye was for good, and she would never see him again. Her tears were thankfully hidden in the rain, but it seemed Edward could still see them, or knew they were there, for his gaze softened as he watched her, before mouthing another, silent, *'goodbye'* before turning and spurring his horse down the path.

Elinor felt Marianne's arm slide around her waist, her sister's head dropping to her shoulder as the sisters held each other, watching Edward disappear down the path before turning to enter the cottage, no longer caring about the rain.

None of the occupants of the cottage mentioned Edward or his visit for the rest of the day, their spoken words very carefully chosen to not mention the man, nor the troubled countenance of Elinor's face as her mind spun with thoughts. That was... until the privacy of their bedroom.

"Despite how long it has been since we last saw him, it was clear to me and to Mama that Edward is as in love with you as ever." Marianne turned to her side, her eyes on the figure in the other bed. "Did he speak of it to you?"

Elinor fell silent, her thoughts on each moment she had spent with Edward in the few hours he had been there. The looks of longing, of pain... the words he had spoken, how broken he looked...

"No." She whispered, her eyes closing against tears that threatened to fall.

Marianne, for once, was silent as she watched her sister's struggle in the moonlight. She held her tongue until Elinor wiped her eyes with a sigh.

"What do you suppose he came here for then, if not to propose to you?"

Elinor turned to her side, curling an arm around her stomach as the other gripped her pillow.

"I don't know." She admitted, her voice low. That was the one thing she had been trying to puzzle out since he had appeared at the cottage.

As Marianne turned to settle in to sleep Elinor let her thoughts wander, her mind easily recalling the vision Edward had made in his wet shirt, his muscles clearly on display as he moved. The Edward in her mind raised his head, his eyes meeting hers and she felt a flush of warmth rush through her. Whomever had said absence weakened the heart was a fool, she found herself more drawn to him now than at Norland Park. She wanted to soothe the pain, to make him smile, to laugh with him, to ki...

With a sigh Elinor tried to push her thoughts to the side. While she had no way of knowing what in truth had brought Edward to answer her mother's letter, she knew there was little sense in letting herself be carried away by thoughts of fantasy. Wishing Edward were hers would not make it so, and she could not let herself cling to hope when there were things to be done around the cottage. No, dreaming was Marianne's realm, one she would let her sister handle with the grace Marianne had.

Yet that didn't stop thoughts of Edward from dancing through her dreams that night, nor the weeks that followed.

CHAPTER SIXTEEN

Several weeks had gone by since Edward's visit, and the family's spirits had yet to be lifted out of the pallor that plagued them. Elinor attributed a good amount of that to the weather, it had been raining for almost the entire time, making it difficult to escape the house and her own thoughts.

Marianne had sat at the piano for hours on end, playing one song over and over again, but whenever Elinor had thought to ask her to please play something, anything, else, she would look over and see her sister's hand on the edge of the sheet music, the first book that Brandon had brought her, and held her tongue.

The only gentleman that had not been spoken of during that period was Willoughby, something that had confused Mary but did not surprise Elinor at all.

"HELLOOOOOO!" The loud voice from outside the window had all three ladies jumping, so lost in their own thoughts they had not heard the commotion on the path. They turned to see Middleton beaming at them from outside before he turned and gestured to others down the path.

"Ugggh are we never to have a moment's peace." Marianne groaned, her head hitting the dining room table, just missing the mending she had been attempting to get right, for the 4th time.

"Oh *there* you all are!" Mrs. Jennings exclaimed as she entered the room, her arms wide for a hug as her eyes twinkled. "I have brought a surprise for you all, my granddaughter Charlotte and her husband Thomas, all the way from London have come to visit." She turned and ushered in a young woman with straight black hair, whose hand was held by a stern faced man with kind eyes, freckles across his nose. "I had no idea that it was them, when I heard the horses I thought it may have been Colonel Brandon returning." Marianne's face lit up at the thought, but then began to fall as Mrs. Jennings continued. "I was delighted to see it was Charlotte and Thomas, and I knew we must immediately bring them over to meet you all."

"It is so wonderful to meet you, I have heard such wonderful things about you all from Grandmother." Charlotte smiled as she reached out and clasped Elinor's hand. "I hope you do not mind but I do hope we will be friends, it is such a delight to have the company of other young women here in the country!"

"My dear, you just left your cousins back at the house." Middleton chuckled as Charlotte made a face, wrapping her arm around Thomas's again.

"Yes but... Anne can be exhausting." Charlotte sighed. "Lucy is lovely, but Anne requires so much energy to keep up with her."

"Yes but Lucy is so looking forward to meeting the Miss Dashwoods." Mrs. Jennings said as she lowered herself into a chair. "It has been all she has spoken about since she arrived."

"Ah, yes, and that brings us to the purpose of our visit!" Middleton grinned, "You are all commanded to the House for dinner tonight!" Before Mary could make any protest, he continued. "Ah ah ah, I shall hear no denials, I shall send the carriage for you at four o'clock, that way we have time for introductions before dinner and will have time for a visit."

"We must be away, much to do to prepare for tonight." Mrs. Jennings pushed herself out of the chair and glanced at the clock on the mantle. "Come along my dears, we will see you all this evening."

The exit of the four visitors was as loud and energetic as their entrance only a few minutes before. Mary opened and closed her mouth several times, at a complete loss for words as she turned to look at her daughters, who both stared back, equally as dumbstruck.

"Shall I lay out new clothing then, Ma'am?" Marta asked hesitantly from the door.

"Yes, I suppose you shall." Mary sighed as she ran her hand over her forehead.

Marianne groaned and let her head fall back to the table. It was going to be a long night.

The carriage, true to form, arrived promptly at a quarter past 4 that afternoon, and Elinor had to tug Marianne's hand to get her to enter the vehicle.

"Do we really have to go?" Marianne whined as Elinor gently pushed her to the cushion.

"Yes," Mary said sternly, before smiling slightly when Marianne crossed her arms with a pout. "Don't be like that Marianne, there will be several young women there for you to speak with and spend time with."

"Who probably won't have a thought in their heads." Marianne muttered.

"Marianne!" Elinor chided as she elbowed her sister. "Charlotte seemed perfectly lovely."

"Fine, Charlotte will be lovely to see and get to know, but I make no promises on the cousins."

"Do try to at least *act* like you are enjoying yourself dear. I know that nothing has really interested you since Willoughby left, but please, try to make an effort." Mary sighed as the horses started to move, shaking the entire carriage.

"It's not Willoughby that I…" Marianne muttered, Elinor only just catching the sound before Marianne's cheeks turned pink as she pursed her lips, stopping her words.

After a few moments of tension building in the silence, Elinor found herself asking: "Why do you suppose Mrs. Jennings said Charlotte's cousins were interested in meeting us?"

"I suppose Mrs. Jennings told her granddaughter about us moving in, and she may have told her cousins." Mary supplied, eying her youngest who continued to grumble in the corner. "We shall find out soon enough." As the main house came into view Mary leaned forward to bat at Marianne's leg with her fan. "And no more grumbling out of you, at least until we are on our way back home."

Marianne sighed as the carriage drew to a close. "Yes Mama."

Middleton smiled as the butler escorted the ladies into the drawing room, a mug of ale in his hand as he gestured to them.

"Ah, Mrs. Dashwood, Miss Dashwood, Miss Marianne Dashwood, allow me to introduce my cousins, the Misses Steele, Lucy and Anne."

Elinor turned to see the two newest members of the group standing side by side as they dropped into a slight curtsey. One girl had the thickest mane of black hair that Elinor had ever seen, shining and falling halfway down her back. The other had hair almost the same brown as Elinor's, the strands intricately arranged atop her head.

"What a fine pair of pretty girls, are they not?" Elinor could hear the pride in Middleton's voice as the girl with brown hair's cheeks began to flush, the pink flattering her complexion.

"Oh Lord Middleton, for shame!" The raven hair woman laughed, pausing only a moment before launching into a very enthusiastic retelling of their experiences in Devonshire since they had arrived earlier that day.

'*That must be Anne*' Elinor found herself thinking when the young woman grabbed Marianne's hand, talking so quickly Marianne could not get a word in edgewise and pulling her towards the sitting area. Marianne threw a quick glance over her shoulder, a plea for help, but was quickly drawn too far away for assistance. Elinor turned her attention to the other cousin, Lucy if she remembered correctly, and found the woman shaking her head slightly in apology before moving to follow her sister.

"How do you like Devonshire, Miss Dashwood?" Anne asked as she settled onto the couch, Marianne taking her chance during Anne's distraction to distance herself from the very energetic girl. "Have you found any smart beaux? I cannot say there are as many here as there are in Sussex, it seems the estates are much larger here so I cannot imagine there is much opportunity for running into anyone."

Elinor started for a moment at Anne's words, unsure of how to respond, but Lucy responded first.

"Anne, why are you always talking of beaux?"

"Well, I know some young ladies do not care for them, but I think they are vastly agreeable, don't you agree Miss Dashwood? Well, that is if they dress smart and behave civilly, there is nothing worse than a beau who is not civil don't you think? Or one who appears dirty and nasty, well, then they are better off not to be a beau."

"I..." Elinor started to respond, only for Anne to interrupt her.

"Now we have heard everything about your sister's conquest, even as far as Sussex. It does appear that Lord Willoughby is thought of as one of the smartest beau that anyone could wish for, handsome, a lord in his own right, even though he is a Fae. It must be exciting, don't you agree, to think of being married so young?"

Marianne let out a huff at those words as she turned and fled to their mother's side, abandoning Elinor to the sisters.

"Well you see..."

"And I hope you may have as good of luck yourself soon, though I do worry about the lack of beau out here, although you may have a friend in the corner already, a lovely woman such as you, I am sure you have a beau from when you were at Norland."

"Oh indeed she has," Middleton interjected, quite familiar with how Anne was when she got going. "And I have heard that he was in the neighborhood quite recently as well."

Elinor's eyes met Marianne's, who gave a little roll of hers as Anne immediately responded.

"Oh do tell! How exciting, what is his name?"

"Well that is a great secret I am afraid," Middleton chuckled, "all we know is that it begins with the letter F."

"We know a young man whose name begins with F, a Mr. Ferrars!" Anne's face lit up as she looked around the room. "I must say he is quite the agreeable young man, we know him very well, very well indeed."

"Anne, how can you say so?" Lucy interrupted, her hand reaching out to clasp her sister's knee. "We have seen Mr. Ferrars what, once or twice in Sussex, but truly that is too much to pretend we know him that well."

"Oh, I always say the wrong thing, do not pay me any mind." Anne giggled, missing the glare her sister threw her way.

"Yes, you do." Lucy's voice was flat, making Elinor tilt her head in curiosity. "Oh look, the rain has let up, and it looks beautiful outside. Miss Dashwood, would you do me the honor of taking a walk with me, I feel that the fresh air may do us well."

"I... well I..." Elinor looked up and saw the pleading in Lucy's eyes. She let her shoulders drop as she responded "of course."

As they exited the house into the gardens, Elinor had to admit that the sun on her face was much appreciated, after several weeks inside she had longed for some sun and fresh air, but it had been her preference to experience it on her own, not with another young lady, other than her sister.

"I wonder, Miss Dashwood, are you acquainted with your sister-in-law's mother, Mrs. Ferrars?" Lucy asked, her hands clasped in front of her as she walked.

"I... no, I have never had the pleasure of meeting her." Elinor responded. "I did not realize that you were connected with their family, I have only met Fanny and Mr. Edward Ferrars."

"Oh Miss Dashwood, if I dared to tell you all, I do think you would be very much surprised." Lucy smiled, a slight chuckle in her tone. "Mrs. Ferrars is nothing to me at present, but I do think there may come a time when we will be very intimately acquainted."

"Oh? Are you acquainted with Mr. Robert Ferrars?" Elinor asked, only half paying attention to the conversation.

"Robert Ferrars? Oh no not with him, I have never met him in my life!" Lucy quickly corrected her as Elinor's attention was drawn fully to the conversation, a ball of ice now forming in her stomach. "I mean his elder brother, Mr. Edward Ferrars."

"Mr. Edward Ferrars...?" Elinor was both curious and at the same time, full of dread at how the conversation had turned, praying that the woman in front of her did not say what Elinor feared...

"We are engaged."

Elinor felt the ball of ice in her stomach strengthen, her entire body frozen in anguish at the words.

"You... are engaged to... Mr. Edward Ferrars?" Elinor whispered, not daring to speak any louder for fear her voice would give away the breaking of her heart. Perhaps she had heard wrong, Lucy could not possibly mean...

"Yes! Oh of course you are surprised because it was always meant to be a great secret." Lucy gushed, the tension in her shoulders visibly easing. "The only one who knows of it is Anne. It would be terrible if it were to reach his mother, I am not sure if she would approve. I have no fortune, and his mother is a very proud woman, who wants only the best for her son."

Elinor could not hear all of Lucy's words through the blood rushing through her head. Thoughts of Edward the last time she had seen him flickered through her mind, the sadness in them, the pain.

'I should not have come.'

Elinor found herself relying on all of her strength to not show the anguish she was feeling to the woman who stood beside her... the woman who had taken away her happiness without ever knowing it. There was only one thought left that Elinor had, one thing she needed to cling to.

"Is your engagement one of long standing?"

"We have been engaged for the past four years." Lucy blushed as she smiled. Her eyes dropped to the ground, and she missed the stunned expression that Elinor could not hide.

"Four years?" Elinor murmured. That was well before she had met Edward, before her brother had even married Fanny.

"We met at my uncle's, he works as a school master, and Edward was sent to learn from him and was under his care." Lucy continued on, oblivious to the pain she was causing her companion. "It has been four years, almost the entire length of the engagement, since we have been able to see each other or spend time together, writing to each other truly is our only comfort. We have very little of each other, I have only a small portrait of him."

Elinor's gaze dropped to the floor. Now it made sense, his discomfort when alone with Elinor. But still, why, if he was engaged for years, had he come to visit their cottage, why would he have answered her mother's letter by coming in person, rather than writing, if that is what he was able to do with his fiance.

"Miss Dashwood, Elinor... Please promise you will not breathe a word of this to any other soul. Please." Lucy took Elinor's hand, clasping it between her own. "Please promise."

Elinor paused, torn. This woman had in a night stolen all the secret hopes that Elinor had for Edward, but at the same time, was a woman in love, worried about that being discovered.

"I never sought your confidence, Miss Steele." Elinor responded, her eyes rising to meet Lucy's. "But your secret is safe with me, I will not tell another soul."

Lucy's eyes lit up as she smiled, wrapping her arm through Elinor's as they continued their walk. The rest of the evening was a blur, Elinor was aware that she had eaten, but could not tell you what had been served or who had said what for the rest of the night. She knew that Marianne and Mary were concerned about how withdrawn she had become, but she could not tell them anything. There was no one she could share her pain with, no one she could rant to because of a promise made to the one who had dashed all her dreams.

This was why she did not want to let herself dream, to think of things that she had known would never come to pass. She had more sense than that, she needed to be practical, to live only in the here and now and not think of what could be or should be, someone needed to hold her family sturdy, and that had always fallen on her. On the carriage ride back she let one tear fall, excusing it away as dust that had gotten into her eye, all while knowing her mother and sister did not believe her, but also that they wouldn't press her.

At least, not right away.

"What was the long conversation you had with Lucy Steele about?" Marianne asked softly as they were preparing for bed, her curiosity and worry about Elinor finally getting the best of her.

"Nothing of consequence." Elinor replied, lifting her face to the ceiling. "She was sharing her hopes and dreams of the future."

Half an answer was still a truthful answer.

"Well that sounds very uninteresting for such a long conversation."

"Yes, quite." Elinor agreed quietly, listening as Marianne quieted into sleep.

It was several hours before she felt herself finally nodding off, her thoughts jumbled with Lucy's confession, Edward's visit to the cottage, and his appearance at Norland.

The next morning Elinor excused herself, claiming she had been longing for the fresh air and sunshine that the day promised, and fled to a small cave she had found nestled by the beach, one she knew that Marianne had no interest in visiting.

Once she reached the cave Elinor made her way towards the back, barely visible in the light, before falling back against the cave wall, unable to stop the stream of tears from her eyes. She needed this moment alone to finally process everything that had been revealed to her, to let herself grieve for the loss of... she didn't even really know what, a dream, a fantasy? That was all that Edward had been to her, the dream of a man she could be happy with, share her days with.

The crashing of the waves against the rocks matched her mood perfectly as she stared out to the sea, her mind filled with everything and yet nothing at the same time. She drew out the small book that Edward had given her, staring at the inscription he had written.

Your affectionate Friend- E. Ferrars.

Elinor sighed as she pushed off of the wall, suddenly aware of the angle of the sun and knowing that her sister would come searching for her soon if she did not return.

Friend. That was all she was, and all she would be.

That was all there was.

CHAPTER SEVENTEEN

The next week saw the Dashwood's as frequent guests of Middleton and the ladies of his household. While Elinor took care to *not* be left alone with Lucy again, the looks from the young woman would both enrage her and fill her with ice at the same time. Elinor had taken great care to school her face, to bury her emotions, there was no point in letting her inner turmoil show.

"Elinor, Marianne, I was thinking of spending a month or two in London." Mrs. Jennings announced one day while the sisters were playing cards with Anne. "I would be very glad to have your company if you both would like to join me."

"Mama!" Marianne cried, her eyes going to her mother's with hope. London was where the *Ton* was, but also where the Crown was, and the Crown meant that there was a chance that...

"You are very kind, ma'am, but I am sure that our mother could not spare us for that long of a time." Elinor said, and Marianne felt her shoulders drop, as excited as she was about the possibility of going to London and having the chance to see... no she could not leave her mother alone for that long.

"Oh, I could," Mary chuckled as she lay her cards down and turned to her daughters, "I could indeed. I think it is an excellent idea."

"I would prefer to stay here with you Mama." Elinor reasoned, her eyes darting from her mother's to meet Lucy's stare.

"And what obstacle is my dear sensible Elinor going to present?" Mary chided, "Do not let it be about the expense of it."

"I would like to go to London." Marianne moved to wrap her arm around her mother's shoulder as she spoke, leaning down to kiss Mary's forehead.

"Well of course you would Miss Marianne," Mrs. Jennings chuckled, "and I think we all know the reason why!" Marianne's smile soured, no, it wasn't for the reason they may think, but... "And I dare say that Miss Elinor has just as good a reason if the truth were known." Mrs. Jennings continued.

"Mama, are you sure?" Elinor was hesitant, but a look at her mother's face had her grimacing inside.

"I insist upon it." Elinor knew there was no challenge or going against her mother's wishes and sighed. She would make the best of it that she could, and perhaps the change of scenery would do her some good, help make new memories to chase away those that haunted her.

"You see Miss Elinor, your sister longs to go, and longs for you to go as well!" Mrs. Jennings smiled as she spoke. "There is no need for any more demurrals, your mother and I have already settled it all between us, and to London you both will go!"

Marianne and Elinor spent the next several days packing, Mary overseeing to make sure they were bringing their best gowns, even though they could not go to the Modiste for new ones to be made.

"I am surprised at you Marianne," Marianne stopped her folding at her sister's words. "You say you do not enjoy the teasing that Mrs. Jennings loves so much, and yet you freely volunteered for more of it."

"I would put up with that and more for the chance of going to London, seeing the town, some distraction, and perhaps seeing the soldiers, if they are still there." Her cheeks flushed as she spoke. "Besides, I am more surprised that you do not seem excited about the thought of seeing Edward, he was heading to London when he left here wasn't he?"

"I... well... perhaps we will be able to see him." Elinor said, proud of how steady her voice was. "He has his family to attend to, and I am sure they have him attending different functions throughout the town."

"Oh, I am sure we will see him, and quite soon." Marianne came to her sister's side and put her hand on Elinor's shoulder as her voice softened. "He loves you Elinor, that is quite obvious. He will find a way to see you, no matter what obligations his family puts him to."

Elinor did not... could not... respond to her sister, her only acknowledgement of the words was to duck her head and step away, folding the last of her linens into her suitcase. She knew better, she knew that Edward would not seek her out, for she was not the one that he loved, but she could not say that to Marianne without breaking Lucy's confidence... and admitting that she was wrong, that her entire family was wrong. No, there would be time for that later, after the pain had eased and more time had passed, when it would make sense for them to have grown apart and she would not have to answer questions from Mary and Marianne.

Thankfully the excitement of the trip to London captured Marianne's attention as Jonathan had loaded up the carriage. Mrs. Jennings had thankfully answered every one of Marianne's questions, chuckling at her wide-eyed excitement as the skyline of London came into view after the end of the day.

"Come my dears, we have arrived." Mrs. Jennings said as the carriage began to slow, before drawing to a stop at a home near the park. Marianne's eyes sparkled as she took in the area, her smile growing at the footmen who approached to open the door. It felt nice to be reminded of what it had been like at Norland, even if it was only for a short while.

"These are the Misses Dashwood," Mrs. Jennings explained to the servants, "I would like them to be treated like royalty while they stay with us. If there is anything you want, please let Trevor know, and he will attend to it for you, won't you Trevor?"

"Indeed ma'am." The gentleman Mrs. Jennings had spoken to nodded to her, and then bowed to Marianne and Elinor.

"Come now, let me show you to your rooms, they were Charlotte's, and her mother's before her, before they both left to wed. I do hope you will both be comfortable here."

Marianne's eyes were wide as she looked around the room before landing on the desk, complete with quill and paper. She let Mrs. Jennings continue to show Elinor around as she quickly sat and began writing. She knew it was a long shot, but if there was a chance that Brandon was in London, it was worth trying wasn't it? That way she could know for sure if she really had missed *him*, or if it was another of her flights of fancy that had been conflated in her mind. Would she have the same reaction to him now that Willoughby was not around, or was it merely that she had enjoyed having the attention of both men?

Though while she was at it... she took another piece of paper and began to compose a second letter, this one addressed to Willoughby. While she hadn't missed him quite as much as others seem to think she had, there were still some unanswered questions in her mind, such as why had he left, what had been said by his clan. While she may not have been completely in love with him, her heart had been engaged, and yes, it stung her pride a bit that he had walked away so easily, but if she could get answers, then she wanted them.

She was so engrossed in her writing she did not see Mrs. Jennings's smirk or hear her whisper to Elinor.

"Trevor..." Marianne called out as she made her way through the house, seeking the servant; she presumed he must be the butler, to see if he would be able to help her. When she did see him she quickened her step, nearly running to the small man. "Would you be so good as to take these to the post for me?"

"Would you prefer the penny post or the two penny post miss?" Trevor asked as he took them from her.

"I.... two penny for this one." Marianne touched the letter that she had addressed to Brandon, "penny post is fine for the second."

"Very good miss, I will take them straight away."

"I do hope the letters reach them." Marianne whispered as she watched Trevor descend the stairs.

"I'm sure they will." Elinor responded, causing Marianne to jump, not having realized her sister was behind her.

"Will you write to Edward?" Marianne asked as she leaned into her sister with a sigh.

"... perhaps." Elinor's eyes slid to the window as she spoke, and Marianne tilted her head at hat.

"You should." Marianne said as she straightened and stepped away. "I'm sure he would answer straight away."

'*At least one of us is sure of that.*' Elinor thought as she followed her sister.

The next few hours passed with Marianne checking the window every few minutes, not quite sure of what she expected... or who.

"Oh do come away from the window, your young man will not come any sooner for having watched every moment. It is getting to be a little late for any visitors to come calling, no matter how much you may want to see them."

"It is not too late," Marianne insisted, even though she reluctantly pulled herself from the window. She knew she was being impatient, but now, weeks after not seeing either gentleman, if there was a chance of getting an answer to her questions, she wanted them, no matter how unreasonable it was.

She froze when she heard a knock at the door.

"There, what was that?" She whispered, knowing Mrs. Jennings could hear her.

"It was for the house next door, I am sure." Mrs. Jennings cautioned, shaking her head as she went back to her cards.

When the knock sounded again all three women sat up straight.

"No, I daresay that was here wasn't it." Mrs. Jennings murmured.

"Marianne." Elinor whispered, her hand coming out to grab her sister's wrist, her eyes filled with concern.

"I know," Marianne whispered back, "it may not be either of them, but Elinor, if it were one of the…"

"Colonel Brandon, Ma'ams." Trevor's voice stopped Marianne's words as she spun, her chocolate eyes meeting the gold that danced through her dreams. As he lifted the hat off his head, his ears twitching to catch the sound in the room, her breath caught.

Images played through Marianne's mind as she took in his appearance, the smile as they walked through the gardens, his ease with his staff, but also the kiss with Willoughby, the times she drew away from Brandon at Willoughby's insistence, Brandon's ears disappearing into his hair as he tore his hat apart.

Her heart began to race as she had to force herself to breathe.

"I…" Marianne began, only to stop. Now, face to face with the one she had hoped to see for *weeks*, her words failed her. "I…" she began again, stopping when forced to swallow around the lump in her throat. She closed her eyes as she felt them begin to fill with tears, tears of regret for how she had behaved but also of shame. She had been so foolish, so caught up in what she thought she should have wanted that she had ignored him, abandoned him time and time again, and now that he was here, now that she could discuss how she felt, she found herself hesitant.

Brandon's head lifted from its slight bow, his eyes meeting hers once again, stunning her with their intensity and what almost looked like… hope buried in them for only a moment. But was that hope that she would say she wanted to spend time with him, or the hope that she was now officially bound to another and the freedom that it would provide him.

"Excuse me." She choked out, quickly fleeing past Brandon, her shoulder brushing against his arm in her haste.

"Is your sister well, Miss Dashwood?" His voice echoed in the halls as Marianne hurried through them, fleeing to the sanctuary of her room.

"I... I believe she is just over tired from the trip, we have only arrived today." Elinor's voice was light,

"Colonel Brandon, it is a delight to see you after so long." Mrs. Jennings interjected, false joy easily heard in her tone as she tried to lighten the mood. "I hope all is well with the Queen?"

"I– ah– yes, the matter is now as resolved as it could be."

"Good, with this nonsense with Napoleon I know she and her husband have come to rely on your advice and counsel." Mrs. Jennings pushed herself up to stand before Brandon, taking his hand in hers. "Your Country owes you a great deal of gratitude, Colonel."

"No gratitude is needed, Mrs. Jennings." Brandon's lips curled slightly, his cheeks taking on a pink hue, and Elinor found herself smiling as she realized it meant he was embarrassed. Her smile faded as he turned his golden gaze to meet hers. "I do wonder if I may have a moment in private with Miss Dashwood though, I hope you do not mind Mrs. Jennings."

Mrs. Jennings's eyes went wide as she glanced at Elinor, confusion apparent in her face. "I, no, of course not, I will let you two be. I believe I, " she paused for a moment before nodding, "yes, I will go and check on Marianne, to be sure she is ok after our journey."

Brandon's claws pierced the edge of his hat as he gave Mrs. Jennings a small nod, his eyes locked on the floor until the door closed behind her. His head then raised, piercing Elinor with the intensity of his gaze. His jaw clenched for a moment before his lips pulled back into a grimace, his fangs glinting in the fading sunlight as he turned to glance out the window.

"Miss Dashwood, I..." he hesitated before letting out a slight growl and shaking his head. "I believe I know the truth, but I still have to ask. Are there congratulations in order for your family?"

"I'm sorry, Colonel, but I am not sure what you mean." Elinor's head tilted in puzzlement as she watched the man before her shift uncomfortably.

"I have heard talk of Miss Marianne's betrothal to Lord Willoughby."

"But, how can that be?" Elinor cried in alarm. "Who would say such a thing?"

"Several people, all of whom made a point to tell me as they saw me, knowing my connection to Middleton and Mrs. Jennings." As Elinor's face settled into a grimace his ears began to emerge from his hair as they fully tuned to Elinor. "Miss Dashwood, is everything finally settled?"

"As far as my mother and I know, we cannot say they are betrothed. Nothing has been said to either of us." Elinor paused, taking in the face of the man she spoke to, unsure of how to respond. "I can say that he had gone to the council of his clan to speak with them and asked for a moment of time with my sister, but he left quickly after speaking with them, and Marianne has said not a word of any formal commitment between them."

Brandon's eyes lost some of their glimmer as she spoke, his face falling at the mention of the council of the Allendale Fae.

"If that is the case, then, I wish your sister all imaginable happiness, and to Lord Willoughby, that he may endeavor to deserve her." His lips curved once again into a grimace as he turned away. "I bid you goodnight."

"Colonel..." Elinor called out, but Brandon never paused as he stormed out of the house. He stopped only for a moment after stepping to the street before striding away, never looking back to see the chocolate eyes that followed him from the upstairs window.

The rest of the evening Marianne was unusually subdued and quiet, leaving Mrs. Jennings to try and fill the silence with humor and discussions of who they would meet around the town and all the people she needed to introduce the sisters to. Eventually, however, she conceded to the mood of the evening, withdrawing to her private chambers and leaving Marianne and Elinor to their thoughts.

"Colonel Brandon was disappointed to not be able to see you." Elinor stated as she prepared herself for bed.

"He did see me." Marianne's voice was soft as she pulled the cover of her bed over herself.

"For all of five seconds Marianne. You know he has a great fondness and regard for you."

"And I for him." Was Marianne's response, her voice barely audible through the blankets.

"Then why did you flee when he arrived?"

"I... I do not know."

"I thought you had wanted to see him."

"I did... I still do."

"Then why?"

"Oh I don't KNOW Elinor." Marianne pulled down the blanket with a groan, uncovering her face. "It was... I just... seeing him again, after so long, after all the wondering, the thoughts that I had, the questioning, all that had happened with Willoughby. It was..."

Marianne paused with a groan, drawing the blanket back over her face.

"It was?" Elinor prompted, sitting beside her sister on the bed and running her hand over the top of exposed ebony hair.

"It was overwhelming" was the muffled reply.

"Overwhelming?" Elinor chuckled slightly, the sound growing in laughter when Marianne uncovered her face to show a pout.

"All the things that I thought I should feel for Willoughby, that I tried to convince myself I felt for Willoughby, never appeared. Until they did, the moment I set eyes on Brandon earlier today." When Elinor's chuckle grew into a laugh Marianne glared at her. "It isn't funny Elinor, he is the opposite of everything I have ever said I would look for, he is stern instead of eased, proper rather than carefree. Yes, there may be butterflies in my chest when he looks at me, and my heart nearly melted in the heat of his golden eyes, but is that enough? He is so stoic all the time when we are near Mrs. Jennings and Middleton, Proper with a capital P. But, oh Elinor, he is so different in private, so very different. When we were at Hartland with my mare, there was a side to him with his servants that I had never seen before, one I want to see more often."

"You need to talk with him, Marianne. You need to let him know where things stand."

"But Elinor... where would I even start?" Marianne sighed.

"What is this, you have never been unsure what to say before?"

"Yes but – this is different."

"Well," Elinor began, sliding into the bed next to her sister, "you could start by confirming to him whether you are or are not engaged to Willoughby."

"WHAT?" Marianne cried, bolting upright in bed. "What are you talking about Elinor?"

"That was why he was here today." Elinor pushed herself up with both hands. "He had been told of your betrothal, and wanted to know if it was true."

"But there is no betrothal!" Marianne declared. "Nor, to be completely honest, do I think there ever would be with Willoughby. Even if his Council were to say he could marry me, I do not think that I would accept."

"I thought you liked Lord Willoughby?"

"I do... in a way. But not in the way I think one would need to like their spouse. It is more that he is an amusing diversion, but I realized the more I spent time with him that we discussed nothing beyond the mere surface. There was no depth, no debate. No... sharing of thoughts like we saw with Mama and Papa. With as much time as I spent with him, I cannot truly say I know anything about him, and I daresay he knows nothing about me."

"Did you find that with Brandon?"

"No," Marianne admitted, "but I wonder if that is because I did not give him a chance. Because there were glimpses of it, moments that made me wonder, that drew me to him." She pulled her knees to her chest and wrapped her arms around them. "I was a fool wasn't I?"

"I…"

"I was Elinor, chasing after the dashing young hero, and not the wise sage with hidden facets to uncover. I just hope I have the chance to get to know him better, and that I haven't ruined any potential."

"I do not think you have Marianne." Elinor leaned over to kiss her sister's forehead before drawing her back down to the bed. "The face I saw today was not one of a man who had given up."

Marianne fell quiet as Elinor blew out the candles, murmuring her goodnights to her sister even as her thoughts kept her awake. The thought that Brandon believed her to be engaged to Willoughby… she frowned as she turned as gently as she could in the bed, not wanting to awaken Elinor. She would need to correct that, to let him know there was no engagement and no words to that effect had been spoken between herself and the crimson eyed Fae.

With the beginnings of her plan in place she let herself drift to sleep, a fanged smirk and molten gold eyes teasing the edges of her consciousness as she gave herself to slumber.

CHAPTER EIGHTEEN

The next week had been a form of quiet hell for Marianne. Every time there was a knock at the door, every time Trevor brought a letter into the hall she felt her heart flutter, only for it to stutter with a small sad frown and slight shake of the butler's head. Everyday she had written a letter to the Colonel, but received no response. In her desperation, she had written to Willoughby, of all people, several times to see if he had any information about Brandon's whereabouts, to see if he was in London still or if he had been called away on Fae business.

And yet he had not responded to her in any way either.

"Why does he not come?" She whispered, her nose pushed against the window to scan the street.

"Marianne, come away from the window." Elinor's voice was soothing as she took her sister's arm and pulled her away from the window.

"I do not understand Elinor, he is in town, I know he is." Marianne sighed as she dropped into a chair.

"Give him time, dearest." Elinor smiled faintly. "I am sure that the Colonel is a busy man, he may not have been home to see your letters."

"Oh, the Colonel is quite the busy man, I do say," Mrs. Jennings chuckled, her face showing her amusement as she sipped her tea, quite entertained by the young sisters. "He seems to only be able to relax at Hartland, here he is always out and about or at the palace at Queen Charlotte's command. And do not get me started on when he has interactions with other Fae, I swear the man has no rest when they are involved."

"Busy... yes..." Marianne whispered as she drew her bottom lip into her teeth. She knew she was being silly, just because she had realized, or started to realize, what she wanted did not mean that Brandon knew or felt the same... she only hoped he could feel the same. "Busy..." she murmured again, as her eyes went wide.

Oh she was being a fool. Brandon would not want some childish girl for a wife, who demanded his attention at all times, no, he would need someone who could stand on her own, to step in when he was busy or at the Crown's disposal. Someone... someone like...

"Elinor!" Marianne gasped, her head snapping to look at her sister's suddenly concerned eyes. "I was wondering if..."

"Excuse me, ladies." Trevor's high voice interrupted, and as the trio of women turned he gave a small bow, presenting a silver platter with a letter.

"Is that..." Marianne jumped from her chair only to pause at the slight shake of his head.

"It is for Mrs. Jennings, Ma'am."

"Well, then, let's see this." Mrs. Jennings took the letter and opened it, taking a moment to pursue its contents. A smile began to grow on her face. "Ah, now here is something, Charlotte and Thomas are back from their trip, and they have arrived in London with the Miss Steeles. And oh, they have asked us to join them at an evening assembly this evening." Her eye twinkled as she looked up at Marianne with a shrewd glance, taking in the young girl's face. "You can expect that the Colonel will be invited," she bit back a chuckle as Marianne's face snapped up, her eyes wide, "and I would expect that your "Mr. F" will be in attendance as well if he is in London, it seems everyone who's anyone will be there." Her gaze slid to Elinor, just to see her cheeks pale at the words.

"Come on Elinor, we need to prepare." Marianne gasped, grasping her sister's arm to drag her out of the sitting room.

"I..." Elinor started, only to stop, the ball of ice she had hoped had eased suddenly back in her stomach.

Lucy Steele and Edward... in the same room.

She had never dreaded an evening more in her life.

London gatherings, even the 'small and intimate' function that Mrs. Jennings claimed this was, greatly exceed anything they had seen at either Norland or in Devonshire. There must have easily been more than 200 people in the grand home as they made their entrance, Marianne's eyes darting about to take in everything, Elinor's focused on the floor, afraid to look up.

"Oh it's beautiful," Marianne sighed as she leaned against her sister's arm.

"Yes, quite." Elinor responded half-heartedly.

"Now my dear, none of that," Mrs. Jennings teased as she took Elinor's other arm. "One never knows what they will find at a soiree like this."

Elinor let her eyes rise from the floor to sweep the room, briefly catching a glimpse of long white hair and golden eyes in the corner that were focused on her sister as she looked around the room, but never saw the man she was seeking.

"Ah, there is Charlotte, please excuse me girls." Mrs. Jennings patted Elinor's hand before crossing towards her daughter and son-in-law.

"And then there were two." Marianne whispered, and Elinor let herself smile at her sister's words.

"Oh, Miss Dashwood, Miss Marianne!" A feminine voice had Elinor's pausing, her eyes going wide a moment before a glove-covered hand touched her shoulder. Elinor's back stiffened as she turned, her eyes catching the brown that had been tormenting her dreams for the past few weeks. Anne continued on, not noticing the tension that now filled Elinor. "I dare say that London is very full of smart beau, though I do declare that some of them have been quite rude and naughty." Anne wrapped her arm through Marianne's, pulling her from her sister to whisper loudly, "Look how they preen and ogle at us here on the side, waiting for their moment to pull us into a dance."

"I do hope you will stay by my side then Miss Dashwood," Lucy said as she took the place that Marianne had, capturing Elinor's arm with hers. "I am in such a fever of anticipation that I do fear I will faint."

"Oh, well, I…"

"Oh, Lemonade, come Miss Marianne, we absolutely must have some." Anne cried, dragging Marianne with her across the room, Marianne's eyes meeting Elinor's beseeching her sister for help only to lose sight of her in the crowd.

"They say that he is here tonight," Lucy whispered, her eyes scanning the room.

Elinor swallowed, the ice growing in her stomach. "Whom do you mean?" She squeaked out, knowing propriety demanded it. Lucy's words were vague, but Elinor had little doubt of who she was speaking of.

"Why, Mr. Ferrars of course. Edward"

"Are you sure?"

"Quite! I was told for certain he would be here." Elinor could feel the slight tremor in the other girl's arm and felt the ball of ice churn into nausea.

"Elinor?" Elinor turned at the voice, starting as she looked into the eyes of her sister-in-law. "Elinor, I did not know you were in London, it is so wonderful to see you out and about in true society."

"Fanny," Elinor gave a slight curtsey, however Lucy at her side stayed upright.

"It is so hot and crowded in this room is it not?" Fanny continued, "I do wonder how I would be able to stay even just a moment longer." A young man with black hair tied at the nape of his neck stepped up beside her, a glass of lemonade in his hand. "Oh, Elinor, I do not believe you have met my younger brother, Mr. Robert Ferrars. Robert, allow me to introduce Miss Elinor Dashwood."

"Miss Elinor, I am delighted to meet you." Robert gave a broad smile as he reached out to take Elinor's hand, leaning down to give a bow over it. "My brother Edward has spoken very highly of your beauty, and while I say on the whole he is a very poor judge of women, I must say that in this instance, he was absolutely correct."

You.. ah…" Elinor stuttered, the man's forwardness taking her aback. "You are very kind, sir." She turned to Lucy, noting the distress on her face. "Fanny, Mr. Ferrars, may I present my companion, Miss Lucy Steele."

Robert's blue eyes turned to Lucy, darting over her figure before he nodded, a small smile on his lips. "Charmed, my lady."

Lucy gave a small curtsey, her cheeks flushing pink as her gaze darted back to Elinor. "Is your brother going to be here tonight, Mr. Ferrars?" She asked, her voice coy, and yet the sound of it made Elinor's stomach turn.

"Edward? Oh God no, I swear our brother shuns society. He may be my older brother, and I hate to speak ill of my own relatives, but Edward is truly something of a homebody, he would much prefer to be alone than among others."

"Oh, Mr. Ferrars, how unkind you are to say that." Elinor struggled not to roll her eyes at Lucy's words and how… simpering she sounded.

"Elinor!" Marianne's loud whisper had Elinor turning a moment before her sister grabbed her arm, pausing only to curtsey to Fanny before dragging Elinor away, not even waiting to see if Fanny had responded.

"Marianne? What is it?"

"Willoughby," Marianne responded as they weaved through the crowd. "He is here."

"Willoughby," Elinor's eyes darted around the room until she saw the figure of the Fae in the other room. "But I thought you did not want to see him."

"We are still friends, or so I thought, and I thought he may know more about where Brandon has been." Willoughby turned at the words, his crimson eyes meeting Marianne's for a moment before his face turned into a grimace and he turned away.

"I do not understand, why does he act that way?" Marianne murmured. No, she was not in love with the Fae, but still his actions seemed rude to her.

"Marianne, please, let it go. I'm sure he has his reasons."

"I do not understand…" Marianne murmured, her eyes trailing the Fae as he climbed a slight set of stairs into an adjoining room. "Elinor, I have to find out if he knows anything."

"Marianne, he will know you are here, and if he is able he will come and find you."

"I… but Elinor, he may be able to tell me if Brandon is still in town or away."

"Marianne…" Elinor cried as her sister pulled away, dashing towards the second room. A firm hand caught her around her waist as she started to stumble, and she caught another brief glimpse of long silver hair before Brandon disappeared into the crowd in the direction her sister had gone.

Marianne struggled through the crowd of the *ton* into the other room, her eyes scanning for sight of either Willoughby or, she hoped, Brandon. A bark of laughter caught her attention from a corner, and her gaze turned to see Willoughby, his back towards her, surrounded by what looked to be a group of Fae.

"WILLOUGHBY!" Her exclamation came just as the musicians had slowed their playing, and her voice carried through the rooms, causing all conversation to pause.

Willoughby's shoulders tightened for a moment before she saw them drop and his head shake slightly. A woman with deep red hair and an emerald green dress turned to eye her, one brow raising as she lifted her fan and made a comment that Marianne could not quite make out, but had those in her group chuckling.

"Excuse me." Willoughby set his jaw as he stepped away from the group, his steps slow towards Marianne. After several long moments he stopped and gave a slight nod. "Miss Dashwood, Miss Dashwood..." he let out a soft cough as if clearing his throat, "your mother is doing well, I hope."

"Yes, sir, thank you for asking." Elinor responded after a few moments of silence.

"That is..." Willoughby coughed, his crimson eyes darting momentarily to Marianne before fixing on the wall behind the sisters, "good. Have you been in town long?"

"Willoughby, what is going on?" Marianne interrupted, her brown eyes puzzled with the man's stiff posture. "I have been writing to you but received no response, were my letters delivered?"

Willoughby's shoulders stiffened at the words, his eyes flashing back to Marianne's, and she almost swore she saw a mixture of anger and pain in them, however he stayed silent.

Marianne felt a pang in her chest at his actions and continued silence. No, she could be honest with herself and admit that while her affections for the Fae had never been as deep as they could have been, she had been dazzled by his charm and attentions, and his stiffness and... curtness hurt her more than she had thought they would.

"Will you not at least shake hands with me?" she whispered as she extended a gloved hand. "We are friends, are we not?"

Willoughby's gaze held hers for another moment before his shoulders dropped, his expression turning guarded as he reached out to briefly touch her hand for a moment before letting his drop as if burned.

"I had the pleasure of receiving your letters, Ms. Dashwood, however I..."

"Willoughby, who is this?" The titan haired woman stepped beside him, her hand coming to rest on his shoulder as she tucked her other hand through his arm. Her crimson eyes drifted over Marianne before snapping back to her face.

"Ah, Sophia." Willoughby's smile didn't quite reach his eyes as he looked at the woman who had tucked herself into his side. "These are some acquaintances of mine from Devonshire, I believe I had told you about them and how kind they were to me these past few months."

"Devonshire," Sophia's voice was light as her gaze met Marianne's. "Ah yes, I remember, that was the poor little family you were trying to help out, wasn't it?"

"I... well..." Willoughby cleared his throat, his pale face taking on a red hue in the candlelight. "Miss Dashwood, Miss Dashwood, it was good to see you both again, if you will excuse us."

With those words he turned, drawing Sophia away from the puzzled sisters, however her voice rose as they crossed the room, the words reaching Marianne's ears.

"That was the plain girl that you said you had entertained yourself with? That is *not* what I would consider plain Willoughby..."

"Plain girl?" Marianne whispered, her brow furrowing at the words. "Elinor, I... I do not understand?" Flashes of the time she had spent with him coursed through her head, the poems, the forward behavior, the *kiss*, had he been playing with her the entire time?

Had she been that much a fool that a kind word and a bright smile had blinded her to his true intentions? No, he had gone to the council... or at least had said he had gone to the council...

The noise in the room began to rise around her as her knees began to go weak. Had she been so caught up in the flash of what she thought love was supposed to be that she had been no more than a mere distraction for him? Her first true taste of the whims and games of the males of the *ton*, and she had fallen, well not entirely fallen she would allow herself, but still far enough, into his schemes.

"Elinor... I..." All her sister's warnings, all the comments that Marianne had pushed aside, defended Willoughby against ran through her mind. What the others must think of her, and that Brandon thought she was engaged to

Willoughby… had she been so blind as to what was going on around her? Her sister was right, she was nothing more than a child pretending to understand how the world worked, and in that moment, she felt everything she had thought she had known crumble.

She took a step towards Elinor, her sister watching her with concern in her eyes before darting them just over Marianne's shoulder and back, her arms raising to hold her sister close.

Marianne's legs gave out before they could meet, the shock of the evening taking its toll on her. Not of Willoughby's behavior, no, while that hurt it did not cause this reaction, but her view of the world had shattered, taking with it everything she thought she had known.

A strong pair of arms caught her, drawing her back against a firm chest as a hand wrapped around her waist. Loose silver hair draped over her shoulder as Brandon curled himself around her back, protecting her and holding her as the room spun.

"Allow me to help you." He whispered, his hand tightening around her waist as he turned to glare at Willoughby and the group of Fae he stood with.

"Colonel…" Marianne whispered as she felt herself sink into his heat, the strength he provided her.

"Ms. Elinor, please take her hand." Brandon instructed, waiting for Elinor to reach Marianne's side before he stepped to Marianne's side, his hand still wrapped around her waist. "Come, I will get you to Mrs. Jennings's."

"Thank you, Colonel." Elinor whispered as Marianne sank into Brandon's side, letting him be the rock in the whirlwind of her mind.

Elinor watched her sister with concern, paying no mind to the ever-hawkish eyes of the *ton*, her ears ignoring all the whispers and speculation. She knew Brandon could hear them all, but he did not let them stop his steadfast movements, the care that he showed Marianne, as they made their way through the ballroom.

When they made it outside into the fresh air he hesitated to step away from Marianne, only removing his arm when Elinor drew her close so he could hail his carriage to the entryway. With sure movements he lifted Marianne into his arms to set her in the seat, waiting for Elinor to take the place beside her before giving instructions to his driver.

Marianne's eyes never lifted from the floor during the quiet carriage ride to Mrs. Jennings's house, despite Elinor's quiet whispers of encouragement. It was only when the carriage drew to a stop that she raised them, meeting the burning amber of Brandon's gaze, churning with a mixture of pride and resignation.

Not even the loud voice of Trevor could pull Marianne's focus from Brandon as he squawked about, ordering the servants of the household to see to the young misses, thanking the good Colonel profusely as he gently directed Marianne into the house, finally breaking the connection.

At the door Marianne paused, looking back to the carriage and the golden eyes that watched her every movement for a moment before the heavy wood closed, separating her once again from the man she had wanted to see for days, but when she had, she had not been able to say a word.

CHAPTER NINETEEN

The next morning Elinor woke to find herself alone in the room she shared with Marianne. Her eyes went wide as she scrambled out of bed, drawing a waist coat around her as she hurried out of the room to find her sister. Marianne *never* rose before her, preferring to sleep well past when she should, lingering in her dreams with a smile on her face until she simply had to leave the bed and face the day.

Finding Marianne dressed and sitting at the breakfast table had not been what Elinor expected, especially given how withdrawn Marianne had been after the ball.

"Good morning Elinor." Marianne's voice was soft as she accepted the soft boiled egg that was placed in front of her.

"Marianne, I..."

Elinor's words were interrupted by the groan of Mrs. Jennings as she stumbled, her eye still blurry with sleep, into the room.

"Well, that truly was an evening to remember." Mrs. Jennings groaned as she slumped into her hair, nodding at Trevor when he brought her a slice of toast. "The shock with Willoughby, it was all anyone could talk about." Elinor's glare stopped Mrs. Jennings's words, and the elderly woman cleared her throat, suddenly aware of Marianne in the room. "Now now dear, it will be fine. Truly, no one was expecting it, but that is not an impression on you by any means."

"Why should Lord Willoughby's actions have any impact on me?" Marianne asked, her voice quiet. "I do not see why they should give anyone an impression of me at all."

"Marianne..."

"Elinor, if you will excuse me." Marianne nodded to Mrs. Jennings, her eyes avoiding Elinor's as she pushed away from the table. Elinor watched her sister move through the door, surprisingly moving towards the kitchen where Trevor had disappeared than to the upstairs bedroom.

"That poor child." Mrs. Jennings sighed as she covered her toast with marmalade.

"Why do you say that Mrs. Jennings?"

"Truly?" Mrs. Jennings sighed. "They were saying that is his new bride, they were married two weeks ago. She is from a Fae clan from Northern regions of England, they say it was a merging of the clans."

"Two weeks? But that would mean..."

"I know." Mrs. Jennings shook her head as she prepared her tea. "It was shocking to me when I heard it as well, but truly, is it not better that you become aware of it now, and not after Marianne had spoken of her engagement?"

"But Mrs. Jennings, there was no engagement."

"Come now child," Mrs. Jennings scoffed, "surely you cannot expect me to believe that. With how those two were carrying on?"

"Truly, Mrs. Jennings, there was no engagement." Elinor's gaze met Mrs. Jennings's, showing the truth of her words. "Whatever attachment others thought there may have been, it was due to the actions of my sister."

"Elinor," Mrs. Jennings chastised, her eyes narrowing as she glared at the young girl, "you forget I saw them together, how they behaved. You cannot deny that they were alone for several hours without a chaperone."

"I…" Elinor paused, Mrs. Jennings was right, Marianne's behavior had been rather scandalous, Elinor herself had thought the same. "I tell you, there was no engagement, nor did my sister's affections truly lie with Lord Willoughby. Yes, I thought the same for a brief moment, however I did not give my sister enough faith, something I would much like to rectify. If you will excuse me."

Elinor tightened the belt around her waist coat as she hurried in the direction she had last seen her sister, pausing at the door to the kitchen at the scene she found.

"It takes that much planning for one dinner then?" Marianne was bent over the table next to Trevor, perusing a list he had laying there.

"This is not even a full dinner Miss, it is just a simple evening for three." Trevor shook his head as he held out his hand and snapped once, waiting only a moment before several sheets of paper were placed in his hand. "This is more in line with a full dinner, with say 10-15 guests."

Elinor rested her shoulder against the doorjamb as Marianne graciously took the offered papers from Trevor to scan through them. "This just looks like the food list though." She murmured, carefully looking through the papers.

"Yes Miss, the list of decorations, candles, flowers, dishes, would be with the housekeeper. It is how we keep things organized, split the tasks between certain staff to oversee when you are talking about a family as grand as this."

"Fascinating. And who is the one that creates these lists in the first place? Is it the staff or the lord?"

"Well, if you excuse me Miss, it is the lady of the house that makes these choices, everything is very carefully selected based on who will be attending."

"Truly?!" Marianne's head darted up, her eyes wide.

Elinor's soft chuckle drew Marianne's attention, and the younger girl's cheeks flushed pink. "Did you never watch our mother when she was preparing for one of Father's gatherings?"

"I... well, no. I was usually lost in my poetry or my music." Marianne admitted, her eyes lowering to the floor. "It seems I have a lot to catch up on."

"What brought this on?" Elinor crossed to Marianne to wrap her arms around her waist, her chin coming to rest on her sister's shoulders to look at the papers on the table.

"I just... I thought..." Marianne sighed as she settled against Elinor, "I realized that I had no clue how a manor actually operates, and wanted to learn. There is more to life than poetry and fantasy."

"Surely there is some time for poetry and fantasy for you though," Elinor tightened her arms slightly, "it would do you no good to become like me, we need someone like you in the family."

"No Elinor," Marianne's voice was soft, almost inaudible, "I think it would do me good to be more like you. You do not get wrapped up into a fantasy until you realize almost too late what it could cost."

"You are still young Miss," Trevor laid his hand on Marianne's free shoulder and patted it gently. "You are the perfect age for dreams and fantasies. You remind those of us who are wizened beyond our years of the joy of youth."

"Thank you, Trevor." Marianne smiled slightly at the man. "I would love to come and learn more from you if that would be alright, and I would not take time away from your duties while we are here."

"Anytime Miss, and if I am not available, I will have someone else help you as well."

A footman scrambling through the door pulled the group from their thoughts, the young boy almost tripping over himself as he offered a small tray filled with letters to Trevor. With a slight bow, and more than a slight flush on his face at the sight of the two sisters, he backed slowly out of the room.

"Well, Miss Marianne, it seems this time one of the letters is yours." Trevor smiled as he drew out the letter and offered it. Marianne paused for a moment, her eyes darting nervously to the letter before Elinor felt her take a deep breath before she reached out to take it into her possession.

"Willoughby." She whispered, her shoulders drooping slightly as she read the name of the sender. "Excuse me." With a small nod to Trevor, she drew free from Elinor's embrace and fled the kitchen, her steps fading as she hurried up the stairs.

"I…" Elinor found herself at a loss as she watched her sister's retreat. With a soft shake of her head, she turned to Trevor and gave him a slight nod of her head. "Thank you, Trevor, for helping her, I hope she was not too much trouble."

"None at all Miss, though I do hope she is going to be alright. She seemed… less… somehow just now."

"I hope so too, Trevor." Elinor sighed as she gave another small nod and hurried after her sister.

Marianne sat on the edge of the bed when Elinor rushed in, her eyes focused on the small paper in her hand.

"Do you think I ever really knew him, or did I only know the image he wanted me to see?" Marianne's voice was low and even tone, a far cry from her normal speaking pattern, and that chilled Elinor deeply.

"What do you mean?"

Marianne shifted the letter towards Elinor and held it still, waiting for Elinor to take it from her. After a moment's hesitation, Elinor stepped closer and took the piece of paper, half of her wanted to know what the man had said, the other half afraid of what she may find.

My dear Madam,

"I have just had the honor of receiving your letters, for which I beg to return my sincere acknowledgements. I am much concerned to find there was anything in my behavior last night that did not meet your approbation; and though I am quite at a loss to discover in what point I could be so unfortunate as to offend you, I entreat your forgiveness of what I can assure you to have been perfectly unintentional. I shall never reflect on my former acquaintance with your family in Devonshire

without the most grateful pleasure and flatter myself that it will not be broken by any mistake or misapprehension of my actions.

My esteem for your whole family is very sincere; but if I have been so unfortunate as to give rise to a belief of more than I felt, or meant to express, I shall reproach myself for not having been more guarded in my professions of that esteem. That I should have meant more, you will allow it to be impossible, when you understand that my affections have been long engaged elsewhere, and it will not be many weeks, I believe, before this engagement is fulfilled. As to the whereabouts of Colonel Brandon, the good Colonel is not one that I find in my circle of company, and as such I am at a loss as to the location of the man, and daresay I will not likely be in his presence in the near future.

I am, dear Madam, your most obedient humble servant,
Willoughby of Allendale

"I do not understand?" Elinor looked quickly up at her sister as she finished the letter.

"Clearly, he seemed to think me more enamored with him than I ever was, but the way he phrased it, Elinor. This is not at all how he spoke, how he presented himself. So, I have to ask again, did I ever know him, or perhaps was it just a facade he wanted me to see?"

"Marianne, if this is what he is truly like, then it is just as well you were not in love with him, and that your relationship had gone no further."

"What a fool I was," Marianne's laugh sounded hollow, "you know that I did fancy him at first, his charm, his smile, here was someone who shared the same interests as me, who shared my love of poetry, of romance."

"What changed then?" Elinor had to know, needed to know. She had also misjudged her sister, and was finding this new mindset unsettling, as it was so at odds with her fanciful sister.

"It was as I told you before." Marianne sighed as she pushed the letters that had fallen to the bed, all but one unopened, onto the floor to lay back. "The conversations never seemed to go beyond the surface, a discussion of everything that was good and pleasurable in life, without any acknowledgement of the challenges or harms that made it more meaningful. The focus was on him, and how I could support or enhance him, rather than on us or what we could grow together. It became... almost vapid in a way, and I would find myself wishing to return to a book or a poem rather than continue the conversation with him.”

“Then why did you allow it to go on so long?”

“It is not as though there were many options at the cottage Elinor.” Marianne sniffed. “There was Colonel Brandon and Lord Willoughby... and then there was only Willoughby.”

“Marianne...”

“Truly? I wanted to give you time, Elinor, time to be able to wait for Edward. I have never seen two people more perfect for each other, I knew that it was only a matter of time before he rode to the cottage to confess to you... But he never came. And by the time he had, I had gotten caught up in the fantasy of my own creation.” A single tear dripped down Marianne’s face, the only one she let fall from her eyes. “And in doing so, it appears I may have fooled everyone, including the man that now fills my thoughts. When he took me in his arms last night, I nearly fainted, Elinor, yet I could not bring myself to tell him, no matter how much I wanted to. And you tell me he thought I was engaged to Willoughby, it is no wonder he does not respond to my letters, does not return to this house.” She curled herself, her arm coming to wrap around her waist as she turned to her side.”

“Please Marianne, do not let yourself think these things.”

“Elinor, you have no idea what I suffer.” Marianne’s voice was deadly soft. “To know that the man you may very well love is possibly lost to you forever.”

Elinor started at the words as she felt the need to hold back a laugh. She found herself, for the first time in months, wanting to blurt out the secret that she knew.

Yes, she knew that feeling only too well, she experienced it every day, knowing that both Lucy and Edward were present in London, that there was a chance that she would encounter either of them on the street, either alone or, a shudder went through her, heaven forbid together.

The thought had a ball of ice constantly freezing and churning in her stomach, nerves she had never thought she had before on edge.

Yes, she knew all too well what it was like to know that you loved someone who would never be yours, who was not free to love you back. And in some ways, that made her pain worse than Marianne's, Marianne could at least have hope, if only she would see it. Yet for Elinor, there was only a lifetime of regret, of wondering, in her future.

It was that thought that had her rising from her position beside Marianne, gathering her clothes for the day in her arms before leaving the room, letting Marianne sit in silence on the bed.

Chapter Twenty

"Oh, what a calamity, I must say, this is truly is a calamity!"

Elinor groaned at the voice that carried up the stairs... she was in no mood to deal with Anne or her sister, who was likely at her side. If only she was able to...

"Miss Dashwood, Oh Miss Dashwood" Elinor's hand tightened on the banister as that hopeful thought was crushed. With a sigh she made her way down the stairs to where Anne stood, her perfect sister poised and quiet beside her. "Please, you must tell us, Miss Marianne, is she much distressed?"

"I ask that you keep your voice down please, Miss Steele, Marianne is still resting in her room." Elinor stepped past the sisters, leading them to follow her away from the staircase, not wanting to disturb her sister... or to see her for that matter, as Elinor was still hurt and reeling from Marianne's unintentional comment.

"But surely she would love to see Lucy and me, you know we would never speak a word about Wil..." Anne paused mid phrase as if catching herself before lowering her voice to a whisper, "Lord Willoughby." Lucy shook her head at her sister's words, but it did not stop Anne from continuing. "I say what filthy beasts men are! Truly! Did you know that there was a gentleman who paid me great favor when we first arrived in London, he helped me from my carriage and was there asking for a dance at the first ball we attended, but now he is nowhere to be found. That as a Mr. Finch if I remember correctly, so it is not only your sister being cast aside like old shoes, these men, no manners or sense of propriety."

"Anne, would you *please* hold your tongue?" Lucy hissed, elbowing her sister's arm. "Honestly, have you no consideration?"

Lucy turned to Elinor, her eyes filled with a warmth that Elinor did not want to see, she did not want to like the woman who stood before her, knowing what she had cost Elinor. "Could you please tell your sister, I truly feel for her distress. To think of being jilted and spurned after giving her affection so freely to another." Elinor's brows rose at the words, her mouth opening to correct Lucy, when the woman continued. "It is fortunate enough that we know a man far too honorable to ever stoop to such conduct, don't we?"

The pointed look Lucy gave her made Elinor freeze. There was a hardness in the other woman's gaze for just a moment that made Elinor wonder if there hadn't been more to Lucy seeking her out, having *her* be her confident. Had she really needed another woman to talk to, or had she been trying to eliminate a potential threat to her relationship?

Did that mean that Elinor *had* been a threat? No, Edward was far too honorable, as Lucy had said, he would never have let himself turn his back once a commitment had been given.

"Yes," Elinor found herself responding in a whisper, "we do."

Lucy watched her face for a moment before nodding, the hardness in her gaze gone as if it had never been as she grabbed her sister's hand.

"Come Anne, let us leave Miss Marianne alone, I am sure she will be feeling better and more up for a visit another day."

"That would be lovely, I would love to go walking with Miss Marianne in the park, she is a very agreeable person I must say." Anne gasped as she clasped Elinor's arm, drawing her reluctantly towards the door. "I do hope she feels better soon, it was so shocking, so very shocking, especially what we had heard of those two from Devonshire, it must have been horrible, simply horrible last night."

"I think Marianne was surprised," Elinor admitted as she finally was able to draw her arm out of Anne's grip, "but she was not as devastated as people seem to think she was, there was a clear misundersta..."

Her words fell off as the door opened to reveal Brandon, hand poised to knock, on the front step.

"Oh, Colonel, it is a surprise to see you," Anne smiled, nudging Elinor briefly as she passed. "My sister and I were just leaving, do give our regards to Miss Marianne."

Elinor and Brandon watched the pair as they moved down the street, Anne talking away with Lucy occasionally interjecting.

"I can't say I am disappointed that they were leaving just as I was arriving." Brandon chuckled as he spoke. "They are quite exhausting."

"Hmm, they are, but their heart is in the right place." Elinor found herself admitting. "Please come in, Colonel, let me go get Marianne for you."

"No, I... well I actually came to see you."

"Me?" Elinor stopped short, turning to face the man. "Sir, I am flattered but..."

"What?" Brandon's face turned puzzled as he blinked down at her before his cheeks flushed. "No, it's nothing like that, I just... there is something that I think you and your sister should know, but I do not know how to tell her directly."

"What is it?" Elinor motioned Brandon into the drawing room, letting the door stay slightly open as she followed him.

"Do you remember a conversation that we had several weeks ago, when I said to you that I only hoped Willoughby would endeavor to deserve your sister?"

"Yes, what did you mean by that?"

Brandon signed as he paced the sitting room. "I have known Willoughby for many years. When we were children we were raised together, his clan often coming to visit my father. When my father died, however, it was no longer politically convenient to associate with me, and the visits stopped. He is a pureblood Fae, there was no place for friendship with a half Fae who is also half human. Now, that is not Willoughby's fault, but it shows how he was raised. He was the prince of his clan, the only son of the leaders, and it was known from the day he was born he would one day inherit the leadership of the southern Fae. They are a proud and ancient clan, here before William the Conqueror came to these lands and created England, beholden to no King or Queen. They are a law unto themselves, with total sovereignty over the lands they hold. They have not participated in any of the fights or wars that this Nation has faced, unless it threatened their lands, and even then, they only joined as an independent nation, the Crown had no control over them."

"You say that as if it is a bad thing?" Elinor whispered, her eyes focused on Brandon as he continued to pace.

"It's more trying to help you understand Willoughby's mindset. As the prince, he never wanted for anything, it was always there, so he never learned the meaning of work, or the value of a challenge before obtaining a prize. His sole purpose became to chase what made him happy, what brought him pleasure. Wine, women, gambling, the hunt, if it made him feel happy, he chased it with little regard for how it would impact others."

"And what of you?"

"Me?" Brandon sighed as he lowered his hands to lean over an armchair. "After my father died, I was left to fend for myself. My mother was human, and did not live much longer after my father's death, my half-brother settled in to rule in my father's place. I was given a choice to join the ranks of his army or leave, and I chose to leave, to make my own way. I know what it is like to struggle, to not know where your next meal will come from or when it will be, to scrape by. I earned my keep first as a mercenary, hired by the English government, before joining their ranks. The training I had received from my father made me useful as a strategist, and they were talents that helped the Crown win battle after battle, war after war. Eventually they honored me with a commission and land. I am officially retired from the army, but I remain at their call in times of war, such as now with Napoleon.”

“So different, despite starting off similar.” Elinor breathed.

“In a way we were never similar. Willoughby was always looking at the surface, the physical beauty, the pleasure, never seeing beyond that. I always looked for the truth of something, what was inside. I had seen him do similar over the centuries with women, he would find one he found beautiful, woo her, seduce her, leave her when he was bored and onto the next woman. It was why it bothered me that he turned his attention to Marianne.”

“But why Marianne? She didn’t ask for his attention?” Elinor’s brow furrowed in concern.

“She didn’t need to. Your sister is...” Brandon cleared his throat as he looked towards the second door of the room, his attention on something beyond it.

“Your sister is beautiful, you both are, but there is something about her, something that draws you in. It's more than just her face, though her face is as lovely as the sun, it's her heart, her passion. She longs for more, has a need to learn, yet still dreams. She is mischievous, caring, intelligent but naive.”

He sighed.

“Willoughby saw only the beauty and the naivety, likely wanting nothing more than a casual amusement. His attentions and affections went further with her than I had seen him ever with another woman, which is why when I was told they were engaged, I had hoped he had changed to be a man who deserved her, but I see he has not.”

He stood then, his stride purposeful as he made his way to the second door, his hand coming out to rest against it for a moment before his shoulders dropped. “I trust you will know best how to tell Marianne, and to determine how much of this she needs to know. I only want what is best for her, she is worthy of all the happiness in the world, and I pray one day there is a man who is able to deserve her."

He lowered his head to the door for a moment before straightening, the only sign of his distress as he stood were the ears that had disappeared into his hair. He turned and gave Elinor a brief nod before striding out of the room, leaving Elinor sitting alone.

The sound of the second door creaking open did not surprise Elinor, nor did Marianne's quiet footfall as she entered the room, her eyes filled with tears. When her sister fell to her knees beside her though with a choked "Oh Elinor," her eyes filled to match, and the sisters fell into each other's embrace, tears streaming down their faces.

CHAPTER TWENTY-ONE

Elinor sighed silently as Brandon and Marianne sat, both silent, in the parlor. It had become a frequent occurrence over the past few weeks. Marianne would undergo her lessons with Trevor and the servants, learning from them what went into truly running a household, not just the events but the day-to-day needs. Her readings had changed from books of poetry and first love to books of exploration, of questions of politics and women's rights.

Yet the moment Brandon came to visit, she became quiet, almost shy, only to groan and feel angry at herself when he left for wasting yet another opportunity to get to know him better. Elinor could see the resignation creeping into Brandon's eyes as he watched Marianne before he took his leave for the day.

"Marianne, will you please honor us with your playing?" Elinor finally could not stand the awkward silence anymore. "You are so skilled with the piano."

"I... yes, of course Elinor." Marianne whispered, her eyes darting up to meet Brandon's for a moment, her face flushing with the brief contact before she escaped to the piano, setting herself down with a deep breath.

The first chords of music danced through the air, the melody light and beautiful, and it took a moment before Brandon's face turned to stare at Marianne with cautious hope.

Marianne's hands flew over the keys, caught in the melody, needing no sheet music to guide her as she played the first song that Brandon had brought her those months prior.

"I..." Brandon began, pausing to clear his throat before his words failed him, and he continued to watch Marianne as she lost herself in the music and the feeling it evoked.

"Colonel..." Elinor whispered as she smiled gently at him with a slight nod, hoping that her sister would finally have some forward motion with her fascination with the man.

"The Lord John Dashwood." Trevor's voice broke the moment, and Brandon's face fell as he stood, gave Elinor a brief bow before shooting a look, full of longing, to Marianne, and striding out of the room, pausing only to give recognition to the girls brother as he entered the room.

"Elinor, Marianne, it is good to see you!" John exclaimed, nodding back to Brandon before focusing on his sisters.

Marianne's hands faltered on the keys for a moment before she changed the tune she was playing, the notes turning darker, more mournful...

And louder.

Elinor forced herself to smile as she greeted her brother, drawing him to the couch to sit, only for him to sit in the only armchair as if he belonged there.

"I see that Colonel Brandon has been here visiting with you a good deal." John said, snapping his fingers for a cup of tea from the staff.

"Well, yes." Elinor responded, shooting the young maid a glance of apology as she scurried into the room with a cup and pot of tea.

"That is good, good." John nodded, waiting until the tea was poured and the servant had left the room. "You should try for him Elinor, yes, he would be a good match for you."

If he heard the discordant notes from the piano, the slight pause in the music, Elinor could not tell, for it did not seem to affect him in the least. Yet she noticed and saw the slight tremor in Marianne's shoulders.

"Yes, yes indeed," John continued as if there had been no reaction, "I do think that you may have a chance there. After all, you have it in you to attract the men, you just..." He paused and let his eyes scan his sister and her simple dress. It was pretty, yes, but simple. "You just need to go about it the right way."

"I assure you John, that is not my intention." Elinor gasped, "I have no designs on Colonel Brandon."

"No, pity. It would be a fine match for you, a fine one." His eyes darted over to Marianne before returning to Elinor. "After all, one of the Dashwood sisters deserves a fine match" His voice lowered, though his whisper was still loud. "I do worry that it may be all over for Marianne, there are too many rumor tying her to Willoughby for anyone to truly look at her now."

"John, there was never anything between Marianne and Lord Willoughby." Elinor groaned, "Surely you know that."

"My dear, it does not matter what *happened*, only what is *said*." John reached out to pat her knee. "And people have been talking."

He stopped to take a sip of his tea, perusing Elinor as he drank.

"As to any... prior attachments that you may have fancied, I do hope you know that it is quite out of the question." John's eyes met Elinor's directly, and she found herself swallowing, knowing exactly what she meant. "Mrs. Ferrars has some very– definite– intentions for your cousin Edward's marriage."

"I... what?" Elinor started, did that mean that Mrs. Ferrars *approved* of Edward's engagement to Lucy? No, it couldn't be, for Lucy was still acting as though it was all to be kept at the utmost level of secrecy.

"Yes, she wishes to form an alliance with the house Morton, Miss Morton is quite an acceptable match, her family has the proper standing, and she the proper upbringing to be Lady Ferrars."

Miss... Miss Morton?" Elinor's voice rose as she spoke, and Marianne paused in her playing, turning to see if Elinor needed assistance. With a slight shake of her head Elinor directed her back to her playing, needing something else to focus on in the background. No, that meant that the family was not aware of the engagement, for they would not be trying to match Edward to another if he was previously engaged... unless they knew but did not approve of Lucy...

"Yes, she is an heiress, set to inherit £30,000, it is a very desirable connection on both sides, and will do well to set Edward on a path to succeed in life." John seemed quite pleased with the thought himself, for a rise in the Ferrars family would also mean a rise in the Dashwood family... well the male side of the Dashwood family. "So, as you see, Colonel Brandon, now that would truly be an excellent match for you, the man makes a fairly decent sum and would be able to help take after your mother and sister. To help facilitate this match, I come with an invitation to dine at the Ferrars residence tomorrow evening, the Colonel will be in attendance, and you would be able to make the acquaintance of my mother-in-law, the esteemed Mrs. Ferrars herself."

"John, I am not sure that w..."

"We accept." Elinor was cut off by Marianne's quick response, the younger girl undaunted by the look that Elinor was sending her. "Thank you and thank Mrs. Ferrars for her hospitality."

"Excellent, then we will see you both, and Lady Mrs. Jennings of course, tomorrow evening. I bid you both good day."

Marianne rose from the piano, grabbing Elinor's hand to hold her in place as John left the room. It was only after the front door closed that Elinor turned to Marianne, her face full of exasperation.

"Marianne, what were you thinking?"

"Elinor, it is the perfect time for you to meet Edward's mother, and to hopefully see Edward himself!"

"You heard John though; his mother seeks to make a match with Miss... Miss Morton."

"That is only because she does not know YOU Elinor!"

"Marianne," Elinor sighed, "it is not always that simple. There are things at work that you have no knowledge of."

"What I know is that you love him, and I am certain that he loves you. And once Mrs. Ferrars gets to know you, she will see what an excellent match you would be for her son and support you. Now, I am going to tell Mrs. Jennings that we are expected for dinner tomorrow."

"No, Marianne," Elinor whispered as her sister ran from the room, "you do not understand anything, anything at all."

And now, thanks to her sister's lack of knowledge, Elinor was facing an evening of torture, close to Edward whom yes, she would admit, *to herself only,* that she loved, yet fully unable to truly be near him.

CHAPTER TWENTY-TWO

Elinor watched the streets of London pass from the carriage window, choosing not to be part of the conversation between Mrs. Jennings and Marianne. Each moment that passed made her heart feel heavier, a sense of dread forming. It was taking all of her considerable will to not let the others know how tense she was becoming.

Yes, she hoped that she would be able to see Edward again, but knowing now what she does, she knew it would never be the same. He would never be free to see her in the same light that she saw him, and the thought made her want to curl into a ball and cry. It was funny, as Marianne became more like her, in some ways she was becoming more like Marianne, full of emotion, and finding it hard to contain and keep it hidden away.

When the carriage drew to a stop she took a deep breath, waiting to exit the carriage last before entering the doorway that seemed to both welcome and reject her at the same time. At least it would be a night free from having to lis...

"How *delightful* that you were able to come!" A voice had Elinor stopping, a gasp breaking free from her lips a moment before another's arm wrapped through hers, and she turned to meet the brown eyes of Lucy. "Can you imagine Elinor, Anne and I only arrived here this afternoon, but we have been invited to stay the whole week!"

"Oh, that's... that's lovely." Elinor choked out, as her heart began to hurt even more. Had Lucy been so accepted already that Mrs. Ferrars had approved of her and Edward's match? Or was this Fanny's doing, who had seemed so taken by Lucy at the ball the weeks before.

"Please have a moment of pity for me, Miss Dashwood," Lucy whispered, her hand stopping Elinor from following the others as they made their way to the dining room. "There is nobody here that can feel for me but you, I am all of a tremble with nerves." Lucy took a breath then leaned closer to lower her voice. "In a moment I shall see the person that all of my future happiness depends on."

Elinor started, her heart beginning to race even as she told herself it couldn't. "Edward is here?"

"No, no, he is not to be present tonight, but that is a good thing." Lucy paused as her hand tightened around Elinor's arm, her gaze turning cunning again. "He cannot conceal the great affection that he has for me when we are together, so it is better that he is not here."

"Oh, I... I see." Elinor responded, drawn helplessly by Lucy as the woman started to slowly move towards the dining room.

"I mean Mrs. Ferrars, whom I do hope to one day call Mother. It is important that she like me, it will make our lives together so much fuller to know we have her blessing." Lucy continued, paying no attention to Elinor's hesitation.

Elinor slid her arm out of Lucy's grip as she smiled, the sentiment not meeting her eyes as she bowed her head slightly. "I hope it goes as well as you hope." Her voice was even, and Elinor was proud of herself for not letting the tremor that threatened to overtake her be present in the sound.

"Thank you, dear Elinor, it truly warms my heart to know I have at least one ally here!"

Elinor let out one sound, half laughter, half sob, as Lucy left her alone in the hallway, and her eyes closed to try and push back the tears that threatened to form. What a quandary she found herself in, wanting Lucy's efforts to fail, yet at

the same time, hoping they succeeded so Edward did not find himself bound to
the Miss Morton she had heard talk of.

At no point, she was determined, would she let herself hope that both Lucy
and Miss Morton failed, and that Edward would return her affection instead.

No, it was better to give that up as a passing dream, a fancy she dared not have
let herself dream of in the first place. They were friends, that was all.

And she would fervently deny that her heart was crying at the thought.

Mrs. Ferrars was both not what Elinor had expected, and perversely, exactly
what she had expected. She had half expected the woman to resemble Edward.
Yet while the coloration was the same, the lady's dark hair only just fading to
gray with age, but Edward's eyes sparkled with mirth, where Mrs. Ferrars's eyes
gleamed with judgment. She resembled her daughter more closely than her eldest
son in that regard, and Elinor found it slightly terrifying when her dark brown,
almost black eyes, focused on her.

Mrs. Ferrars took a sip of her wine, her gaze scanning the table before settling
on Marianne. Marianne had just raised her head, smiling at Brandon, who sat
across the table from her, when Mrs. Ferrars spoke.

"So, I hear Lord Willoughby has taken a bride at last, that he has finally joined
with the Fae from the Northern lands."

"Oh yes indeed, Mamma." Fanny quickly responded, her eyes also darting to
Marianne with almost undisguised glee.

"I understand that it was quite the upset to... certain... young ladies." Mrs.
Ferrars's brow raised as she considered Marianne, who sat before her, unaffected
by the words being spoken, and not giving her the reaction she had expected.

"You know how it was with him, Mamma," Robert responded from his chair at the table, "he had several ladies who hoped to catch him, but he clearly was above those games, turning it around to play with them instead." He chuckled as he ripped off a piece of his roll and buttered it. "That man would not be caught by anything but another full Fae and one with a fortune at that. Like keeps with like and all."

"Will Mr. Edward Ferrars be joining us this evening, Ma'am." Brandon interjected, a heated glare at Robert before his eyes turned back to meet Marianne's.

"No," Mrs. Ferrars responded, "I have arranged for my eldest to be staying with the Mortons for the next few days. Have you met the Mortons, Colonel?"

"No, I cannot say that I have ever had that pleasure, Ma'am." Brandon's lips curled in a way that could show amusement, but Marianne could tell it was exasperation. "I am sure they do not run in the same company that I do."

"Hnnn. True, they are a very distinguished family." Mrs. Ferrars responded, either unaware of or uncaring of how her response sounded to others. "I must say, the good Miss Morton is truly an exceptionally charming young lady, and very accomplished."

Mrs. Ferrars's eyes shifted to rest on Elinor, watching her closely for a response. Lucy shifted in her seat, her gaze darting to her sister for a moment as she bit her lip.

"It is nice to finally meet you Mr. Ferrars." Mrs. Jennings's effort to ease the tension was obvious as she turned to speak to Robert, but many at the table seemed relieved at the change of topic. "I am familiar with your brother but have not had the pleasure of meeting you before."

"Yes, I apologize," Robert responded, "I am not enamored with the country Lady Mrs. Jennings. While I do find country manners pleasing in their own way, I find I often choose not to travel outside the city and the comforts it provides."

"I hope you do not take us for country bumpkins then Mr. Robert," Anne protested, "We have some very fine people in the country, and fine people. And I am sure that your brother Edward has always enjoyed the country and his time there, don't you agree Lucy?"

"I... Anne! How should I possibly know that?" Lucy sputtered halfheartedly, her gaze darting to Elinor before turning back to her sister.

"You know, now that you mention it, I have heard Edward say that he was never happier than he was when he was with us at Norland." Marianne interjected, causing all attention to turn to her. Marianne lifted her head as Mrs. Ferrars's gaze met hers, and let her lips curl into a half smile. "This is truly an excellent meal, I do say."

Mrs. Ferrars's jaw set as she tried to stare down Marianne, throwing her napkin to the side when her efforts failed. With an annoyed sound she pushed back from the table, the sign that she, and therefore all the guests, were now done with their meals.

"Ladies, if you would all care to join me." Her voice was cold as her eyes never left Marianne's, waiting for the other women to stand before stalking out of the room.

"Oh Ma'am," Lucy rushed ahead of the other women to trail Mrs. Ferrars, "please, you must make sure to sit out of the draft from the windows. We do not want you to catch a chill." Lucy's eyes lit on a settee covered with pillows, and led Mrs. Ferrars to it. "Let me arrange the cushion for you, to make sure you have a comfortable seat for the evening."

Elinor let out a slight huff of irritation as Mrs. Ferrars smiled at Lucy, accepting the offer and the seat as if it were her due.

"I thank you child. Please, what did you say your name was?"

"Lucy, Lucy Steele, ma'am." Lucy gave a deep curtsey, and Elinor watched as Mrs. Ferrars preened under the attention.

"She seems to be a decent, earnest girl, Fanny." Mrs. Ferrars nodded to her daughter who quickly agreed with her.

"I do believe she is." Fanny agreed, before turning her gaze to Marianne. "Marianne, dear, would you play for us?"

"I..." Marianne shot a look to Elinor who gave her a slight nod. "If you wish."

"I do. Mamma, Marianne is quite the accomplished musician."

"Ah, then we welcome your playing." Marianne made her way to the piano in the room, her fingers beginning to move over the keys when Mrs. Ferrars continued. "I have heard that Miss Morton also plays the piano quite well, as well as the harp. Quite the accomplished musician." Her gaze snapped to Elinor. "Does Miss Elinor Dashwood play?"

"I... no ma'am." Elinor admitted, her eyes falling from the almost triumphant look in Mrs. Ferrars's.

"Oh, that is a pity."

"Elinor is more of an artist, Mamma," Fanny informed her mother, "she drew that most excellent miniature of Norland Park that I have told you that I adore."

"Ah, yes. I believe I recall you showing that to me." Mrs. Ferrars nodded, her brow lifting. "I believe her style is very reminiscent of Miss Morton's do you not think? Miss Morton is also a gifted artist, but then I say she does everything well, does she not."

Marianne's fingers faltered on the keys, her pinky hitting a discordant note that had everyone turning to her.

"Excuse me, Ma'am," Marianne said softly, only Elinor able to see the slight twitch in her eye that gave away Marianne's temper, "but please, could you explain what Miss Morton is to us? You have mentioned her off and on all evening, especially when we were discussing Elinor."

"Marianne..." Elinor whispered, only to be ignored by the other women in the room.

"Dear Elinor, do not mind them, do not let them make you unhappy."

Elinor held back her wry laughter, oh, of the people in the room that made her *unhappy*, she could not say that it was Mrs. Ferrars that currently led the list, although she was rapidly moving up the ranks.

"You are quite opinionated are you not, Miss Dashwood?" Mrs. Ferrars sneered, her gaze hardening as Marianne resumed her playing. "Have you no respect for your elders and betters?"

"I have immense respect for my elders, but I withhold judgment on who is my 'better' until after the first meeting, which we are still in, are we not?"

"Well, then, it is time for this meeting to end. I thank you ladies for your attendance." Mrs. Ferrars pushed herself to her feet, turning on her heel, a clear sign of dismissal, which Elinor was only too happy to obey.

"Elinor, do not." Marianne warned as Elinor opened her mouth to speak once they were in the carriage, and Elinor chose to honor her sister's request, returning her gaze to the passing scenery as they rode home in silence.

Elinor could not help but think that as much as she had appreciated her sister stepping in to speak on her behalf, her actions may have caused more trouble than Marianne knew.

CHAPTER TWENTY-THREE

Elinor had just finished breakfast the next morning when a slight knock was heard at the door, and Marianne conveniently disappeared, leaving Elinor to face their guest, Lucy, alone.

"My dear dear friend, I am so happy!!" Lucy exclaimed as she rushed into the room and took Elinor's hands in hers, drawing her to the closest couch. "I was so afraid last night but I must say, Edward's mother was absolutely charming! I think she took quite a fancy to me with her comments!"

"I…" Elinor started, then had to stop and force herself to swallow to wet a throat that had suddenly gone dry. "She was certainly very civil towards you."

"Civil?" Lucy started, her smile dropping slightly as her eyes narrowed. "Did you honestly see nothing more than civility? I saw a great deal more than just 'civility'." Her smile grew again as she almost bounced in the seat. "I honestly believe we are more than halfway to securing his mother's consent already!"

"I am happy for you, and glad you think so." Elinor bit her lip before continuing. "But I do have to say that I fear that Miss Morton may prove to be a stumbling block, given how his mother spoke of her. Is she not the one she seeks to have as his bride?"

"Miss Morton." Lucy dropped Elinor's hands and sat back on the couch. "No, you will not dampen my spirits by speaking of her. Miss Morton may be the one that his mother speaks of and praises, but I remind you it is ME that he had made his promise to." Lucy's voice turned darker, losing her happy tone as she reiterated, staring directly into Elinor's eyes. "Me, not her, nor anyone else."

"Yes, you are right, I am so…"

A soft knock on the parlor door had Elinor's words fading as Trevor stepped in to announce a new guest.

"Mr. Edward Ferrars."

Elinor's eyes darted to Lucy's, whose own were wide, and a slight tremor began to shake the other woman's shoulders.

Elinor scrambled to her feet to rush to the door, intent on telling Trevor not to admit him when Edward himself walked through the door, his Cobalt eyes meeting Elinor's as she stopped, frozen in his gaze.

"Miss Dashwood…" Edward started, then his tone changed, became softer, more intimate as he stepped forward and took her hands in his, lifting them towards his chest. "Elinor."

Elinor let eyes trace over his familiar and beloved face, relishing the warmth of his hand against her, the heat of his skin almost scalding. He gave a small sound and began to draw her closer, his eyes darting between hers and her lips as his own parted.

"I am glad to see you, I need to ex…"

"Mr. Ferrars…" Elinor whispered, interrupting his words, pausing to clear her throat. She could not allow this, not when… "You know Miss Lucy Steele, I believe."

Elinor drew her hands out of his grip, pausing for a moment to let her fingers linger before she fisted her hands behind her back, away from the temptation that he posed. She stepped to the side just as Lucy rose from the couch, and the look of confusion in Edward's eyes that merged into almost pure male panic had Elinor closing her eyes as a shaft of pain went through her heart.

"Ah....." Edward let out a choked sound as his gaze met Lucy's, and Elinor swore that she heard hesitation and regret in the one sound, but forced herself to let go of such fanciful thoughts. "Yes, of course." Edward continued, his voice decidedly more forced than when he had first spoke. His mouth opened and closed for a few moments, as if he were unsure how to continue until he composed himself, offering Lucy a slight bow. "How do you do, Miss Steele?"

"I am well, thank you Sir." Lucy's tone in contrast was playful, flirtatious, yet the sound was grating in Elinor's ears.

"Good... good, and yourself, Miss Dashwood?" Elinor lifted her eyes to Edward's, and there was no mistaking the regret and the longing that lingered in them, but which was directed at her and which was for Lucy, she had no way of knowing.

"I am well, thank you." Elinor responded softly, expecting Edward to look back to his fiancé, but was quite surprised when he almost refused to.

"I am very glad to hear that, and Marianne... is she well?"

"Marianne will be very happy to see you." Elinor quickly told him. "In fact, I will go and tell her you are here, please, excuse me."

She had taken two steps to the door, intending to escape the situation she found herself in, when it opened, and Marianne stepped in, a smile on her face.

"Edward, I thought I heard your voice! I knew you would come to visit us."

"Marianne." Edward began, but trailed off.

"We had hoped to see you last night, we were visiting with your family for dinner. Why did you not join us?" Marianne shot Elinor a look before turning her attention back to Edward, completely ignoring the other person in the room.

"I... well, I was... engaged elsewhere." Edward choked out, his eyes darting to the floor.

"Engaged elsewhere?" Marianne laughed, "Oh but Edward, that will not do when there were dear friends to be met."

Elinor shifted uncomfortably as she saw Lucy's face turning red at both being ignored and the very casual and yet intimate way that Marianne was speaking with Edward. Marianne was unknowingly making the situation that much more volatile, but had no knowledge of what she was doing.

"Perhaps, Miss Marianne," Lucy interrupted, unable to stay silent any longer, "you think young men should never stand upon engagements, if they have no mind to keep them."

Elinor watched as Edward's attention darted between Lucy and Marianne. He knew he was in the crosshairs, but was unsure how he had gotten there, and the position slightly terrified him.

"No, indeed." Marianne responded to Lucy before shifting to look back at Edward. "I am sure that whatever it was that kept him from being there, it was a matter of conscience for Edward, as he is truly a man who would keep and honor his engagements. He would always keep his word, once he has given it."

Elinor's eyes closed at the hurt those words caused. Yes, Marianne was accurate, Edward was indeed a man who would keep any and all engagements, it was purely thus her misfortune to have met him after his affections had already been promised to another. There was nothing she could have done against time, and if Lucy and Edward had grown up together, they had a bond that she could never have hoped to match.

She opened her eyes to watch as Edward's shoulders dropped slightly, as if he felt the weight of the world suddenly rest on his shoulders. Elinor halfway wondered whether he had come to the same realization she had, especially when his gaze shifted to meet hers, lingering for a moment longer than was proper.

"Yes." His voice was hoarse as he responded, his tone almost resigned as he tore his eyes away from Elinor. "Yes," he repeated, his voice steadying, "and that being so, I regret that I must leave you, for I am promised to my sister." He shifted his jacket as he looked between the three women "I must go there directly."

"But you will come again, soon?" Marianne questioned.

Her words had only just faded when Edward interjected to tell her "very soon, I hope." He gave her a small smile as he bowed his head to her. "Miss Marianne, Miss Dashwood, Miss Steele."

He quickly made to escape the tension in the room, but Lucy's voice stopped him.

"If you are going towards your sister's, good sir, perhaps you would be kind enough to escort me? I am expected there, you see, and still do not know the way."

Elinor glanced at Lucy and caught the smug smile on her lips before the other girl's face changed into a flirtatious and innocent expression.

"I... of... course?" Edward's voice rose slightly as he spoke, and Elinor saw him give a nervous swallow before he nodded to Lucy with a slight smile. "It would be my pleasure."

Lucy smiled softly as she curtsied to him and made her way to the door, nodding briefly at Marianne. When she reached Elinor she gave another small curtsey, her eyes locked on Elinor's as her smile turned smug before she swept out of the room. Edward let out a deep breath as he turned to look at Elinor, pausing for a moment as his smile softened and his eyes met hers. After a moment he tore his gaze away and his smile turned rueful as he followed Lucy out the door.

"What could possibly bring her here so often?" Marianne groaned as they heard the front door close. "Could she not see that we wanted her gone?"

"Marianne, we are all his friends, and Lucy has known him longer than any of us. She has every right to want to see him, same as we do." Elinor's head was beginning to pound, a combination of the nerves from the evening before and the morning's activities.

Marianne eyed her sister, noting the tension in her shoulders and how she held herself. "You know, Elinor, it is that kind of talk that I cannot bear. If you want your statement to be challenged, I am the last person to do so. If that is how you truly feel, then so be it."

As Marianne flounced from the room Elinor allowed herself to collapse into a chair, unable to bear the weight of everything. Elinor could not tell Marianne what had caused the tension, nor truly what existed between Lucy and Edward. She was bound to secrecy from a promise she had never wanted to truly make to Lucy to help keep the engagement secret, and while the entire situation may cause her pain, she was bound by her honor to keep it.

In the solitude of the parlor, Elinor let her head tip back as her eyes closed, silver tears trailing down her face as she thought of Edward, and how it had felt when his hand had held hers.

CHAPTER TWENTY-FOUR

It had been several weeks since Elinor had last seen Edward, though she had heard plenty of him from Lucy, who had taken it upon herself to come to visit every two to three days, just to advise Elinor of how her relationship was growing... not with Edward, no, though that would have been painful enough, but with Fanny and Mrs. Ferrars.

Yet when she suddenly *stopped* arriving, Elinor thought little of it, other than to sigh in relief at not having to be faced with the truth of her situation. In all honesty, if Edward had not been involved, Lucy is someone that Elinor thought she could find herself being true friends with, unfortunately, though, Elinor felt a slight resentment towards the girl, one she knew she should not feel, but she found herself unable to quell it.

That was, until Mrs. Jennings came rushing in, Charlotte at her side one morning.

"Well, Miss Dashwood, have you heard the news?" Charlotte bubbled, interrupting Mrs. Jennings who had just opened her mouth to speak.

"I... well, I am not sure what you are talking about, so I would suppose not." Elinor puzzled, looking between the two women as Marianne stepped up beside her.

"Oh, it is quite the scandal! I am surprised it has not made it here to you, London is all abuzz about it."

"Charlotte, my dear," Mrs. Jennings coughed, and her daughter went silent, her cheeks flushing slightly.

"What are you talking about?" Marianne demanded, her attention focused on Mrs. Jennings.

"Well, I had met Charlotte for our weekly promenade, and I heard several of the families around, speaking about Mrs. Dashwood's despair."

"My mother?" Elinor was puzzled, for last she had known her mother was still in Devonshire, far from London.

"No, the *other* Mrs. Dashwood." Charlotte was bouncing as she stood in her excitement.

"Fanny? Is she alright?" Marianne gasped, her hand coming to Elinor's shoulder. While neither sister held much love for their brother's wife, that did not mean they wanted any ill to befall her.

"That is what I asked my dear," Mrs. Jennings nodded, "is Mrs. Fanny Dashwood ill? And the answer was such a shock I tell you."

"Wait until you hear it, Miss Dashwood, Marianne." Charlotte bubbled.

"Yes, yes, please do go on." Now that her concern for Fanny had passed, Marianne's irritation at the length of time the story was taking was beginning to show.

"Well, it seems that the family has found out that Mr. Edward Ferrars, the same Mr. Ferrars that I used to tease you about my dear," Mrs. Jennings nodded to Elinor before continuing, has been engaged to Miss Lucy Metzer for these past FOUR YEARS!"

Elinor froze, stunned, as Marianne gasped behind her, a whispered "no" falling from her lips.

"Oh yes!" Charlotte continued for her grandmother, "And apparently not a creature knew except the two of them and her sister, but you know how Anne is with talking! Apparently when she was over for lunch one day, Lucy out and about town, Anne accidentally let it slip to both Mrs. Dashwood and Mrs. Ferrars! The rumor on the street is that Anne was chased out of the house, Fanny threatening her with a shoe as she ran!"

"It is even more than that," Mrs. Jennings picked up the tale, "for as she left the house in a rush, Anne ran right into Lucy, who was ascending the steps, knocking both sisters right to the ground."

"I heard that Mrs. Fanny Dashwood was screaming at them both, uncaring that they were now on the street, about charlatans and harlots, coming to steal her brother's future and their fortune." Charlotte giggled, excited to share the latest gossip with the two women, unaware of how the news was impacting them both.

Marianne's hand came to rest on Elinor's back, her fingers clasping at her sister's gown as Elinor forced herself to breathe.

"Everyone was talking about how the Steele's are now no longer welcome at the Ferrars residence, and given how powerful the family is, that means almost no other family will take them in and they are having to move to an inn. An INN, can you imagine?" Charlotte continued as she turned to her mother. "I am waiting for them to come to us to ask us to take them in, could you imagine?"

"What of Edward Ferrars?" Elinor whispered as she looked to Charlotte for a response.

"That's the thing. No one has seen him. But I cannot say he will be happy, with his love being treated so poorly by his own family. Indeed, they were forced to stay on the street under the guard of the butler while the maids quickly packed their belongings and threw them onto the street with them."

"Those poor girls." Marianne whispered as her head lowered to Elinor's shoulder. Elinor found herself unable to think of any response, anything to say.

"I suppose they will move back to their Uncle's house now," Mrs. Jennings considered, "I do not believe they would be willing to show their face in public now."

"Oh but surely, Mamma, they will be staying at least until things are resolved with Mr. Ferrars, if he and Lucy *were* to marry then they would have to be accepted at the house." Charlotte gasped.

"Would they though?" Mrs. Jennings lifted a brow at the thought. "Knowing Mrs. Ferrars as I do, I cannot say that it may end well if Lucy were to try and force that."

"You aren't suggesting..."

"Indeed I am. Not everyone would be as thrilled at their child making a love match as I was with you my dear." Mrs. Jennings noted. "And it is well known that Mrs. Ferrars is focused primarily on standing and wealth, and if you have neither you are beneath her attention. Now, Lucy is well able to make do, and I cannot see any reason why she and Mr. Ferrars would not continue their plans, no matter what his mother says. Now, I do not think that she would completely cut him off, but she may drastically reduce his income."

"How dreadful," Charlotte sighed. "They may need to move to a cottage Mamma, we should help them to find one, you know of all the cottages available around Devonshire, let's start there. Please excuse us, Miss Dashwood, Miss Dashwood."

Elinor stood, frozen, as Mrs. Jennings and Charlotte exited as quickly as they had appeared. Her mind was reeling with the information.

Part of her was relieved that she no longer had to keep such a terrible secret, to feel it eat away at her, but the other part of her was upset with how Edward's family had reacted. Would it have been the same if it had been her, rather than Lucy? No, she couldn't let herself think that, to go down that line of questioning.

But she could not help but wonder how Edward would handle the news. Would he disavow Lucy now that his family had objected? No, she knew him better than that. He would stay at her side, honoring his own commitment, no matter what happened or what repercussion it would have.

"You knew."

Marianne's soft voice pulled Elinor out of her state, as she turned, her eyes wide to meet her sister's.

"Yes." she whispered back, her voice barely audible.

"For how long?"

Elinor gave a soft laugh. "Four months. Lucy informed me the first night we met."

"FOUR MONTHS!" Marianne almost shouted before catching herself. "Four months, and yet you have carried on as if you knew nothing, oh, and Elinor, all the things I have said, all the hopes I had expressed on your own behalf."

"Oh Marianne, I was glad to spare you from knowing what I did, and how much I felt. Now, I can think back and speak of it truly without any great distress." She paused, "I wish him to be very happy."

"You can say that?" Marianne questioned, her eyes scanning her sister's for some hint as to Elinor's true feelings.

"Yes," Elinor nodded, "I can."

Marianne stepped away, her hand rising to her mouth as she thought before pausing, looking back at Elinor.

"Then perhaps you did not feel as much for him as I thought after all."

Elinor let out a small laugh, but there was no mirth in the sound.

"You think I did not feel that much for him? Truly? Marianne, for four months I have had this... this knowledge hanging on my mind, unable to speak of it to a single person." Her voice started to break as she spoke, but she could not find herself caring. "I have had to listen to Lucy's talk of her hopes and dreams of her life with Edward again, and again and again. I have known myself to be divided from Edward forever in the way that I had hoped, while dealing with unkindness from his sister and the snide remarks of his mother."

Marianne made a soft sound as tears began to fall from Elinor's eyes, but Elinor continued, unable to stop herself from venting the hurt and anguish that had been churning over the previous four months.

"I have suffered all the punishment of an attachment without enjoying any... any of the advantages." Her voice broke as tears began to stream in earnest. "I may not have shown it Marianne, at least not in the way you had hoped I would, but I felt it so much, so very much. I have been unhappy, so truly unhappy, and I just..."

Elinor's hands lifted to cover her face as she crouched to the floor, overcome with tears. Marianne stood, stunned, unable to move for several seconds as she watched her strong, brave, and steadfast sister crumble, before rushing to take her into her arms and hold her, letting Elinor sob into her shoulder.

"I have been so horrible to you, without knowing, and I am so sorry if I had made your suffering any worse." Marianne whispered, placing a kiss on Elinor's hair as Elinor wept in her arms.

CHAPTER TWENTY-FIVE

Elinor's eyes were still swollen from the tears she had shed the next morning, but there was little she could do about that.

Or so she thought.

Marianne brought her two spoons, the bowls almost icy cold, and placed them over Elinor's eyes.

"Where did you…"

"It was a tip from one of the maids," Marianne said soothingly as she ran her hand over her sister's hair. "It is how they help the swelling of the eyes before they go to work." Marianne shifted one of the spoons to rest more fully on Elinor's eyes. "If you place them in the ice box for a few minutes they chill, and the cool temperature helps with the swelling."

"It feels wonderful." Elinor sighed, a slight smile turning her lips despite everything from the past day. "It does feel a strange turn of our roles though, you with the practical advice and me overcome with emotion."

"That is true," Marianne chuckled, tapping her finger on Elinor's nose, "but I think you should cherish it while it happens."

"I do, believe me Marianne, I do."

The sisters sat together, Marianne's head on Elinor's shoulder, in silence. Neither wanted to break the peace of the moment, a peace they had not felt since their father had died nearly a year before.

And yet as the world did not cherish the time as they did, a soft knock at the door ended their peace.

"Excuse me misses, Mr. John Dashwood is here to see you both."

"Please, see him in Trevor." Marianne stated, lifting the spoons from Elinor's eyes before looking her over and nodding. She was pleased to see that the swelling had gone down, it would not do to have their brother seeing how impacted Elinor was by the news.

"Elinor, Marianne…" John started, pausing as he stopped by the chair, waiting until Elinor gestured for him to sit. "I am sorry it took me so long to come, I… I assume you have heard the news?"

"Yes, we have." Marianne responded, shooting a glance at Elinor who sat still, her eyes cast to the floor.

"I must say I am quite amazed. I had believed that he was a man of sense, and this was all unexpected of him."

"What is to be done now?" Marianne laid her hand on Elinor's arm, not wanting Elinor to have to ask the questions that she may not want the answer too.

"Now? Well, now there is nothing to be done." John sighed. "When Edward came to the house last evening Miss Lucy Steele was waiting for him by the door, crying. When he entered the drawing room his mother confronted him, demanded that he end the engagement." Elinor's head snapped up at the words, but John was lost in his own thoughts and did not notice. "Edward, to both his honor and his detriment, refused, and asked for his mother's blessing to their union. She, of course, did not give it, and threatened to disinherit him if he continued his folly."

"To his detriment?" Marianne echoed softly when John paused.

"Quite." John let his shoulders slump, as if burdened by a great weight. "He still refused, insisting on honoring his word, and his mother cast him out of the house, removed his inheritance and left him with nothing other than the clothing he had on his back. I will give him credit, he did not back down, instead he looked her straight in the eye, offered his arm to Miss Steele, and left with her on his arm, never once giving deference to his mother."

"How awful, I feel so sorry for him." Marianne murmured, her hand stroking Elinor's arm as Elinor took a shuddering breath.

"Elinor..." John paused, waiting for Elinor to lift her eyes to him. "Mrs. Ferrars was good enough to say that– whatever objections there may have been to– another attachment– it would have been by far the least evil of the two, and she would be glad now if it had been the proposal instead." Elinor drew in a deep breath, the only outward sign of how the news affected her. John gave her a small smile as he rose from the chair to leave but paused at the door.

"She is, in truth, an excellent woman, and it grieves me to see her so distressed. I am sorry for burdening you with this, but I thought it would be better to come from me, rather than for you to hear it from the gossip mill that is running rampant through the town."

"Thank you, John," Elinor whispered, "it is most appreciated."

"I bid you both a good day, then. I must hurry back to Fanny, who is quite beside herself. This reflects on all our family now."

The loud clomping of his footsteps faded before either girl spoke.

"I think we have had enough of London, don't you Elinor?" Marianne sighed as she sat back against the couch, letting her head fall backward.

"Quite." Elinor responded softly.

She was not surprised by Edward's actions, she knew he had more honor than his mother had accounted for, and that he would not turn his back on his promise, even if it was made in error. But to know that he was cast out, shunned from his family, cut off from the lifestyle that he had been accustomed to, that hurt her heart just as much as knowing he was soon to wed another.

What was he to do? He had been trained to be a Lord, to join the ranks of the politicians, but it was not the lifestyle he had wanted for himself. He had no training, no vocation set up, that he could step into to earn his way.

"I think I would like to go for a walk..." Elinor murmured as she rose from the couch, gesturing for Marianne to stay where she was. "If you could talk to Mrs. Jennings, ask her if we could return home, I will be back shortly. I need just a moment to clear my head." She shook her head when Marianne began to protest. "A moment alone Marianne, I will be no more than a quarter of an hour."

"Elinor, are you sure?"

"Very sure." Elinor gave a small smile. "The fresh air will help me clear the melancholy in my mind, you know how I enjoyed the cliffs at the cottage."

Yes, the fresh air would do her some good. True, it would not be as clean and as crisp as the air by the sea, there were too many people and animals in London for that, but she still stopped and took a deep breath as soon as the breeze caressed her face.

It was a decidedly different feeling, walking the streets alone as everyone whispered among themselves at seeing her. While true, she was not directly part of the current goings on, as far as anyone outside of her family knew, she was still attached to the Ferrars family through marriage, a fact that had been shared through the *ton* at the events they had attended.

"...s Dashwood... Miss Dashwood." It took several moments before Elinor realized that someone was addressing her directly, and a few more before her eyes landed on Colonel Brandon, who stood off to the side of the street, his golden eyes watching her with concern.

"Oh Colonel, I did not see you there, I apologize."

"There is no need for apologies, Miss Dashwood, I wanted to see how you were fairing."

"I am... well, all things considered, thank you Colonel."

"Good, and... and your sister?"

Elinor's smile turned warmer as she saw the nerves in his gaze. "She is good, Sir. I do think that she is in need of some company, however, should you wish to indulge her."

"I..." he gave a small laugh. "I suppose I am that obvious, aren't I?"

"To one who knows you both, I would say yes." Elinor's eyes danced with merriment for the first time in three days.

"Ah... yes... well." Brandon seemed more flustered than Elinor had ever seen him, and it genuinely amused her, how her sister had reduced this strong, stoic Fae to resembling a youth in the first blushes of love. "I may come to visit you both, but I was hoping for a moment with you, if you do not mind. I have a... a favor to ask of you, and I do not know how best to suggest it."

"Is everything alright?" Elinor stepped closer to him in concern and he quickly raised his hands to let her know everything was fine.

"Yes, everything is fine, it is more I have a... proposal... that I would like you to relay for me. You see..."

Elinor was thoughtful as she stood in the parlor of Mrs. Jennings's home, waiting for her guest. It had not surprised her how quickly Mrs. Jennings had agreed with the sisters about the need to leave London, as the woman was missing the quiet of her country estate. They would be leaving in three days' time, but first, there was a request that Elinor needed to relay, one that could change the course of another's future.

Trevor's soft knock had her spinning, her heart beginning to race as she saw the ebony hair and Cobalt eyes of Edward as he slowly entered the room.

"Miss Dashwood..." His voice was low, strained, and she noticed the rigidity of his jaw, the new lines around his eyes. He appeared to have aged 10 years in the days since she had seen him.

"Mr. Ferrars, it is good of you to come."

"I am not sure if I am Mr. Ferrars anymore." Edward sighed. "I am sure that you have heard tha..."

"Yes, sir, I have. And that is what I wanted to talk to you about."

"Elinor you have to know that..." Edward started, but Elinor's words stopped him mid sentence.

"I have an offer, if you will, from Colonel Brandon."

"From Colonel Brandon?"

"Yes, you see– He has a rectory on Hartland that has sat open, he has not been able to find anyone that he would like to fill that position." Elinor was proud of herself for how even she was able to keep her expression.

"But..." Edward started and then paused, considering her statement. "He knows I have no formal training in the Church, doesn't he?"

"He does, but he knows you from your reputation, has heard both Marianne and myself speak of you, and how much we– we think of you. He felt that you would be the best person to oversee the parishioners of his estate. He says it comes with a sum of £400 per year, and while that is less than you are accustomed to..."

"It is more than generous..." Edward stammered. "Colonel Brandon is offering me a living... do I have you to thank for this."

"No." Elinor shook her head, not wanting him to think it was due to her intervention. "It has to do with your own merit, and the type of person that you are."

Edward's eyes scanned her face for a moment before the tension around his eyes began to ease. "I am then profoundly grateful to him... and to you, no matter what you say."

Elinor gave a small nod, grateful that she was able to help ease his concerns, though the thought of him being close to their cottage on Hartland with his new bride filled her heart with ice.

"Elinor…" Edward's soft voice drew her out of her thoughts as he stepped closer, his hands clenching at his side. "Every time we have met it has seemed impossible to tell you what I really think and feel."

"Yes." Elinor's voice was just as light as her gaze met his, and she easily read the longing that lingered in his.

"Now… now more than ever."

"Yes." She let her eyes drift shut, not able to be faced with her own longing reflected back to her.

"Why do you not think badly of me Elinor?" Edward's voice held a tone of pleading, one that Elinor was helpless but to respond to.

"Because you never deceived me." She responded frankly, opening her eyes to meet his to show him her sincerity. "When I heard… when I was told of your engagement," she paused for a moment before continuing, watching a look of pain course over Edward's face, "everything became clear. You did nothing wrong, truly. I wouldn't think so highly of you had you acted any differently."

The emotions, hope, resignation, regret… longing that passed over his face was hard for Elinor to witness, but she held his gaze until his eyes closed and he whispered "thank you" to her, his voice broken.

After a few moments cobalt eyes met her warm brown as he opened his mouth several times, as if he longed to say more, but kept stopping himself from expressing it. Eventually his lips settled into a sad smile as he watched her, before he turned his face from hers with a sigh.

"Goodbye."

Elinor knew what he meant. It was not goodbye forever, not when they would live so close once he accepted the Rectory from Colonel Brandon, but this was a goodbye to everything that could have been between them. And as much as she did not want to admit it...

"Goodbye." She whispered, and watched as his smile fell and his eyes closed as if in pain before he turned and shuffled out of the room as if his feet had lead weights in them. She let out her breath as she heard the door close, letting herself take a moment before she turned to help Marianne finish the packing.

It was time to leave London, and the memories it now held.

CHAPTER TWENTY-SIX

The carriage ride to Devonshire was markedly different from the one that had brought them to London. The carriage was no longer filled with chatter and excitement, and that honestly suited Marianne more than she had realized it would. Too much had happened in London, and she had outgrown her fascination with the town. She longed for the simplicity of the cottage, the thunder of the sea against the cliffs, and the comfort of her mother's presence.

"We will need to stop at my estates for a few days, before we continue onto the cottage." Mrs. Jennings advised quietly, also not wanting to disturb the silence in the carriage. A soft murmur of agreement fell from Marianne's lips as she turned her attention to the countryside, watching as the miles of trees gave way to the familiar cliffs of what she now thought of as home.

As the carriage began to slow to a stop she suddenly bolted upright, gasping as she saw Brandon standing by the door.

"Ah, good, I was hoping he would be able to make it." Mrs. Jennings nodded as she too caught sight of the man. "I had worried his business in London would keep him too long."

"I didn't realize he was coming home as well." Marianne breathed as she ran her hand down her hair, which caused Elinor to chuckle.

"Yes indeed, he said he wanted to be sure the rectory house was in good shape before the new tenants moved in."

Marianne's eyes flew to Elinor, catching the slight grimace on her sister's face before Elinor schooled her expression, once again showing no signs that she was bothered by the upcoming addition to their area.

As the carriage pulled to a stop Brandon stepped forward, offering his hand first to Mrs. Jennings and then Elinor, helping them out of the carriage. When he offered it to Marianne, she took a deep, calming breath and laid her hand against his, but curled her fingers so she slightly held his, rather than merely using it for balance. His soft inhale and the way his body froze had her looking to him, and she found herself captured by his golden gaze.

How had she ever found his eyes to be cold? They burned like the sun, shifting with his emotions, deepening when he was lost in thought, brightening when he was happy. She found herself smiling as she stepped out of the carriage, never shifting her gaze as she took in every shift of his ears, the shift of colors within his eyes.

"Thank you." She whispered, and his ears quivered as they shifted to focus solely on her. As she let her hand drop from his she heard his exhale, and realized that from the moment she had touched him he had not allowed himself to breathe.

This was the feeling that she had wanted, that she had hoped for, why had she been so stubborn, so blind as to deny it? Her hand felt cold now that it was no longer against his, and she found herself wanting to lace her fingers through his, to trace the claws that tipped his fingers, to feel his breath against her skin, his lips against hers...

"Come Marianne, it has been a long journey and we should get you settled." Mrs. Jennings drew Marianne away from Brandon, shuffling her towards the door of the manor. Just before entering Marianne looked back at the carriage to find Brandon's entire attention was focused on her, and Marianne smiled, nodding her head to him as she bit her bottom lip. Brandon stiffened as his mouth dropped open, but before he could say a word Mrs. Jennings had whisked Marianne inside, the solid wood closing between them.

That look occupied her thoughts for the remainder of the day as she went through the motions of eating dinner and preparing for bed. It wasn't until she lay under the blanket, curled up next to Elinor that she allowed herself to give in to the questions that had run through her mind.

"What do you think they want from us?" She whispered, and felt Elinor turn to face her.

"Who?"

"The gentlemen. I keep thinking of Willoughby, and what we found about him."

"I do not know." Elinor sighed.

"Perhaps they see us not as people, but merely as playthings." Marianne mused, worrying her bottom lip with her teeth.

"That may be true for Willoughby, and John to some extent, but I do not see that being how Brandon or Edward truly think."

"I suppose." Marianne turned to her back, lowering the blanket to stare at the ceiling through the darkness. "But it makes you wonder, do they see us as women as their equals, or are we just a doll, property, to them?

"I wish I knew for certain." Elinor sighed as she let her head rest against Marianne's. "I truly do."

The question lingered on Marianne's mind as she slid to sleep, and was the first thought she had upon awakening. Her quiet demeanor was noted by both Mrs. Jennings and Elinor, but she could not pull herself out of her own thoughts to calm their worries.

"I need to go for a walk." Marianne mused, her gaze lingering out of the window the gardens of Mrs. Jennings's estate.

"Marianne?" Elinor questioned.

"A walk," Marianne responded. "I need some fresh air to help settle my thoughts."

"But it is going to rain my dear," Mrs. Jennings protested, "look how gray it is outside."

"I know, but I promise I will be back long before the rain hits."

"Well, alright, but keep yourself away from the cliffs, and be careful in the meadow, there are dips and twists that are hidden by the flowers." Mrs. Jennings cautioned, earning her the first bright smile from Marianne in weeks.

"Thank you Mrs. Jennings." Marianne exclaimed as she threw her arms around the older woman, and dashed out of the house before any further protest could be raised.

Marianne let the salt brined air fill her lungs as she tipped her head to the sky, letting the mottled light from the clouds wash over her face.

It amused her, at Norland she had never wished to be alone, always wanting to be near others, even if she was lost in her book or her poetry. Now, she found more comfort in her own thoughts than in the silly gossip of others her own age. She was on the verge of turning 18, and now more keenly felt the difference between being a girl and being a woman.

Ironically, she was not sure if she would have had that revelation if she had not actually met Willoughby and Brandon. Had she stayed at Norland Park, she could honestly say that she would still have been the same, a spoiled child who did not know what she wanted, but expected it to come to her.

Oh how her parents had spoiled her. She had always been more drawn to flights of fancy than Elinor had, and her parents, especially her father, had always let her. Elinor had been the one to step in where Marianne hadn't strengthened, so she had never really realized how much she had needed to grow to become her own person.

At the very least, she was thankful to Willoughby for opening her eyes to that.

The soft rumble of thunder suited her mood as she continued to walk, lost in her thoughts. She nodded briefly to the gardener she passed, working on a hedge, who cast a glance at her and the darkening sky, but Marianne had disappeared around a corner before he was able to give her any caution.

When had she gone from someone who dreamed of fancy things and softly spoken words? When had she begun to long for a deeper connection, of a true partnership? She had said, so many months before, that it was what she had sought but she had not realized what it really meant. Her only knowledge of love had been her parents, and her father had been around 20 years older than her mother, so while they had been loving towards each other, it hadn't been the flash of love spoken about in her poetry books. Her mother had lived for her father, that was true, and while Marianne had thought that was what she wanted, had she really expected to give up all her own personal pursuits when she married?

If so, why had she started to turn from Willoughby?

He had been comfortable, easy. A quick smile, a well placed word. Granted, in the end she had been wise to turn from him when she had, to not let herself fall head over heels for him, but at the time... how had he not been what she wanted?

Brandon... Brandon was not comfortable. He didn't put her at ease when he was near. He was like a lightning bolt, one that strangely both irritated and soothed her. The bright flash of the sky accented her thoughts as she continued her journey, no set destination in mind.

No, Brandon made her *feel*, and that was what had made her uncomfortable at first. The touch of his hand against hers made her heart beat faster than Willoughby's lips had against hers. Brandon made her angry, but at the same time, made her feel safe, protected, and cherished. He acted as though he cared about *her* thoughts, *her* vision for things, and it made her smile to think of how he had changed his garden merely at her suggestion. It was the first time anyone had listened to her, taken her advice.

It wasn't though she hadn't had suitors at Norland, though there had not been that many. Too many of the men in the area had been boring, merely looking at her beauty and not her mind, her personality.

But wasn't that what Willoughby had done as well?

Willoughby was always looking at the surface, the physical beauty, the pleasure, never seeing beyond that. I always looked for the truth of something, what was inside.

Marianne let her head tip back into the softly falling rain as she remembered Brandon's words from only a few weeks before.

Yes, Willoughby had been flash, and he had been *safe,* never challenging her to think beyond the surface. But Brandon made her *feel*, made her think, challenged her to be her best, to do her best, not because he wanted her to, but because she wanted to for herself.

He's too...too proper.

Oh the thoughts of youth. Marianne groaned as she remembered her passionate vow to Elinor to never be alone with Brandon, and to only be near him in a crowd. She had gotten exactly what she wished, even when she realized she no longer had wished it. By the time he had taken her mare to stable at Hartland, she had found herself looking forward to spending time with him, to speaking with him. Not about poetry, but about his estate, the lives of those who lived on it.

Things of substance– that had actual value.

It was amazing to her how someone else finding value in her thoughts had helped her to find the value in herself.

A loud crack of thunder was her only warning before the soft rain became a torrential downpour. Marianne let out a loud gasp as she spun, trying to determine where she was and which was she needed to go to make her way back to the manor. The rain was heavy enough that it obscured everything more than a few feet in front of her, and she quickly tried to scramble back the way she had come.

The flashes of lightning were blinding as the storm shrieked its fury across the skies, the thunder deafening as it roared almost continuously with each flash. Marianne felt the hair at the back of her neck start to rise and ducked, instinctively screaming as the tree she had just passed exploded as electricity coursed through it, its heavy branches giving up the ability to hang on under the strain. Marianne ran as quickly as she could to avoid the falling limb, and in her haste, was not watching her feet as carefully as she had been. Her foot hit a slick of soil, now slippery mud with the rain coursing over it and lost its purchase, tipping her onto the ground.

Her head hit a rock, and the world around her went black, her small pink clad completely still form a stark contrast to the anger of the storm.

CHAPTER TWENTY-SEVEN

Elinor sat at the window, trying to focus on her book while still scanning the grounds for any sign of her sister. Approximately 15 minutes after Marianne had left for her walk Colonel Brandon had arrived, a small bouquet of flowers in hand, and Elinor knew that Marianne would not want to miss him.

That had been nearly an hour before, and now the skies raged as she had not experienced in quite some time.

Perhaps she had missed her return, and Marianne was hiding somewhere in the house with her thoughts. It would not be the first time Marianne had found a quiet nook to read, but typically she would at least alert her that she had returned,

"Where is your sister?" Brandon's voice startled Elinor out of her thoughts, voicing the same question that she had just been thinking.

"I'm sure she has returned by now, most likely she has discovered the library." Mrs. Jennings mused, as she sipped from her cup of tea.

"No, she is not." Brandon's voice gave no reason to question it, but Elinor found she had to.

"Are you sure?"

"I..." Brandon's cheeks flushed slightly before he shook his head. "I can scent everyone in the house, and her scent is old, as if she hasn't been here for more than

an hour." Elinor had forgotten that Fae senses were more keen than a humans...
but that meant...

"You don't think..." Mrs. Jennings gasped as Elinor turned, her eyes wide with
fear.

"No..."

"What is it? Where is she?" Brandon demanded, his voice deepening as he
stalked towards Elinor.

"She went for a walk, but she promised she would be back before the rain hit..."

A bright flash of lightning blinded the room, the thunder booming before
the light had even faded. Between one breath and the next Brandon was gone
from the room, the slamming of the front door the only indication of where
he had gone. Elinor spun back to the window to watch Brandon as he raced to
the stables, emerging with his horse, free from its tack, and leapt onto its back,
disappearing into the rain.

"She couldn't be, could she...?" Elinor's eyes were wide as she spun around,
her face showing her fear.

"Come now, let us prepare, if anyone could find her, it would be the good
Colonel." Mrs. Jennings's voice was grim as she rose, a quick nod to the hovering
servants who ran to prepare for the worst.

Elinor watched them bustle about with her heart in her throat... Why hadn't
Marianne returned when the weather began to turn? She turned back to the
window and placed her hand against it, trying to peer through the sheets of rain,
but knowing she would not find anything.

A slight groan of pain tore from Marianne's lips as the rain lashed against her, the
sound lost against the cracks of thunder. She had no idea how long she had been

laying there, but her dress and hair were completely plastered against her, and water was pooling in ways she did not remember just before her fall.

But her head... oh her head. Another grimace turned into a groan as she attempted to move, and agony coursed through her.

"... arianne!" A hint of sound broke through the cacophony that surrounded her, so faint she was almost sure she had imagined it.

"Marianne!" No, she had not imagined it... there it was again, as if someone were searching for her, but she couldn't find the strength to move, all she wanted to do was sleep...

"Marianne, oh thank god." A familiar voice choked as she felt hands against her hair, her shoulders.

She struggled to open her eyes, moaning as the world spun around her with the movement, and a gentle hand was placed under her head, helping lift her carefully out of the rain. She managed to lift her head, and when her vision cleared she saw the frantic golden gaze of Brandon as he scanned her face.

"Marianne," his whisper broke as he drew her close, his silver hair falling over around her, shielding her from the elements as she felt his chest shaking, as if he were overcome by emotions.

"Co... Colonel..." She whispered, her eyes drifting shut as her head met his shoulder... "Brandon..."

The rain that had been pelting her constantly eased, and Marianne found herself surrounded by warmth, mixed with the gentle scent of Brandon. Her body relaxed, tension she hadn't realized she had easing as she felt herself lifted off the ground, cradled gently against a strong, slightly trembling chest.

"I've got you, I've got you." Brandon soothed, carefully settling her onto his horse, his coat wrapped securely around her to shield her from the storm. When she felt his warmth settle at her back, one arm securing her around his waist she let herself drift, her head once again coming to his shoulder, and she surrendered herself to the pulsing darkness once again.

"Oh gods!" Elinor gasped as she saw the horse appearing out of the storm, Brandon hunched over a small form cradled in his arms. "MRS. JENNINGS!"

A groomsman ran to meet Brandon's horse, holding the mane while Brandon used all his strength and grace to keep Marianne from being jarred as he slid off its back. Elinor rushed to open the door wide, letting Brandon through with Marianne cradled in his arms.

"She is chilled, make a fire in her room." Brandon commanded as he hurried through the manner, letting Marianne's scent lead him to her room.

"We already started one." Mrs. Jennings assured him as she scurried after him, Elinor's hand clasped in hers as they followed down the hall.

"Good, she will need to be stripped and chafed all over, there is a rasp forming in her lungs, we must get her warm." He lay Marianne down on the bed, his coat flung to the side in his haste. Without thinking Brandon removed his outer jacket, not wanting the wet garment near her. "I have seen this too many times on the battlefield, build the fire up some more, and bring her some additional blankets, we must get her temperature up."

Brandon bent over Marianne's figure, his hands reaching for her gown, when he paused. Marianne's eyes fluttered open at that moment, chocolate eyes dulled with pain meeting his gold, as his hands began to shake.

"Colonel..." Elinor whispered as she took a blanket from a maid, stepping forward as Brandon stepped back, his eyes still locked with Marianne's."

"I... I should leave you." He swallowed, and Elinor noticed his hands never ceased their tremors. "Please, be sure to make haste, time is of the essence, she hit her head, it had ceased bleeding by the time I arrived, but it may need attention as well."

"Thank you sir," Mrs. Jennings nodded, stepping in front of Brandon to usher him out of the room. She turned to a hovering groomsman and ordered "have someone fetch the doctor immediately."

"Yes Ma'am."

Brandon's eyes were still on Marianne as the door to the bedroom shut, and Elinor swore she heard a muffled sob from the other side.

"Hurry, we must get her out of her wet clothing." Mrs. Jennings commanded, and Elinor jumped into action, quickly working with the other woman to remove Marianne's gown and under clothes, gently dressing her in a flannel nightdress that had been left by Charlotte.

Marianne's focus had gone in and out during the commotion, she had scanned the room each time she had a moment of lucidity, only to fade a moment later.

"Brandon..." Marianne whispered, her eyes drifting shut as she sighed at the warmth now surrounding her.

"He's here Marianne, he did not want to leave until he knew how you were. He is downstairs, waiting for the doctor." Elinor murmured, her voice low.

"I want to see him." Marianne's voice was soft, the words almost too faint to be heard.

Mrs. Jennings nodded to Elinor as the elderly woman sat on the side of the bed, taking Marianne's hand in hers as Elinor rose to make her way downstairs to summon Brandon.

"How is she?" She had barely made it halfway down the stairs when Brandon rushed to her, his eyes darting back upstairs towards Marianne's room.

"She is a little recovered," Elinor assured him, "resting now as she tries to shake off the chill."

"Good, good, that is good."

Elinor let herself take in Brandon's figure, the tension in his shoulders, his hair still dripping down his back, how his hands were opening and closing as if he couldn't keep himself still.

"She has asked to see you, Colonel." Her soft words made Brandon pause, his eyes wide, before he rushed past Elinor, darting back up the stairs to Marianne's side.

Marianne's head turned towards the door at the quiet knock, her lips curving the best they could as the door opened and Brandon stepped through, his ears quivering as he moved towards her. The hustle and bustle of the other occupants of the room faded as he sat on the edge of the bed, his fingers brushing against her hand as it lay beside her. Brandon's mouth turned up into a small smile as he watched her, the panic in his eyes fading.

Slowly, deliberately, her eyes locked onto him the entire time, Marianne shifted her hand, letting her fingers rest over his. Brandon's breath caught as he quickly looked down to their hands, watching as Marianne slightly laced her fingers through his, before his attention turned back to her face. Marianne gave him a slight smile as her head turned towards him on the pillow, her eyes drifted closed and she let herself drift to sleep, knowing he was there to watch over her.

When Elinor came to check on Marianne some time later, Brandon still sat by her side, her hand linked with his.

CHAPTER TWENTY-EIGHT

I t was early in the morning when Elinor rose, making her way down the hallway to the room Marianne rested in. Brandon had stayed for dinner, insisting on eating by Marianne's bed to watch her, but they had finally convinced him to rest . He had promised to return in the morning to check on Marianne, and Elinor found herself smiling that her sister may finally be getting the happy ending she wanted after all.

A soft moan of pain had her quickening her steps, and as she opened the bedroom door the wheezing gasp of breath she heard from the room had a chill running through her.

"Marianne?" She whispered, watching as her sister's head tossed back and forth. "Marianne??" Her voice was louder as she came to sit at Marianne's side, a hand moving to push back Marianne's hair.

The heat coming off of Marianne's skin made her pause, as Elinor's eyes went wide. With a gasp she tore out of the room, running down the hallway until she nearly crashed into the Butler, who had been drawn by the sounds of her footsteps.

"Please, get the doctor…" Elinor gasped, and the man snapped to attention, calling down for a footman to run at once.

"Whatever is the matter?" Mrs. Jennings grumbled, her door opening as she blinked her one eye against the remnants of sleep.

"Marianne, she is burning up." Elinor cried, "She is gasping for air, she needs the doctor right away."

"I thought the doctor said she was fine yesterday." Elinor heard one of the maids whisper as they two began to collect in the hallway.

"I was worried about that," Mrs. Jennings sighed, belting a robe over her nightgown. "Lord knows how long she was outside in that rain."

"I hope the doctor is able to hurry." Elinor murmured as she followed Mrs. Jennings back down the hallway to Marianne.

"He will, or I daresay we will send Colonel Brandon to get him, that is not a man who will tolerate dilly-dallying, especially when it comes to her."

Indeed, when Brandon arrived before the Doctor, he had only taken one step into Marianne's room before his eyes had darkened. In a flash he had jumped down the stairs, intent on dragging the doctor there, involuntarily if needed. It was only the fact that the man was stepping down from his carriage that stopped Brandon's rage, but not his worry. His growl was audible when the doctor had ushered everyone out of the room but one maid and Elinor, but Elinor knew it came from a place of fear. The panic in his eyes had been visible when he had heard Marianne's breathing, and given his own experiences with soldiers, it made perfect sense.

The doctor's movements seemed torturously slow, even though Elinor knew he was moving at the pace he needed to in order to examine Marianne.

It did not make watching it any easier, especially when each moment Marianne's breathing sounded more and more labored. Her cheeks had long turned pink, but it did nothing to ease the pallor of her face, the deep pink shade emphasizing how pale she was. Elinor started at a loud gasp from her sister and had to hold back tears as Marianne's back bowed briefly before she went dangerously still. It was only the ragged sound of her breathing that kept Elinor from completely breaking down.

An eternity had passed before the doctor motioned Elinor to follow him, the man staying silent as he made his way down the stairs, undaunted by the group that followed him, and the golden eyes boring through his head, a slight pink tint coloring the whites of Brandon's eyes.

"I am afraid that it has moved to her lungs." The doctor sighed when he reached the foyer. "Unfortunately, it appears to be putrid in nature, there is little medication that I would be able to give her other than a mild sedative to give her body time to fight it."

"What does that mean?" Elinor whispered, her attention darting up the stairs and then back to the doctor.

"It means there is little any of us can do, it is all up to your sister now." The doctor set his bag on a small table, digging through it for a moment before drawing out a small vial. "This will help her to sleep should she need it, there is little else I would be able to assist with. Keep the room warm, but it should also be aired out regularly, to give her fresh air if possible."

"Thank you, Doctor." Mrs. Jennings stepped forward, to take the vial, before she turned and placed it in Elinor's hand.

"I will be available should she take a turn for the worse, but..." the doctor trailed off as he removed his glasses with a sigh. "Let us hope she does not."

Elinor stood, lost in thought, as she looked at the small vial. The murmurs of sound barely registered to her as she assumed Mrs. Jennings escorted the doctor out.

Could she give this to her sister?

Would it help her?

"Laudanum." Brandon growled after a single sniff of the bottle.

"Isn't that a good thing though?" Elinor whispered.

"I... I have concerns." Brandon sighed, "I have seen too many times the effects of this medication, and the harms that it can cause. Yet on the other hand..." his head lowered. "I don't want her to suffer. It is no simple thing she is facing, and gods I wish I could help her, to make her better."

"You have, Colonel, you got her back here, you helped her rest last night." Elinor murmured as she watched Brandon shake his head.

"But not quickly enough." He groaned. "There is no knowing how long she was there, laying in the rain."

"Brandon..." Elinor's use of his name had his attention focused on her as she gave a small smile, in spite of her own fears. "You got her here, you found her, and got her back to the house."

"It's not enough..." He growled.

Elinor reached out and captured his hand, drawing his focus back to her. "It is. It will be. I have faith in Marianne, you must too."

"I have all the faith in the world in her." He sighed, then let out a wry laugh "the doctor, perhaps not as much."

"She will get through this." Elinor said firmly, whether to convince Brandon or herself... she wasn't quite sure.

By the third day of the fever though, it was hard for her to keep that optimism. Brandon had all but moved into Mrs. Jennings's home, sleeping in fits in the parlor, relieving Elinor when she needed to sleep of the ever constant vigil at Marianne's bedside.

If there had ever been a doubt in Elinor's mind how deeply Brandon cared for Marianne, it had been firmly stamped out by his care of her. His worry lingered in his eyes, the tremor of his hand, yet when she needed help with Marianne, he was there, steady, lifting Marianne with such gentleness it brought a tear to Elinor's eye. His experience with others who were infirmed was truly a godsend, helping Elinor and Mrs. Jennings in ensuring that Marianne was able to drink the broth they brought her to help keep her strength up. Propriety was long forgotten in his care, and Brandon sat at Marianne's bedside, the cuffs of his sleeves pushed to his elbows, his coat long shed over the back of a chair.

"If only I was able to do more." Brandon's voice was deep with fatigue as he groaned, letting his head fall back.

"I think…" Elinor paused, letting her long hair fall over her shoulder. "If you could send a man to the cottage, to bring our mother here. I feel she may need to be here as soon as possible."

"No, no, I will go myself, I can get there faster than any of my men can." Brandon stumbled slightly as he stood, his eyes darting to Marianne's still form on the bed. "I will be back by the end of the day tomorrow," his tone softened, and Elinor knew he was saying it for *Marianne's* sake, not her own.

Elinor kept her vigil at Marianne's side after he had gone, taking the meals brought to her by the servants in the room, afraid to leave her sister's side. Each gasp from Marianne, her hands clutching the sheets, had Elinor rushing to the bed, her heart in her throat, only for Marianne to calm, falling back into unconsciousness.

By the seventh time it happened Elinor was unable to hold back her own fears, and in the silence of the room, began to crumble.

"Please Marianne," she pleaded, tears streaming down her face as she lowered her head, resting her forehead on her sister's hand, "please recover. I do not know what I would do without you." Her voice cracked as her tears became sobs, "Please do not leave me alone."

The soft movement against her cheek failed to comfort her as she wept her stress into the bed, but a soft, broken voice had her stilling, daring not to draw another breath.

"Silly Elinor, I could never leave you alone."

Elinor let out a cry as her head lifted, her eyes meeting Marianne's who, for the first time in days, looked *at* her, rather than through her.

"Marianne, oh Marianne!" Elinor repeated, lifting Marianne's hand to place a kiss on the back before bringing it to her cheek, her tears turning from fear to joy as Marianne took a deep, unlabored breath.

Mrs. Jennings, drawn by Elinor's cry, stood in the doorway, her hand held over her heart as the two sisters watched each other.

CHAPTER TWENTY-NINE

E linor helped Marianne settle into her pillows, helping her to sit more upright but still supported, a book of poetry in her hands to help pass the time until Brandon returned with their mother.

"Does it have to be poetry?" Marianne groaned, and Elinor smiled at the sound, faint as it was.

"Well, I daresay you are not up for Gulliver's Travels," Elinor chuckled, tapping Marianne on her nose. "And the other novels available I would say are not appropriate for me to read to you. Besides, I thought you *liked* poetry."

"I did... once." Marianne pouted, "at least tell me it contains Robert Herrick, and *not* Willoughby Blake."

"Ah, well, sorry to disappoint you, but... no." Elinor laughed as Marianne let out a little sound of annoyance.

"I remember when Blake was your favorite poet, after those times with Papa."

"He used to be." Marianne grumbled. "And then I discovered *Hesperides*, and much prefer Herrick's work now."

"Gather ye rosebuds while ye may?" Elinor grinned when Marianne's cheeks flushed pink, but this time a healthy glow rather than the frightening they had been.

"Something like that..."

"Excuse me, Ma'ams." A maid knocked hesitantly, stilling the interaction between the two, "but there is a gentleman here below, asking to see Miss Elinor."

"A gentleman?" Elinor repeated.

"Yes, ma'am."

"Tell him that I am not avail..."

"Oh go, Elinor." Marianne poked her with a finger. "It will save me from hearing some of Blake's poetry."

"Yes, all right." Elinor stood with a sigh, bending to place a kiss on Marianne's forehead. "I will not be long."

"Trust me," Marianne gave a small smile, "I will still be right here."

Elinor let the maid lead her to the entryway, unable to answer Elinor's question of *who* the gentleman caller was. She would be lying if she said she didn't hope it was Edward, even though she knew that was out of the question.

The last man she expected to see step out of the shadows, however, was the black haired, crimson eyed Fae.

"Miss Dashwood." Willoughby began, as he took another step closer.

"Excuse me, I have no time for this, or you." Elinor's voice had chilled, she had no pretense of warmth anymore for the Fae, not after what they had learned.

"Please, I want to explain." Willoughby grimaced, as if the words were hard for him to say, and Elinor thought to herself that in a way, they very well may have been, he was not someone that she could see using the word 'please' all that often. Though if those words were hard for him, the way his voice faltered on his next showed Elinor exactly how infrequently they were used.

"I want to apologize..." Willoughby's voice dropped as he spoke, "to... to ask for your forgiveness."

"I'm sorry, Lord Willoughby, but you are not welcome here." Elinor was firm. Marianne was still recovering from being ill, there was no way she would let the man disturb her.

"Miss Dashwood, at the risk of you thinking even worse of me than you likely do, it is still worth me trying." Willoughby's voice was harsh, so unlike his even and cultured tone. "I need you to know that…"

Willoughby growled, his fist clenching as he stopped.

"When I first came to Devonshire, and met your sister, I admit, I was taken by her beauty. I have had a history of pursuing things that interest me, and there is little doubt that Mario… that Miss Dashwood did interest me." His eyes narrowed as he spoke. "She was beautiful, young, full of life, and smelled of sunshine. I found myself unable to do anything other than be drawn to her side. And before I knew, I had… fallen." Willoughby gave a soft laugh. "Yes, Miss Dashwood, if you can believe that, I had truly fallen in love with your sister."

Elinor let out a small scoff as her arms crossed over her chest, the look in her eyes one of disbelief.

"I swear to you it is the truth." Willoughby vowed. "I had made up my mind, this is the woman I was going to marry, this was the woman I wanted at my side leading my clan. And then… then I went to the council, who were not as keen on the idea as I myself was."

"Of course, your "council." Elinor repeated harshly. It was what they had thought, it seemed. The council had not been willing to accept Marianne.

"Yes, I may rule the clan but they have the authority to remove me from that position." Willoughby snarled, "and they took it upon themselves to issue an ultimatum. I could marry Marianne, yes, I can see that surprises you, but they did give me that option. However I would have lost my clan, been cast out, no longer the leader, no longer under their protection."

"Or?" Elinor's brow rose as she asked, knowing that it was not the only choice he had been given.

"Or…" he acknowledged, "I could walk away, to leave my heart behind and follow the path they had set for me. To marry into the Northern Clan, to Sophia, the princess of their clan, and join our two clans together, to increase their strength.”

“And so you set off to London to what end, to find and court this princess?”

“What else could I have done?” The words burst out of Willoughby as he watched Elinor carefully.

“You could have told us, told my Sister, the truth. I think you owed her at least that much.”

“As if any of you would have believed me.”

“You don’t know, because you didn’t try.”

“No, Miss Dashwood, you could not have believed me because you do not understand. I have lived my *entire* life within the clan, we work together as one unit, one family, because we all are family. You do not understand what it would have cost me to have walked away, to have lost everything and everyone that I loved, for the sake of what, a dalliance?”

“That sounds to me as if you did not love my sister.” Elinor countered.

“NO.” Willoughby growled. “I did, I still do. But I will outlive her. And I would have turned my back on everything if I had followed my heart. Do you have any idea how much I would have suffered when I was alone?”

“You speak as though you had no choice.”

“I had no choice.” Willoughby roared, ignoring Elinor when she tried to quiet him down. “I am controlled by the council, by the will of the clan. So do you now pity me, Miss Dashwood? Or has this all been in vain?”

“You speak of your loneliness, your loss, your inability to manage. I notice nowhere in your words did you think of my sister, or of her feelings, or of a potential future you may have had.” Elinor responded after a moment.

“You despise me now, don’t you?” Willoughby asked harshly.

Elinor considered the man for a moment, a man so lost in his love of comfort, of pleasure, that he gave no thought to anything beyond that.

"No, Lord Willoughby," she said softly, and watched the tension in his body ease at her words, only to tense again as she continued. "I should be grateful you never truly had my sister's love. She can never be more lost to you than she is now."

Willoughby growled as he took a step forward, and then froze, his eyes darting up the stairs to the figure that stood at the top. Marianne looked down upon him, her body wrapped in a blue blanket, the crest of Hartland visible at her shoulder, her eyes cold and unforgiving as she considered him.

All the fight seemed to leach out of Willoughby after a few moments, his eyes closing as if in pain. Without another sound he turned and strode out of the door, out of their lives for good.

"Marianne?" Elinor called up as she turned towards the stairs.

"I am fine, Elinor." Marianne responded as she let herself lean against the wall. "You may not pity him, but I do." Elinor hurried up the stairs to help Marianne back into the bedroom, sliding her arm around Marianne's waist as her sister continued. "Someone who has no idea of who he is, or what he wants? Can you imagine an existence as meaningless as that?"

"No, I cannot." Elinor agreed as she helped Marianne slide back into the bed. She helped slide the red blanket off Marianne's shoulders and settled it back into its place across her lap.

"Where did this come from?" Marianne murmured, letting her fingers trace the embroidered crest.

"Colonel Brandon brought it." Elinor smiled as Marianne gripped the fabric tighter. "He felt you did not have enough blankets, and brought it a few days ago to help you to stay what he felt was warm enough."

"He found me, I remember his eyes through the rain..." Marianne murmured, half to herself.

"Mmmm, yes. And he has been here, almost afraid to leave your side since." Elinor tapped the blanket with her hand. "He went home only once, and that was when he brought this back, the rest of the time he had stayed here, unwilling to leave."

"What, he's here? Elinor, WHY DIDN'T YOU SAY ANYTHING?" Marianne cried as she tried to push herself back upright, only for Elinor to chuckle and push her back down.

"He left to go pick up Mama. It was at my request, Marianne, he will be back by day's end."

"Oh…" Marianne's voice trailed off as her eyes began to drift closed. "How long will that be?"

"I am not sure," Elinor soothed as she ran a hand over Marianne's hair. "But you should get some rest, and it will help the time pass faster."

"Nnnn…" Marianne agreed, already half asleep.

The sky was beginning to shine with the pinks and purples of sunset when Elinor heard a carriage outside the window. With a quick look at the slumbering Marianne she ran out of the room, dashing down the stairs to meet her frantic mother before she could get to far from the carriage.

"She is well, she woke and she is out of danger." Elinor ran to her mother's arms, letting Mary enfold her in her embrace as mother and daughter clung together. Mary began to tremble in Elinor's arms as she let her tears fall, Elinor's eyes lifting to meet the relieved gaze of Brandon.

"Come, she is sleeping, just sleeping, but should awaken soon." Elinor shifted Mary, leaving her arm around her mother's waist as she led her into the manor, Brandon close behind them.

By the time they had reached Marianne's room she had begun to stir, her eyes opening to see her mother standing in the door, her hand over her mouth as her eyes filled with tears.

"Mama," Marianne whispered as she reached out a hand, which Mary quickly rushed forward to grab.

Brandon stood in the hallway, his own eyes shimmering with emotion as he watched Mary slip onto the bed and take Marianne into her arms. Marianne's gaze turned to meet his, and after a few moments she smiled, mouthing the words 'thank you' to him, as she let herself sink into her mother's embrace.

"Lord Willoughby," Mary sighed as she rested her head against Marianne's, having just been informed of all that had happened and all that had been learned since her daughters had left for London. "I find it almost hard to believe. We were all deceived by him, weren't we?"

"I believe he deceived himself, more than any other." Marianne's voice was thoughtful. "He wanted to believe in his own fine words, more afraid of losing what he perceived to be his status, his comforts, than to know who he truly was on his own." She sighed, her fingers running over the red blanket that was never far from her touch. "I am so glad you are here, Mama."

"I know my darling, I am glad to be here as well. And as soon as you are well enough, we will begin our journey home."

"Home," Marianne sighed, "I think I shall truly be glad to be at home." She tucked the blanket closer around herself, and her hand came to rest over the embroidered crest at the corner.

CHAPTER THIRTY

The journey back to the cottage was quiet, but it was also more peaceful than the first portion of their trip to Mrs. Jennings's. While Brandon did not choose to join the ladies in the carriage, he rode beside it, escorting it the entire length of the journey.

Marianne found her eyes wandering from the scenery to his profile, appreciating his figure as he seemed to be one with his horse through long years of riding. She often found herself distracted by the shifting of his shoulders as he reigned the horse in, the sun reflecting off his silvery hair, the flick of his ears as he picked up sounds she could only imagine hearing.

On rare occasions his eyes would turn and meet hers, their amber depths glowing in the sunlight. Where before, as young and immature as she had been even six months before, Marianne would have averted her eyes with a blush, now she met his gaze full on, letting a smile curve her lips, an answering one forming on his handsome face.

Elinor smiled as she would catch Marianne looking at Brandon, it was much more entertaining than the book that she had brought with her. Not that she would let Marianne know she was watching, it would have embarrassed her sister. When her gaze met her mother's, she saw a similar smile returned, both women thoroughly amused watching the pair poorly pretending not to watch the other.

"It will be good to have both of my daughters home." Mary finally broke the silence, hiding her smirk when Marianne started and quickly turned from the window.

"Yes, while London was lovely, I missed the quiet of the country. There is such interesting scenery here." Elinor responded, winking to Mary as Marianne's cheeks flushed pink.

"I hate you..." Marianne huffed as she settled back into the bench, her arms crossing over her chest.

"No, you don't." Elinor nudged her with her shoulder, which made Marianne's lips curve before she responded with a harder nudge of her own.

"It would serve you right if I did." Marianne laughed, letting her head hit Elinor's shoulder.

"Oh, I have missed you both." Tears shone in Mary's eyes as she watched her daughters. While she had enjoyed the quiet... for a day... she had truly missed the energy that her daughters brought to the house.

"We missed you as well Mama." Elinor reached out a hand, waiting for Mary take it before Elinor squeezed. A mischievous smile turned her lips as she glanced down at Marianne, a matching expression on her sister.

"OH, STOP!" Mary laughed as Elinor and Marianne launched themselves at their mother, both crowding her on her bench, their arms scrambling to come around her.

When Brandon next looked into the carriage, he saw the pile of three women, arms around each other, as they dozed lightly together.

Marianne let her hand trace the keys of the familiar piano at the cottage, her thoughts on the hours she had sat at it, learning new music, challenging herself at Brandon's encouragement. How she had changed, how she had grown, she felt like a wholly different person than the child who had left the cottage only a few months before. While she still appreciated the beauty of the instrument, she knew the work that it took to maintain it, to keep it properly tuned.

She smiled as she heard Jonathan and Martha chatter with her mother in the kitchen, making plans for the week, what was to be served, tasks to be completed. She had a new appreciation for them, without them, she knew she would have been lost when it came to preparing any food. Lord, she hadn't even known how to light a fire when they had moved here.

How many things had she taken for granted, accepted without a thought? How many people had she overlooked? Could she even name any of the servants at Norland? She wasn't quite sure if she could.

But now she would make sure to know everyone who worked with her, to know their lives, their families. To truly work with them, rather than ordering others around without regard for their own needs and time.

She let her thoughts carry her to the window, her fingers coming to rest on the pain as she saw Brandon speaking with the driver from the carriage. His smile flashed, a glint off the slight fangs, and even though she could not hear what he said, she could just imagine the humor in his voice.

"Colonel Brandon is a good man, I think." Marianne's tone was pensive as she watched him.

"He is." Elinor responded as she stepped up behind Marianne to wrap her arms around her sister's waist. Her chin hit Marianne's shoulder as she too considered the man through the window.

"What a life he has known. He stayed faithful to the first woman he loved, even after he had lost her. His struggles, his journey, what he has had to endure, and yet he still seeks to find moments of happiness in life." She sighed and let her head drift to meet Elinor's. "I daresay *he* is the true romantic."

"Hmmm." Elinor murmured, letting Marianne continue her thoughts.

"It is not what we say... or what we feel that makes us what we are, it is what we do." Marianne mused, pausing for a moment before continuing. "Or fail to do."

"Do you still find him too proper?" Elinor teased as she swayed with Marianne in her arms.

"Hmmm, no, I can't say I do. Oh, he is proper, very proper, but have you noticed that he only keeps that stiff propriety in company of those he is not familiar with?"

"I can't say that I have."

"He does." Marianne smiled as she spoke. "His eyes lose that coolness that he had when we first met, and you can see the warmth that he hides. You can see it when he speaks with those that work for him."

Marianne straightened when Brandon turned from the groomsman and made his way to the door, giving him a soft smile as he entered.

"I must leave you for now, Adam wants to get the horses back to the stable for a rest, and I need to see to the mountain of paperwork that no doubt awaits me."

Elinor smiled as she released her arms from around Marianne and quickly made her way into the kitchen... to politely eavesdrop next to her mother and Martha.

"Why is he leaving now when he has the advantage?" Mary whispered softly.

Elinor noticed Brandon's lips curl into a faint smile, and knew he had heard them, but did not make a move to stop their conversation.

"I have heard that the great tamers of horses do it by being gentle, then walking away." Elinor whispered even more quietly into her mother's ear. "Nine times out of ten, the wild horse will follow."

"Are you comparing your sister to a wild horse?" Mary teased quietly as she glanced at Elinor.

"She is a proud wild mare, destined to find her own path." Elinor smiled as Marianne took a step to follow Brandon as he bowed slightly then made his way out to Adam and the waiting horses and carriage outside.

Marianne sighed as she watched Brandon and Adam disappear down the path, barely acknowledging that her mother and sister had come to her side.

"Elinor," Marianne sighed, and Elinor realized Marianne must have realized more than she had thought. "I look back at my conduct last autumn. I truly was a fool wasn't I, to myself, and inconsiderate of everyone else as I tried to pursue a flight of fancy."

"Marianne, please do not compare your conduct with Lord Willoughby." Elinor's eyes narrowed as she spoke.

"I don't." Marianne shrugged. "I compare it with what it should have been." She turned to meet Elinor's eyes full on "I compare it with yours. I only hope that I am wiser now."

"You have always been wise, my dear." Mary wrapped her arm around Marianne as she spoke, causing Marianne to smile.

"You know, I have determined to enter into a course of serious study." Marianne grinned as she spoke, "Colonel Brandon has promised me that I am welcome at Hartland as often as I would like to borrow books and to play the beautiful piano that he has."

"Hmmm, he is quite generous." Elinor laughed.

"Oh, I daresay he is." Mary chuckled, "but I do have to ask Marianne, would you be going to study the books... or to study the good Colonel?"

"MAMA!" Marianne cried in outrage, making both Mary and Elinor still, worried they had misread Marianne's intention, only to relax as Marianne burst out laughing. "Who is to say I cannot do both?"

Indeed, Marianne waited only two days to walk to Hartland, Martha walking behind her with a knowing grin.

"Stop it." Marianne groaned as she caught sight of Martha's grin, before offering her arm for the woman to take.

"I do not know what you are talking about Miss." Martha giggled as she hesitantly took the offered arm, her smile growing when Marianne laughed.

"As if I haven't seen you, Elinor and Mama buzzing about together, whispering in corners."

"There is a lot of planning to do Miss." Martha's face was the look of innocence.

"Not when you stop talking the moment I enter the room!" Marianne exclaimed, shooting the other woman a mock glare. "Thus, I know you were speaking of me, I just wish to know about what."

"Well......" Martha bit her cheek as Marianne pouted, her face turning to face away from her. "We were taking bets on how long it would take you to visit Hartland... to visit your mare of course." Martha laughed as Marianne's face whipped back to her, her eyes wide.

"You didn't!"

"Oh, I daresay we did Miss, in fact it was at your mother's suggestion."

"Oh, well now I have to know, who won?"

"I did, if you would believe it." Martha laughed. "Your mother was sure you would march after him less than an hour after he left, your sister said your stubborn streak would mean you would wait at least a week. Jonathan, bless his soul, was confused as to why you would visit Hartland at all when you had only just returned to the cottage, but I said, I give it two days, and then she will visit."

"And how did you select the two days?" Marianne was curious.

"Knowing you as long as I have Miss Marianne, I know how curious and also how headstrong you are. You wouldn't want to go immediately, yet at the same time, you want to know what is in those books, and to see your young man again."

"He isn't my young man…" Marianne grumbled, her eyes dropping to the floor. True, no matter how well she thought of him, and how he seemed to enjoy being around her, that didn't make him her anything… did it?

"Come now Miss, none of that." Martha slowed them to a stop, waiting for Marianne to look back at her face. "I have seen him around you since you met him, and Elinor told your mother and I how he cared for you when you were sick. If he isn't *your* young man, I will eat my shoe."

"I hope you are right." Marianne sighed as she resumed walking with Martha, her pace quickening as they approached Hartland.

As soon as she saw the formal gardens, the hydrangea beginning to flower with their mix of pink and blue, her heart began to race. It may have made no sense to anyone else how seeing the flowers mixed into the gardens would make her heart race, but to her, it was the first time someone had asked her opinion and listened, truly listened, and followed it. And how beautiful it looked, the hydrangeas were much more fluid, adding a sense of harmony to the garden that the roses had lacked.

Beyond the garden movement caught her eye, drawing her gaze to the entryway, and the man that stood in it. She couldn't see his face, but somehow knew that his whole attention was on her as she made her way closer. She was so entranced watching him come into more focus that she did not even notice Martha stepping away, nor hear the delighted giggle of the other woman.

"Miss Marianne," Brandon bowed as the two women came closer, "I welcome you again to Hartland. I hope you find it as… inviting as I do."

"I am sure I will, Colonel." Marianne's cheeks warmed as she spoke.

"Come, let me show you to the library, there are a great many books that I am sure will capture your attention."

"I… Thank you sir." Marianne found herself stammering as Brandon offered his arm, but stepped forward to take it, letting her fingers trail down the sleeve of his jacket as she did, relishing the slight shiver she felt him give at the movement.

What the inside of the home looked like, Marianne could not tell you, the only thing she saw was the man beside her, and his smile when he looked at her and grinned.

"Here we are." His voice was deeper, his eyes a darker hue of amber as he opened a door, letting Marianne step in before him. Marianne reluctantly turned her attention to the new room... and gasped as soon as she saw her surroundings.

While some libraries seemed dark, cold almost, this was warm, and just as Brandon had said, inviting. There were shelves, floor to the tall ceiling, filled with books of all sizes and colors. A settee sat by the window, the blanket draped over its back telling her it was a well-loved and well-used piece of furniture. Beside it sat one of the grandest pianos she had ever had the pleasure of seeing, its polished mahogany gleaming, along with its gilded golden accents.

A desk sat against a side wall, its wood showing its years of use, polished till it shone, a sturdy, yet somehow also comfortable looking, leather chair behind it.

"I... ah... had a desk put in here for work, it is not my usual study, but I do find I work here most of the time." Brandon ran a hand over his neck as he spoke, his cheeks taking on a ruddy hue with the words.

"It is beautiful, I do not blame you for wanting to work here." Marianne smiled at him as she turned, taking in the majesty of the room. "I would never want to leave either."

Brandon's mouth opened for a moment, only to close again, his cheeks flushing deeper at whatever thought had gone through his head.

"The books are organized by topic." He cleared his throat as he crossed into the room. "At the far wall, closest to the window, you will find books on the sciences, the studies of Galileo, Aristotle, Leonardo da Vinci." He stopped at the second wall and tapped a book. "These are literature, novels, poetry, of various ages. Some of the books are quite heavy, those are all found on the bottom shelves, if you would like one of those please call for either me or for my staff to come and help you with it."

"I thank you, Colonel."

"Brandon..." Marianne's eyes darted to meet his as he spoke. "Please... call me Brandon."

"If you will call me Marianne." she smiled, thrilled at his request.

"Perfect... Marianne." He grinned back at her, but a slight sound from Martha had him starting, his eyes closing as he suddenly remembered they were not alone. "I will leave you to your studies then."

"I... Brandon..." Marianne called out as he began to take a step, and he paused, his ears flicking back to her. "I did not know if you still had work to do, but if this is your primary place for doing it... you are more than welcome to join me."

Brandon's ears quivered as he turned to see Marianne, the sun from the window framing her perfectly, and smiled.

"I would love to."

CHAPTER THIRTY-ONE

Over the next few weeks Marianne was a frequent visitor at Hartland, often dragging Elinor with her to pour over the books... at least that was the reason Marianne gave.

Elinor smiled as Marianne shifted in her chair, moving it ever so slowly closer to Brandon's desk, and Brandon's shifting of his own chair towards Marianne.

It made her heart happy to see Marianne laugh at a comment Brandon had made, his ears twitching to catch her response. They looked good together, but more than that, they looked comfortable with each other.

It truly was remarkable seeing the difference in Brandon's demeanor between his public and his private behavior. Now Elinor could see what Marianne had months prior, the casual warmth that Brandon had when he was around those he trusted. The man had infinite patience, especially where Marianne was concerned, and frequently would put aside his own paperwork to help her understand a portion of a book, or a concept that was raised.

Of course, Elinor was sure, the fact that he would get to stand behind Marianne, his hand on her shoulder or next to hers as it held the book may have had something to do with how eager he was.

But what really made her smile as she hid her face in her own book was not when Brandon would help Marianne, but when Marianne would help him with his work. It had started subtly, he would be muttering to himself about a problem that had arisen, and Marianne would offer a short response, which made him pause and reconsider the problem at hand. Now, he would just motion her closer to his desk and show her the report or the ledgers, asking her for her input or advice on how to handle various situations.

And more importantly, at least to Marianne, he often would take her advice into consideration and often implemented it or a version of it.

"Hmmm, so if we were to rotate the planting of wheat, peas, and you said, I believe, turnips, each year it could actually help improve the production of the fields?" Brandon questioned as he considered the letter from his farmers carefully. Field productions had dropped, which was causing concern for some of his tenants, and none of the newest fertilizers that had been acquired in trade had helped.

"I think so," Marianne bit her lip as she read the document again. "One of the new trades you have on the shelf talks about a process of... I think they said 'crop rotation,' and that it increased the yield for each subsequent year."

"Which one was it?" Brandon pushed himself up, waiting for Marianne to stand quickly before she moved to one of the bookshelves, her fingers scanning the spines until she found a small paper pamphlet. She quickly pulled it out and scanned it, nodding as she read before turning back to Brandon, pointing to a section.

"Here, this is where they recommended it, along with something called fallow, but I am not sure what that is."

"It's leaving a field untilled for a season." Brandon murmured as he scanned the pamphlet, his hand moving to grasp it. His pinky brushed Marianne's hand by accident, causing them both to freeze for a moment, Brandon quickly pulling his finger away, his cheeks tinged with pink.

When Marianne shifted her pinky to rest against his, however, the movement was slow, deliberate. The casual contact made her heart race, and she gasped when Brandon shifted his finger to twine it with hers, hidden behind the pamphlet.

"Thank you, I think this will help solve the tenants' concern and ultimately help increase production." Brandon's voice was soft as he spoke, which only increased the air of intimacy between them.

"Even with the untilled field?" Marianne looked up at him, her own cheeks flushing at the expression in his eyes.

"I believe so. I will go out and discuss it with them all, would you... would you like to go with me? It was your suggestion after all."

"I..." the feel of his finger sliding against hers made Marianne lose her train of thought as she lost herself in his eyes. It was only Elinor's soft cough that drew her out of her daze, and with great reluctance she let her hand fall from the paper, missing the warmth of his hand already. "I do not want to be in the way."

"You would never be in the way, Marianne." Brandon whispered, as he reached out to tuck one of her curls behind her ear. She automatically leaned her face into his hand, sighing as his fingers trailed along her cheek.

"It is getting late, so I do not think it would be proper for me to go with you, if you were going today."

Brandon groaned as she stepped away. "I probably should, we are about to begin planting season, and we need to determine the best rotation for the next yield."

"Then, we will leave you to it." Marianne gave a small smile before she turned, her eyes meeting Elinor's, who rose immediately from her own chair.

Both sisters gave Brandon a slight curtsey before stepping out of the library, Marianne's arm wrapped through Elinor's as they made their way through the home.

"Marianne..." Brandon's voice made Marianne pause as she turned to see him holding the door jamb from the library, his golden eyes shining. "If I were to come by... tomorrow... would I be able to speak with your mother and... and then with you?"

Marianne's smile blinded the sun as it lit her face.

"I will tell her to expect you."

"Oh Elinor, wasn't it wonderful?" Marianne gushed as she fell backwards on the bed after dinner that evening.

"Yes, I dare say that Jonathan outdid himself with dinner." Elinor chuckled even as Marianne shot her a glare.

"You know that is not what I meant." Marianne groused before her face broke into another smile. "I cannot believe that Brandon would not only listen to my suggestion but actually go to take it to his tenants."

"It's not the first time he has listened to your suggestions, Marianne, so is it that surprising?"

"For something this big? Yes." Marianne pushed herself up onto her elbows. "It made me... I don't know Elinor, as if I was his partner, an equal worthy of listening to." She groaned as she fell back against the bed. "Lord, I hope I didn't read too much into his question. Its just – it's been so nice, no, so *wonderful* being able to spend time with him, the real him. Do I want him to ask one particular question so much that I cannot see anything else?"

"Marianne," Elinor chuckled as she sat beside her sister on the bed. "No one looking at him, at you both, could ever think that he wasn't inferring exactly what you thought."

"AHHHHHHHHHHHHHHHHHHHHHHHHHHH." Marianne grabbed her pillow and held it over her face as she screamed into it, her legs bouncing off the bed. All of a sudden she froze, the pillow shifting down to reveal one brown eye as she looked at her sister.

"What is it, Marianne?" Elinor's brow rose as she met her sister's gaze.

"I'm a horrible person." The response was muffled by the pillow, but Elinor was able to hear it clearly.

"Why on earth would you say that, Marianne?" Elinor chided as she leaned over to poke Marianne's arm.

"I just…"

"Marianne, if you are going to talk, I think you should remove the pillow from your face." Elinor laughed as she grabbed the pillow away, revealing Marianne's concerned face. "Now what is it?"

"It just struck me, I'm here, excited about the possibility of Brandon and a future with him, while you…" Marianne sighed, "I feel like I got so caught up in my own world I did not think about what it would be doing to you."

"It is doing *nothing* to me dearest," Elinor smiled as she reached out and took Marianne's hand. "Being excited for you has nothing to do with Edward or Lucy or anything of my situation, I can be over the moon for you without it affecting me at all."

"Dearest Elinor, I do not want to be the cause of any further heartache for you. Please forgive me."

"Marianne, there is nothing to forgive." Elinor squeezed Marianne's hand. "I am happy for you, truly, Brandon is a good man who I believe will make you happy."

"I know he will." Marianne grinned before her smile turned downwards. "But what if he doesn't ask, how would I ever face him again?"

"With your head held high, showing him again and again why he would be mad to let you slip through his fingers." Elinor let herself lay down next to Marianne, her head resting against hers on the bed. "Though I do think you should wear your blue muslin dress tomorrow, it is so pretty against your skin, and I dare say the Colonel does seem to like blue."

"Hmmm, he does, doesn't he." Marianne nudged Elinor with her shoulder.

"Oh he truly does," Elinor chuckled, "though we must be careful not to do your hair too well, or let Martha set your bodice too low, you want him to have enough wits to ask his question of Mama."

"Colonel Brandon speechless, now there is a sight I long to see."

"I am sure you will, perhaps on your wedding night?" Elinor teased.

"Perhaps, but... Elinor?" Marianne asked as she turned to her side, facing her sister, but waited to speak until Elinor turned as well. "I... well... what happens on a wedding night?"

"I – I, actually, I do not know." Elinor said wryly, as she realized she had no idea either.

"I hear all this talk about the wedding night, and the girls we knew at Norland who all wed would blush and begin to fan themselves, or grimace and refuse to talk about it. I just was curious what a wedding night entailed."

"Well... I am sure it involves sleeping in the same bed as your new husband." Elinor mused.

"Oh, well... that doesn't seem like something to blush about though." Marianne huffed as she flopped back again, grimacing when her head smacked the bed instead of the pillow. "And I doubt Mama would want to tell me, I remember her getting flustered when John had asked Fanny to marry him, and he is a *man*, who I am sure is more worldly than you or I." Marianne's eyes brightened as she had a thought. "OH, I COULD ASK MARTHA!"

"You coul... Marianne!!" Elinor grabbed Marianne's hand as she began to jump out of the bed. "Martha is ASLEEP. You can ask her in the morning if you feel the need."

"Don't think I won't." Marianne grumbled as she lay back down, making sure to grab the pillow from the floor. "Oh Elinor, I daresay I will not be able to sleep tonight."

"You will, though." Elinor ran her hand down Marianne's hair, stopping at her sister's cheek. "Because the sooner you fall asleep, the sooner tomorrow will be here."

"Hnnnn." Marianne hummed, relaxing under the Elinor's movements. "I am going to ask Martha though…"

"Oh, I have no doubt." Elinor grinned as Marianne let out a little sigh and, despite her statement, slid to sleep.

CHAPTER THIRTY-TWO

"N o."

Marianne's mouth dropped open as she stared at Martha, unable to process what she had heard.

"But..."

"No." Martha's face was beet red as she hurried away from Marianne, but Marianne was determined to follow her.

"Martha, please. I just want to know."

"No Miss Marianne, there are some things that one does not talk about in polite company."

"But Martha, it is just us! I asked Elinor, and she did not know any..."

"Well, I would hope not!"

"And I can't ask Mama but you are married, so I am sure that you know."

"Why this sudden interest in... indecent topics Miss?"

"Indecent? What is indecent?" Marianne's head tilted as her lips pursed together. "Elinor said you slept in the same bed as your husband, is that what is indecent?"

"Miss Marianne, this is a better topic for your husband!"

"Yes, but seeing as I do not *have* one of those yet, I am trying to learn." Marianne reasoned, and Martha found it very hard to keep her lips from twitching.

"I am not telling you where babies come from Lady Marianne."

"What does a wedding night have to do with where babies come from?" Marianne puzzled, and Martha turned, wide eyed, to stare at her. "I mean, babies are brought by the stork, at least that's what Mama said."

"I... oh Miss Marianne." Martha sputtered, torn between outrage and pure amusement at the sheer confusion on Marianne's face.

"Now I am even more curious, what exactly does a wedding night have to do with having babies?"

A deep cough from behind her had Marianne's cheeks flushing. No, that was not Jonathan, the cough was much too deep, that sounded more like...

"I have to say this is the most... amusing conversation I have walked in on."

Marianne turned slowly, her cheeks warming even more when she met the molten gold gaze of the Fae standing outside her mother's parlor, Mary behind him with her hand over her mouth.

"C...colonel." Marianne croaked as she gave a small curtsey, hoping at that moment that the ground would open and swallow her.

"Despite how – intriguing – I find this conversation, I was wondering if I may have a moment of your time, Miss Marianne." Brandon grinned.

With a slight bow, Brandon held out his hand to Marianne, whose eyes snapped to her mother's. When her mother's eyes softened and she nodded, Marianne let her embarrassment fade as she reached out and placed her hand in Brandon's. When his hand closed over hers, the warmth from it seemed to envelop her as he led her out of the cottage and towards the willow tree that graced the property, its boughs sweeping the ground. Beneath its branches lay a red blanket, the Hartland crest embroidered on the edge, a basket of pink hydrangea resting against the trunk with a single white rose in the center.

"I... Colonel..."

"Brandon." He murmured as he turned her to face him.

"Brandon..." she breathed, her heart beginning to pound. "I..." she paused, suddenly finding herself without any words.

"Marianne." Brandon took a deep breath, as if to center himself before continuing. "I think... I hope you know why I wanted to speak with you. I ask that you let me finish, before you respond." When Marianne slowly nodded she saw his shoulders ease as his eyes closed. "When we first met, you were told that I had my heart broken, and that because of that, I had not let my heart be swayed by any other, do you remember?"

Marianne began to answer, then remembered his request and nodded, not wanting to interrupt him.

"I was – lonely, as a child. My father had unfortunately passed away when I was a child, and my half-brother stepped up to rule his lands in his place. After his passing, my mother was not well with her health. The village I grew up in, however, welcomed us, and did their best to help. There was a girl who lived in town, Winifried, who was around my same age. We spent all of our time together, growing, even though I began to age more slowly than she was by the time we were 15. By the time we were 20, I still looked the same as I had 5 years before, while she had grown into being a woman."

Marianne shifted as he spoke, her teeth catching her bottom lip as she listened. Brandon paused as he gave a soft smile and stepped closer, teasing her bottom lip with his thumb as she released it with a gasp.

"Let me finish Marianne," his voice was solemn as he watched her, "I want you to know the full story before I ask my question."

"Alright." She whispered, and his hand thumb shifted, caressing her cheek before his hand fell away.

"You see, I am not full Fae, my father was a very strong and noble Fae and my mother a human, but they fell in love, a true, deep love. But because of that, many felt uncomfortable around me. But not Winifred. She was my only friend, and the only person of the opposite gender that would truly spend time with me for me. Others would seek me out for my strength, or my speed, but Winifried was the only one that I felt spent time with me because she chose to. And, at the time, I felt fondness for her, fondness that at the tender age of 20, I felt was love. She had protested, saying that by the time we were 50 I would just then be looking like I was 20, and she would have been an old maid." He sighed and then continued. "There is a ritual... a... binding if you will, that a Fae can perform, even a half Fae like me, that will tie the life of their partner to them, something stronger than human marriage, more lasting than any other vow."

"And you wanted that with her?" Marianne whispered, her heart hurting for Brandon, but also for herself.

"I... I thought I did." He admitted, his head lowered, unable to meet her gaze. "She was safe, she was comfortable, and I thought that was what love was. But... she did not agree. When I first brought up the thought of the two of us being together, she laughed. Oh, she didn't mean it maliciously, but the thought was so amusing to her because she had never once thought of me in that manner. Her heart belonged to a medicine apprentice in the next town , who came to our village to trade with us. The next time the apprentice came to visit, she left with him as his wife and never looked behind at me."

"Oh Brandon." Tears had formed in Marianne's eyes as he had spoken, and he lifted his head to hers, his gaze scanning hers.

"That was more than 400 years ago. At that time, Samuel, my full-blooded half-brother, , approached me and gave me a choice, join his military and stay in the same village I had grown up in, or leave."

"And those were your only choices?" Marianne gasped.

"Not every family is as close as yours is Marianne." Brandon gave a sad smile. "I chose to leave, to find my own place, my own path, one not burdened by memories and people who only knew me as the half-prince. To not be forced to relive memories that now hurt and burned."

He turned to the side, his gaze drawn by the basket of flowers. "I made my way, fighting where I could, learning, providing aid, building a wall around my heart to keep myself from being hurt again. And then I found myself in charge of Hartland. The property and its land were failing when I took it over 50 years ago, but it has begun to thrive, and most importantly to me, the people who live and work there are happy."

"But are you happy?" Marianne found herself asking, and Brandon turned to capture her gaze with his.

"I thought I was." He nodded but paused before he continued. "I think honestly it was more I was content, and yes, I know it is not the same, but it was the best I had. And then..." Marianne found herself holding her breath as his smile grew. "Then a little spitfire entered into my life, playing the piano so passionately that it took me by surprise. A spitfire with locks of raven hair, and eyes the color of molten chocolate that saw the world in a way I had never seen it before. I watched that girl, the woman, grow, to come into her own, saw her stand on her own two feet when society sought to tear her down. She made me realize that what I had felt before was only the fondness of friendship."

He took a step closer, and Marianne found herself tilting her head back to keep her gaze on his.

"This woman showed me what it meant to truly have a partner," he continued, "to have someone you can talk to, to be yourself around. She is shrewd, so bright that she deserves all the accolades that can be given, she is joyful, bringing a smile to everyone who meets her or is honored to know her. And that woman has bewitched me, body and soul." His fingers swept across her cheek, carrying the moisture that had begun to fall at his words. "This beautiful, precious woman, she has shown me what it means to love, and to love desperately. There is a question, one that has been burning in my heart to ask her, but I hesitated, waiting to know where her own heart lay because gods above, she deserves nothing but true happiness and joy in her life.”

“And...” Marianne swallowed, trying to ease the butterflies in her stomach at his words, “and do you now know?”

“I hope so, no, I pray so.” He took another step closer, close enough that Marianne could feel the heat of his body reaching out to her. “Marianne...” his voice softened, for her ears only. “I spoke with your mother, and informed her of my intentions, to ask her permission to approach you. But there is only one answer, one person’s answer, that truly matters. I love you, I love you most ardently.”

“Brandon...” Marianne whispered, her eyes closing at his words.

“Marianne, I would be forever honored if you would consent to be not just my wife, but my partner for life, to grow old with me, raise a family together, and to spend centuries letting me learn with you.” His hand took hers, lifting it gently to his mouth as he placed a kiss on the back of it, his eyes capturing hers as they reopened. “Marry me Marianne, make me the happiest man in England, no, the world.”

“Oh Brandon,” Marianne smiled even as tears fell from her eyes. “How could you think the answer would be anything but yes?”

A small, choked sound that was suspiciously like a sob broke from his lips as his arms came around her, drawing her into his chest as his nose buried itself in her hair.

“I swear I will make you happy.” He vowed, his words whispered, but heartfelt.

“We will make each other happy.” She whispered back, her own voice deep with emotion.

Brandon lifted his head for a moment, his golden eyes swimming with his own tears before he slowly bent, placing his lips against hers.

Marianne let out a soft gasp as a shiver ran through her at the feel of his lips against hers. Oh... oh this was what she had expected a kiss to feel like, the heat, the longing, the...

Her soft sound of disappointment as he lifted his head had Brandon chuckling before he wrapped his arms around her waist and lifted her, spinning her around in his joy.

When he finally let her leave his arms, he bent and took the basket of flowers, his face almost bashful as he handed them to her.

"Flowers have a language," he murmured, "and in case you knew it, I wanted to make sure I chose ones that showed you how I felt."

"I don't know it," Marianne smiled as she sniffed the rose, "but I would love to hear what they mean."

"I... the pink hydrangea means love, sincere emotion. And... they are from my... well our... garden, the hydrangea that I planted after your first visit. And the white rose, that is you, what you are to me, and it means eternal love."

"Eternal love, I like the sound of that." Marianne smiled as she again lifted the basket to catch the scent of the rose. "An eternity by your side."

Brandon's arm snuck around her waist to hold her close to him, his eyes closed as he relished the feeling. Marianne let her own arms circle his waist, holding him as close as he held her, as she breathed in his scent, forever imprinting the scent of sandalwood and musk that surrounded him.

"I do have another question though." Brandon mused, an eyebrow raising as he drew slightly back, putting a small bit of distance between himself and Marianne.

"Hmmm?" Marianne hummed, to happy to give it much thought.

"Why were you asking about what a wedding night had to do with having children?"

Marianne's face turned bright red as she tried to pull out of his arms, only for them to tighten around her as he grinned. "Oh no, I want an answer, Marianne." he chuckled.

Marianne pouted, the gesture making Brandon's grip around her waist tense as he groaned before she answered.

"It was... it was just a comment that Elinor made last night, about something happening on the wedding night... and..." her voice trailed off as she buried her face in his chest.

"And..."

"AndneitherElinororiknewwhatwouldhappenandiwantedtoknow."

Brandon went still as he tried to make sense of her words, and then his shoulders began to shake before he broke out into full body laughter.

"It wasn't that funny." Marianne groaned.

"It is, and one day you will realize why." Brandon's laughter faded to chuckles as he lifted her chin to meet his gaze.

"Why won't anyone tell me though?"

The smile that curved his lips sent sensation through Marianne, one she had felt around Brandon before, but never quite as strong. When he bent down, his breath hit her ear and she found herself shivering, not with cold, but with the sensation that it caused.

"Because, Marianne," he breathed her name slowly as she gasped, "some things are better experienced in the moment, it just isn't the same when you are told."

A soft nip of teeth against her ear had her trembling, her knees threatening to buckle as Brandon straightened, his eyes shimmering with a deep copper.

"I..." She stammered, her breathing ragged.

"I can give you a small preview, if you would like," Brandon's voice was husky, the sound sending another wave of sensation through Marianne, making her entire body pulse. "Just a taste... because god your mouth is a temptation."

At his words Marianne's breath caught, and her teeth began to worry her bottom lip.

"Just a taste..." Brandon growled as he watched her lips, and then he descended, his mouth capturing hers as he pulled her close against him.

If she thought their first kiss was everything a kiss was supposed to be, she was wrong, oh so wrong. The basket of flowers fell, forgotten, to the ground as her hands caught at his shoulders. The slant of his mouth changed and she felt herself whimper, her body caught in a sea of flames as his tongue teased the seam of her mouth. When she opened it tentatively Brandon groaned and pulled himself away from her, placing his forehead against hers as he panted, struggling to bring his emotions under control.

"That is what it will be like on our wedding night, and every night thereafter." He groaned, his eyes opening to meet hers. "That and more, so much more."

"Oh..." Marianne whispered, her own eyes closing as she tried to get her breathing back under control.

"Come, let us tell your family the good news, and then I will head to the church, to ask that the bans be read."

Marianne nodded, letting Brandon claim her hand, her fingers tightly wound around his, as he knelt to put the flowers back in the basket and handed it to her.

As Elinor, Mary and Martha chattered excitedly around her, Marianne kept her gaze on Brandon, and the happy twinkle in his eye. No, the wedding night was no longer something to be feared, but something to be anticipated.

She was going to be his wife. Brandon's wife.

When her smile formed, she tipped her head back and laughed. *She was going to be Brandon's wife!*

CHAPTER THIRTY-THREE

Oh, the organized chaos that came with planning a wedding.

Elinor smiled as she watched her mother and Mrs. Jennings, now thick as thieves, whispering in the corner over guests to invite and discussing trips to the modiste with Mrs. Jennings's assistance. Middleton had been by earlier to express his congratulations, and to help take credit for the match. Mrs. Jennings had scowled at the man and shooed him out of the house, his laughter trailing behind him as he cheerfully let himself out.

Marianne herself sat with Martha, continuing her lessons about running a household. They had gone to the nearby village that sat as part of Hartland's estate, Marianne swore it was for informational purposes, yet Elinor felt it was in part to get a moment to breathe with how excited Mary and Mrs. Jennings both were.

Jonathan seemed to be the only one who was not caught up in the comings and goings, content to keep the cottage running as it was. In a way, Elinor blessed the man, he was the one ensuring there was food for the table and they had fresh fabric for the never-ending mending. He and Elinor had gone over the budget for the week only the day prior, and he had made his way to Exeter for some of the items they would need only that morning.

In spite of all the excitement and cheer that had taken over the cottage though, Elinor could not help but find herself internally to be at odds.

While she was pleased, oh so very happy for her sister, it made her wonder about Edward, and whether his nuptials to Lucy had, in fact, gone forward. They had had little word from London in the weeks since their departure, and while on the one hand it was a blessing, on the other, the unknowing made Elinor's heart hurt.

She knew it did little to think about it… to think about him. No matter how she felt, nor how she would have liked to hope Edward felt, they were as separated now as any could be, for he was now tied to another.

She let herself take a moment, stepping away from the kitchen and the ever-present buzz of conversation, and made her way to the room she would soon no longer share with Marianne. Once alone she let herself take out the small book she had been given oh so many months ago when they had left Norland. Her hand shook as she opened it, her fingers tracing the familiar signature that it contained.

Your affectionate Friend- E. Ferrars.

While it hurt, she found herself giving a small smile. Even if she only had him as a friend, and not as a partner as her heart had secretly wished, Elinor could not say that she was not grateful for Edward's presence in her life. Indeed, friendship in and of itself was a beautiful thing, and with how often she was likely to visit Hartland, a friendship with the Rector of the estate would be a blessing. While it would pain her to see Edward and Lucy settle into their married life together, she would value the friendship and companionship they would provide.

"I hate him, you know." Marianne mused from the door, knowing exactly what Elinor was looking at, with how pensive her sister was.

"No, you don't. Nor should you." Elinor smiled despite her pain, loving her sister for her support.

"Well, because you say I should not then I don't, but I am not happy about how you were hurt."

"It is a way of life, Marianne. We do not all get our happy endings."

"Oh Elinor," Marianne said softly as she crossed the room to sit beside her sister, her arms wrapping around Elinor's waist. "If anyone should though, it is you."

"I get to see your happy ending though, Marianne." Elinor smiled as she closed the small book, setting it on the nightstand with a soft finality before turning to Marianne. "Mine will come, if it is meant to be."

"Is it bad of me to want you to have it now?" Marianne mussed. "I feel as though I am abandoning you and Mama, and I want to see you as happy as I am."

"Marianne, I am perfectly content." Elinor's brow rose as she spoke. "And it is not as though you are leaving to the other side of England. We shall see each other almost every day, if not every day still."

"It won't be the same though."

"No, it won't." Elinor agreed. "But that is how life works, it doesn't stay the same, people move, move on, that is normal. Look at John, when he moved to London."

"Yes, but that was a change we all wanted, I mean… could you imagine living with *Fanny* all the time? I nearly lost my mind in the time we shared at Norland."

Elinor laughed. "Sadly, I must agree with you there." Her laughter faded as her thoughts turned once again to Edward. "But there are others that she brought into our lives that were worth it."

"I can still say I hate him though." Marianne shot a glance at her sister, before both girls fell into laughter again.

"Marianne," Mary called from the kitchen, her voice tinged with her own laughter, "the Colonel is approaching, would you want to say hello?"

"YES!" Marianne scrambled from the bed to race down the stairs, Elinor following more slowly behind her, her humor continuing over Marianne's actions.

Elinor slid into the kitchen with Mary and Mrs. Jennings as Marianne rushed out the door to meet Brandon. The three women stood at the window and watched as he handed her a white rose, Marianne's face turning pink at the gesture, before he bent to place a kiss on her cheek.

"Do you remember when she swore to never be alone in his presence again Mama?" Elinor smiled as she watched the couple.

"Oh, indeed I do." Mary sighed. "I am glad she finally saw him for who he is."

"She is good for him." Mrs. Jennings agreed, all three women sighing when Brandon reached out to take Marianne's hand in his. "I have never in all my years knowing him seen him smile as much as he has this past week."

"It will be hard to part with her in three weeks," Mary admitted, "I know she will not be far, but there is something bittersweet about a child leaving the home."

"Was it the same with John?" Elinor pondered, only for Mary to shake her head.

"John was not mine, so it is not the same. One day, when you are a mother, you will see what I mean."

"It was the same with Charlotte's mother." Mrs. Jennings sighed, both of the elder women so lost in thought they did not see Elinor stiffening with the line of the conversation. "She was my only child, so it was hard when she moved out, harder still when she and her husband passed away. And then I felt it all again when Charlotte married Thomas."

"Oh, I believe I see Jonathan," Elinor latched on to the figure she saw approaching from a distance. "I will see if he needs any help."

"Alright my dear." Mary's voice trailed behind her as Elinor fled the room. While she may one day know what it would be to be a mother, right then, it was still too painful a discussion for her to be part of, as her heart hurt for what could have been, but would never be.

"Please let me know if there is anything that you all need, Marianne, I mean it." She heard Brandon say to her sister but could not make out Marianne's response as she hurried up the path to the approaching cart.

"Ah Miss Elinor, you didn't need to come to meet me, I would have been at the cottage soon enough." Jonathan said as he drew to a stop, waiting for Elinor to hop onto the cart beside him.

"Yes, I did." She murmured, causing Jonathan to chuckle.

"The women driving you crazy?"

"In a way." She admitted, smiling when he signaled the horse to continue, although at a much slower pace, continuing the short trip in blessed silence.

By the time they made it down to the cottage doors, Brandon waited astride his horse, nodding as Jonathan drew the cart to a stop.

"Jonathan, Miss Elinor."

"Ah Colonel," Jonathan greeted him, "leaving so soon?"

"Unfortunately, there is some business to attend to at Hartland, and I am working with the staff to prepare the house for the arrival of its new lady."

Marianne gave him a small but happy smile at his words, and Elinor saw him respond to her expression with a wink.

"Good," Jonathan nodded as he stepped down from the cart and offered his hand to Elinor, "though we are sorry to see Miss Marianne go."

"You are all welcome to Hartland at any time, I know how important her family are to her, and that includes you and Martha, Jonathan." Brandon's horse pranced in place as Brandon reigned him in. "Unfortunately, I must go, some of our farmers are discussing the crop rotation plan that Miss Marianne suggested."

"They decided to implement it?" Marianne gasped.

"It looks like we will be, it seems like it will help resolve the farmers' concern. But I must go, it would not do to be late."

"Take care, Sir, and godspeed." Jonathan nodded to him as he grabbed one of the wooden boxes from the back cart. Brandon responded with a nod to him, then to both Elinor and finally Marianne before he reluctantly turned his horse towards the path, nudging it into motion.

"Here Jonathan, let us help with that." Elinor took a basket from the cart, passing it to Marianne before grabbing one for herself.

"Thank you, Misses," Jonathan smiled, "I am grateful for the help."

"How was your trip, Jonathan?" Elinor continued as she stepped away from the cart, her basket carried in both hands.

"It was good, Miss Elinor," Jonathan nodded. "It was thankfully an easy trip, everything we were seeking was available at the market. Oh, that reminds me, Mrs. Ferrars sends her regards."

The simple statement stopped all movement as Marianne's head snapped to Elinor's, her eyes wide.

"Mrs... Mrs. Ferrars?" Elinor's voice was strained as she repeated it back to Jonathan. "Was Fanny's mother in Exeter then?"

"Oh, not the elder Mrs. Ferrars, the new Mrs. Ferrars, I believe you knew her as Miss Steele."

"Oh, I... I see." Marianne reached out to clasp Elinor's arm as Elinor spoke, a small, sad smile forming on her lips.

"She seemed quite excited to see me, she had only just arrived, she said, her and her husband, before they carried on to their new home. It seems they married, oh I think she said it was a week ago or so." Jonathan groaned as he hefted another box to his shoulders. "Let me run these in Misses, then I will be back for the rest, the baskets can go straight to Martha."

"Thank you, Jonathan." Marianne said when Elinor stayed quiet, but her eyes stayed locked on her sister.

After a few moments Elinor let her eyes close, and a gentle shudder ran through her body, making Marianne's eyes mist with tears.

"Oh Elinor..."

"It is fine Marianne, it is as we expected." Elinor forced her eyes open as she pushed her hurt to the side, there would be time to give in to it later, when she was alone, she would not break here, even though she knew Marianne would be there for support. "There is nothing to surprise or upset us. And, in a little while, it will be as if nothing had happened, and we can go back to speaking as friends."

"Are you sure Elinor?" Marianne stepped closer, bending down to place her basket on the ground before wrapping her arms around Elinor.

"Well, I expect I will not be visiting the rectory for a time, but yes, I do believe that after a while I will be able to act as though nothing occurred, because in truth, nothing did, after all."

"I know but, I still hate him for you." Marianne sighed as Elinor gave a small laugh and wrapped an arm back around her sister.

"Very well then, but only for a day, then we must carry on, after all, he truly did no wrong to us. Now come, we need to get these into Martha before she comes out to scold us for dilly-dallying outside."

"I suppose." Marianne gruffed, and Elinor chuckled as Marianne grabbed her basket from the ground and trudged into the cottage.

Elinor kept her half smile on her face as Marianne made it to the door, but as soon as she went through the smile fell, and Elinor let out a small sob.

No, he had done nothing wrong, truly he hadn't, but it did not make it any easier knowing once and for all that any hopes or secret dreams had died. She took a deep breath, forcing herself to draw back the tears that threatened to fall, before she slid a smile back onto her face and followed Marianne into the cottage.

After all, one never looked behind the smile to see the tears. At least she hoped.

CHAPTER THIRTY-FOUR

It was strange how easily one fell back into life in the country. Despite all the changes, and the changes that were still to come, very little had truly changed for Elinor. She still walked the cliffs to enjoy the crashing of the ocean, still met with the fishermen to add some variety to their meals and still teased Marianne about her inability to wake easily.

It was, in many ways, as if they had never left, everything was exactly the same, and yet Elinor knew it was very different.

She settled against a rock overlooking the cliffs and took a drawing pad out of her purse, a gift from Brandon after Marianne had told him how Elinor loved to draw. It had now become part of her routine, drawing the stormy seas and misty countryside. Yes, they were a far cry from her prior works, which focused more on the bright days of Norland and the beauty of those around her, but there was something so compelling in these that she found herself drawn to create more and more as the days went on.

It had only been the other day she had finally taken the drawing she had completed of Norland off the wall, packing it away as a memory to be treasured, but not one that needed to be on display. In its place she had put a drawing of the cottage, Middleton's manor peaking from the back of the trees. She was quite pleased with the shading she had managed, the drawing had a realism to it that she had not found in her own work before.

Yet where she usually found solace in her drawing and her seas, since Jonathan had brought the news of Edward's nuptials she had found herself restless, unable to concentrate. With a sigh she pushed herself off the rock, carefully tucking her drawing book into her purse, before she began the slow process of returning to the cottage.

"Elinor, good, I was wondering if you would be able to help me to shell the peas." Mary called out as she drew close to home. Elinor smiled in return and nodded. It seemed something so mundane, but here at least was proof that they had changed, in some small way. Elinor could not recall her mother ever shelling peas when they were at Norland.

She slid on the apron she kept by the kitchen door, tying it around her waist as she and her mother settled onto the bay window in the kitchen that overlooked the path and the cliffs.

They worked in silence for a few moments, and the familiar, repetitive motion calmed Elinor's thoughts, allowing her to find her calm.

"Elinor?" Mary asked hesitantly and Elinor lifted her head with a hum to meet her mother's concerned gaze.

"What is it?" She asked, her head tipping as she waited for Mary to speak. Mary only watched her, and Elinor found herself fidgeting, losing the calm the shelling had lulled her into. "I promise I am well, Mama. I am happy."

"Are you?" Mary murmured, which caused Elinor to flinch.

Elinor dropped her gaze back to the bowl of peas as she considered her next words. Her mother truly saw through her, seeing the unhappiness behind her smiles where others would not.

"I am… content." Elinor finally responded.

"Dear Elinor, I wish more for you than to be merely content." Mary let her hand cover Elinor's, and Elinor turned hers to clasp her mother's hand tightly.

"I know. And I will be, I know it. It may just... take some time."

A commotion at the door had both women jolting, as Jonathan rushed in, Martha quick behind him, both panting.

"Excuse me Ma'ams, but I felt you may want to know... Mr. Edward Ferrars is coming up the path."

Elinor and Mary's eyes went wide as they met over the bowl of peas.

"Oh my dear..." Mary whispered, as Elinor suddenly sprang into motion, quickly untying her apron to throw it to Martha, Mary following right behind her.

"Mama." Elinor's eyes went wide as a hand went to her hair to soothe it down, and Mary quickly nudged it out of the way to smooth it herself.

"The sitting room, hurry." Mary shooed Elinor out of the kitchen, both women darting to the couch in the sitting room just as a knock was heard at the door.

"Mr. Edward Ferrars." Jonathan said calmly, giving no indication of the scramble the entire household had been in before.

A second later Edward hesitated in the doorway for a moment, before removing his hat and stepping into the sitting room.

"Edward, we are delighted to see you." Mary welcomed him, her voice slightly cooler than it had been on past visits, but Elinor was sure she was the only one who would notice. "May I wish you joy?"

Edward paused and shifted his shoulders, a slight look of discomfort visible on his face, and Elinor wondered if she really wasn't the only one who would notice.

"I...ah." Edward cleared his throat. "Thank you." His cobalt eyes were drawn to Elinor, and she found herself meeting them briefly before lowering her own.

She did not want to see the happiness reflected in his eyes, nor let him see the sadness that still resided in hers. Yes, she wished him well, she truly did, but she did not want to give him the satisfaction of seeing how it affected her.

"I hope you left Mrs. Ferrars well?" Mary continued, emphasizing the 'Mrs.' in her statement, and Elinor let her eyes lift to watch Edward's reaction.

"Yes, yes, she is quite well." Edward responded, his gaze darting to Mary briefly before snapping back to Elinor. He opened his mouth to say something but Elinor jumped in, interrupting him.

"Is Mrs. Ferrars at Devonshire then?"

"No..." Edward paused, then shook his head, "My mother is still in London... she does not typically choose to come to the countryside."

"No, I...ah... I meant Mrs. Edward Ferrars." Elinor's voice cracked as she spoke, and she had to swallow past the lump in her throat that the title had put there.

Edward's expression turned puzzled as he looked between Mary and Elinor, his brow furrowing at the expectant look on their faces.

"I... do you mean Mrs. Robert Ferrars?"

"I–, I'm sorry?" Mary gasped as Elinor froze, her eyes wide as Edward's face changed to one of shock.

"Oh, you have not heard then." His face turned to Elinor, the Cobalt of his eyes focused on her as he spoke. "My brother is recently married to Miss Lucy Steele." Elinor gasped as her mother's hand shot out to clasp her elbow, their expressions encouraging Edward to continue. "After my mother threw me out and gave my inheritance to Robert, Miss Steele also changed her affections. Her actions... freed me from my engagement to her, as she chose to follow the title, rather than the person."

As she spoke Elinor found it harder and harder to breathe, and at the last of his words she could not hold back her sob.

"So now you can marry Elinor..." Marianne gasped, and Edward spun to see her standing on the stairs, a hand over her mouth as Elinor rushed past him, fleeing the room. With a quick glance to Mary and Marianne, and seeing the stunned expression on their faces, Edward turned on his heel, darting after Elinor, following her into the kitchen.

"Miss Dashwood… no Elinor… Please, I have no expectations, I know after everything you have every right to turn me away this instant. If you did, I truly would not be surprised, and if you told me to stay away, I would listen if that was what you wanted." Edward stepped closer to Elinor, reaching for her shaking shoulders but hesitating to touch her. "But truly, I cannot leave here without finally being able to convey my feelings for you."

Elinor gasped as her hand came to her chest and tears began to openly fall from her eyes, her breath coming in gasping sobs as he spoke.

"Elinor, I loved you at Norland, almost from the first moment I met you. I longed to express it then, but as you know now I was bound by my promise to Lucy. I know that was a promise that should never have been made in the first place but had been at her insistence. I thought… I thought you felt it as well, and I know I have puzzled and hurt you by not being open with you, for not telling you then of my feelings."

His hands came to her shoulder, the pressure light, but enough to make Elinor's knees feel weak.

"Let me be open now." Edward's voice had deepened even as his tone softened. "Every day since I first saw you, you have been the only one in my thoughts. The flame that caught the first time I saw you has grown, and I love you, deeply, truly. Elinor, I…" his hands slid from her shoulders to clasp her hands, his chest mere inches from her back as he continued. "I have no right to hope, but I came here today because I could not wait any longer to ask. Can you forgive me?" Elinor felt her breath stop as he stepped closer, and she felt his heat against her. "Could you find it in you to love me?" She took in a shuddering breath as he whispered to her, "Will you marry me?"

At his words she felt as though the sun had finally come out from behind the clouds, bathing her in its heat. She closed her eyes, uncaring that tears still fell, as her lips curled into a smile so happy it would lift the heart.

Her sobs turned to sounds of joy as she slowly turned, her brown eyes meeting his, so close to her she could see the small specks of light blue and gold that were reflected in them. She opened her mouth several times to respond, but the joy that coursed through her was so great it had robbed her of her ability to speak. One hand rose to her mouth as she let out another sob, nodding, and Edward's expression turned from nerves to wonder and finally elation as his arms closed around her, pulling her against him, her own winding around his neck.

Elinor clutched him to her as she felt both of their bodies quivering with the emotion and energy between them. With a small laugh she drew away from him, her hand coming stroke through his hair as she smiled. When Edward started to lean forward Elinor wove her hand through his hair and pushed herself onto her toes, meeting his mouth with hers for the first time.

She felt his arm tighten around her waist as he changed the angle of the kiss, deepening it, and Elinor happily followed his lead. Her other hand clutched his back as sensation coursed through her, leaving her heated and desperate for more, but at the same time making her feel cherished, adored, and above all... loved.

When she finally shifted away to lay her head on his shoulder, she saw Mary and Marianne, their arms around each other as both smiled, tears streaming down their faces.

Now, Elinor knew, she was truly happy.

CHAPTER THIRTY-FIVE

"I still wish we could get married on the same day." Marianne sighed as she packed the last of her dresses into a trunk. Tomorrow she would be marrying Brandon, and he had promised to send a carriage for her things that evening so the staff could have everything waiting for her when they returned from their honeymoon.

"My day will be here before you know it." Elinor smiled at Marianne. "Besides, it would not do for the Rector and his wife to be married without the proper banns being read."

"But still..."

"Marianne, I do not believe you would want to truly share your wedding day with anyone," Elinor laughed, "and my wedding is merely three weeks behind yours, you will be well and truly back from your honeymoon in time."

"I suppose." Marianne mused, before giving in to giggles as Elinor grabbed her by the waist and began to tickle her.

"Besides, you will then be able to tell me what to expect on a wedding night." Elinor laughed as Marianne shrieked and tried to get away.

"NO!!!" Marianne cried out, laughter coloring her voice. "I had to suffer, so you will suffer, after all, it is not a topic for polite conversation."

Both girls stilled as Marianne's words faded, then burst into giggles again.

"Oh, how I shall miss you two." Mary stood in the doorway to their bedroom, her smile swimming with tears. "I cannot believe both of my babies are getting married, oh how your father would have loved to see this day."

"Mama," Marianne whispered as she pulled away from Elinor to sit on the edge of the bed, holding her arms out for their mother, who happily came to join them. "Will you be alright here, Mama?" Marianne asked as Mary wrapped both girls into a hug. "I can talk to Brandon, Hartland is large enough I am sure there would be room for you."

"Oh nonsense." Mary chided, "you should focus on being a new bride, learning your new home and estate, not on moving your mother. I am quite happy here with Martha and Jonathan, and Mrs. Jennings has offered to let me come and stay as often as I wish. I will be perfectly fine here."

"Are you sure Mama?" Elinor raised an eyebrow. "Afterall, I do seem to recall that you do not know how to start a fire."

"Oh, hush you," Mary grumbled, "none of us did in the beginning and we got along fine didn't we?"

"We did, Mama, we did." Elinor agreed as she lay her head on Mary's shoulder.

"Did you ever think that moving here from Norland that our lives would end up like this?" Marianne questioned, and Mary thought for a moment.

"No, my dear, but I can honestly say that this is much better than I had thought it would be. I was so scared with us all leaving Norland and the comforts that it offered that I did not think beyond that. But today is not a day for reminiscing, it is a day for celebration." Mary squeezed both girls before releasing them. "Jonathan said that Brandon's man was on the path to the cottage, are you all packed Marianne?"

"Yes Mama." Marianne nodded as she stood. "Everything is in these trunks except what I am wearing and my clothing for tomorrow. Brandon had the modiste ship the remainder of my new trousseau to Hartland, so they will already be at the manor when we arrive."

"Good, then I will get Jonathan to help bring everything down so it can be loaded into the carriage."

As Mary left the room Marianne turned to Elinor, her eyes filled with tears. "This is our last night together…"

"Yes." Elinor nodded. When Marianne's mouth fell open at how nonchalant Elinor's response had been Elinor could not help but laugh. "It is a rite of passage though, today we are daughters and sisters, and tomorrow you will be a wife. It is to be expected that things will be different."

"Is it bad of me to be so glad though that we will still be living in the same area?" Marianne sniffed back her tears. "When I think of Fanny moving with John to Norland, leaving her family behind in London, I would not be able to bear being that far from you and Mama."

"No, it is not bad at all!" Elinor smiled. "Truly, I am glad for the same reason, I know we will be able to see each other any day we want, we are not really being parted, just we will be residing in different homes."

The girls fell silent as Jonathan and Brandon's man Brandon stepped into the room, each taking a trunk with them after a small nod to the ladies.

"Elinor…" Marianne whispered as the men made their way down the stairs, "I'm getting married tomorrow."

"You are."

"It's funny, I have been dreaming about getting married almost my entire life, but now that it's here…"

"Are you scared?" Elinor asked as she reached out to take Marianne's hand.

"No," Marianne let out a laugh, "strangely, no. I'm excited. But it's different than I felt it would be."

"How so?"

Marianne turned her face to glance at her sister. "For so many years I thought about what my wedding would be like, picturing it down to the type of flowers and food that would be served, and I saw that as the perfect day, but that's not what I am excited about."

"Oh?"

"I'm excited for the day *after* tomorrow. When it is just me and Brandon, and the beginning of our lives together. Isn't that funny? I have always wanted to get married, but the focus was on the day itself, with no thoughts for what comes after. But now, I want that over and done, and I am looking forward to every day after it more."

"That's not strange at all," Elinor smiled as her eyes drifted closed, Edward's face clear in her mind. "That is what I think being truly in love means. Being excited not to just bind your life with another, but to truly live that life with them."

"And here I always thought I was the one led by sensibility, driven to fanciful thinking." Marianne teased as she nudged Elinor with her shoulder.

"Hmm, no, I thought you were always the one who showed perfect sense in every setting." Elinor smirked as her eyes opened to meet Marianne's and both sisters burst into laughter.

"Oh, it is good we will not be far from each other, I imagine we will drive Brandon and Edward mad." Marianne wiped her eyes as tears of joy formed.

"I have a feeling they will enjoy every moment of it though," Elinor smiled, "and I imagine we will often be having dinner at Hartland."

"As if I would accept anything less." Marianne nodded, her voice serious as she gave her best impression of Fanny, only to ruin the effect by crossing her eyes, making Elinor burst out into another peal of laughter.

"Oh Marianne, Fanny you are not, and oh how thankful I am for that." Elinor gasped through her laughter.

"Elinor, I do believe you are right." Marianne laughed as she made her way to her bed and the simple nightgown that was laid out. Her laughter faded as she reached out to touch it, it was one of the garments she had chosen to leave behind as she had new ones that the Modiste had made for her. It was silly, she knew, the thought that in the morning she would be shedding the last remnant of childhood and becoming a full woman of society. Not just a woman but a wife, and *Brandon's* wife.

She felt the butterflies that had been churning in her stomach ease with the thought, his golden eyes flitting through her mind, a smile with the hint of a fang, his mouth moving against hers and making her long for more...

Yes, she was looking forward to spending the rest of her days, however long those may be, at Brandon's side. She had already agreed to become Brandon's wife and bonded match, wanting to never leave him alone and unloved again. She knew that there would be pain one day when her mother and finally her sister passed long before she would, but she would have the memories of them, those of childhood and memories they had yet to make, that she would tell her children about centuries from now.

Tears began to swim in her eyes one last time as Elinor's arms wrapped around her waist, and the sisters took a moment to hold each other, to treasure the last moments of their childhood and adolescence. Soon, both would be part of another family, but they would also remain the closest of sisters.

Marianne smiled through her tears.

She looked forward to seeing the trouble they would get into.

"We are almost done, Miss Marianne, and oh, how beautiful a bride you are!" Martha gushed as she wound Marianne's hair into an intricate twist, miniature white roses woven into the design.

Marianne was truly a vision clad in her deep green silk dress, her hair accented with white. Her skin glowed against the color of the dress, the shade highlighting her alabaster skin.

"Thank you, Martha." Marianne smiled, her gaze drawn to the small bouquet that rested in a jar by the window. The pink hydrangea and white roses were absolutely beautiful. She had specifically chosen the flowers in memory of Brandon's proposal, and she knew they would be well suited to match her gown. She had chosen a deeper color than she had previously worn to highlight her new maturity, the pastels and shallowness of youth no longer drew her, for she knew how deep and beautiful life could be, and found beauty beyond the surface.

That and she had been told Brandon would be in his red military coat with its golden braids, and had seen the deep green against a red silk at the modiste, and had immediately known it was perfect for her wedding gown.

"Marianne, are you almost ready? We need to hurry to the chur... oh Marianne." Mary began, only to sigh as she saw her daughter turn to the door and saw her in her full wedding regalia. When she stood and Martha handed her the bouquet, Mary found her eyes filled with tears. "You are truly beautiful my dear."

"You always think that Mama." Marianne's cheeks had pinked with the compliment, even though she had expected it from her mother.

"And it will always be true." Mary stepped close and placed a kiss on Marianne's forehead. "Are you ready?"

Marianne nodded, a smile on her face, before it turned slightly teasing as she took in the tears in her mother's eye. "Are you?"

"To give up my baby? I am not sure I ever would be." Mary gave a quiet laugh as she wiped her eyes. "But I know I am giving her to the care of a wonderful man, one who is thankfully not spiriting her away to the other side of England to live."

"He is a wonderful man, isn't he?" Marianne sighed.

"Yes, Brandon is a wonderful man, one I know would wait forever for you Marianne but I do not think the Pastor has his patience." Elinor chided from the door, her own eyes misty with emotion as she saw her sister turn, her smile broad across her face.

"Well, then let us be off. It would not do to start my time as a wife with a lecture from the Pastor." Marianne laughed as she wrapped her arm through her mother's and led her through the door, Elinor and Martha following closely behind.

The drive to the church was quiet, but not due to melancholy or nerves, but because Marianne was afraid she would not be able to contain her own joy if she were to speak. By the time the carriage came to a stop in front of the church she was practically vibrating with her excitement. When she entered the church, her mother and sister on either side to escort her, her heart began to race. It was at that moment that her nerves had frayed, was she ready, would she be a good wife, was she who Brandon would need by his side...

When golden eyes turned and met hers from the altar, she felt her nerves begin to settle. When his eyes went wide and his breath caught, his expression showing his awe as she walked towards him, she knew. They would always be enough. Whatever life threw at them, they would be by each other's side.

Martha and Jonathan sat with Middleton and Mrs. Jennings, the women already wiping tears from their eyes as Brandon took two steps from the altar to meet Marianne, Elinor and Mary, greeting them with a small bow, even as his eyes remained on Marianne. Brandon's staff looked on as Marianne placed her hand in the crook of his arm, letting him escort her to the Pastor. While it wasn't the norm, she knew, she was happy at his action, they were approaching as partners, as equals, to be joined before God.

When the Pastor cleared his through Marianne let her hand drop reluctantly from Brandon's arm. During the sermon, she felt the soft brush of his finger against hers, and with a small smile let her pinky curl around his, holding it in place as he drew in a sudden breath. She dared to sneak a look at him, her brown eyes meeting his golden as everything around them fell away. They both spoke when directed by the Pastor, but nothing could draw their gazes apart. When Brandon turned to her and took her left hand, raising it to slide a golden ring with an emerald deep enough to match her gown, surrounded by gleaming yellow topaz she felt herself tremble, not with nerves, but with the full meaning of the moment.

She was his, and he was hers. His lips curled into a pleased smile as she heard the Pastor announce them as Husband and Wife, and before the Pastor could finish the direction to kiss the bride Brandon was already in motion, his lips gentle on Marianne's as his thumb caressed the ring she now wore.

"I love you." He whispered against her lips, before giving her another chaste kiss.

"I love you too." She responded, and Brandon's eyes deepened as he seized her lips in a decidedly less chaste kiss.

The cheers from the pews did not break through the spell that held them, but the loud clearing of the Pastor's throat finally had Brandon drawing back, a heated smile on his face as he raised his hand to Marianne's cheek. Marianne dared to raise herself on her toes, placing another kiss against his lips as she whispered to him "My Brandon."

"Marianne." Brandon groaned as he lowered his forehead to touch hers. "Finally, you are mine."

"We are each other's." Marianne smiled as she lifted his hand from her cheek and laced her fingers through his. Brandon nodded, his eyes closing at the thought, as they took a moment together, unaware of the jubilation that surrounded them.

They would celebrate with those they had come to wish them well, and then their lives together would start.

CHAPTER THIRTY-SIX

Three weeks had come and gone, and now it was Elinor who was in a panic.

"Where has the time gone?" Elinor cried as she frantically packed her clothing in a trunk.

"Oh that is very decidedly not like you Elinor." A teasing voice from behind her made Elinor spin, a gasp coming from her as she saw Marianne behind her. "I would have thought you would be packed the moment I left."

"Marianne, oh Marianne!" Elinor laughed as the sisters ran to wrap their arms around each other. It had been nearly three weeks since Marianne's wedding, and she and Brandon had only returned the night before.

"Elinor I have missed you." Marianne gasped as her arms tightened around Elinor.

"And I you, oh you must tell me everything."

"There is so much to tell," Marianne sighed happily, "but let us also get you packed, what time is someone coming for your trunk?" She drew away from her sister, crossing to pick up a dress that lay across the bed, folding it carefully before placing it in the trunk.

"Edward should be here by sunset." Elinor grinned. "I only have the one trunk that I am taking."

"That is only a few hours away!" Marianne gasped. "Even if it is *just* one trunk, we must still get you packed." Marianne shot Elinor a glance from the side of her eyes. "And do not think that I am not annoyed at your insinuation that I could not contain myself to one trunk."

"It was no insinuation at all." Elinor laughed. "You always had more clothing and belongings that you could not be parted with than I."

"Hmmm, first you have seen me in almost three weeks and you are already teasing me, why did I miss you again?"

"Because I am your best friend and you are mine, dear sister." Elinor smiled even as her eyes turned misty. "Even though I now share you with someone, you will always be my sister."

"Oh Elinor," Marianne whispered as she wrapped Elinor in a hug.

"I'm sorry, I do not mean to be so emotional." Elinor sniffed.

"Elinor, you are getting married *tomorrow*, it is ok to be emotional."

"You weren't."

"As we said, I have always been the sensible sister." Marianne nodded sagely, before grinning at the glare Elinor sent her. "But truly, it is understandable to be emotional, you are marrying the man you love, but it also does bring some changes."

"It is funny, I have been working with Edward to get him settled into the Rectory, but somehow it never quite hit me that I would be leaving the cottage until today."

"What is it you told me?" Marianne mused. "It is a rite of passage. Tomorrow, you go from being daughter to wife, with everything that it entails, and beyond that, you will be a Rector's wife. Far better that be you than me, I would never be able to have the patience for that."

Elinor thought for a moment before letting out a chuckle. "That I can agree with you on."

"Come now, let us get you packed, and if you would like, I can stay the night here with you."

"Brandon would be alright with that?" Elinor asked, amused at the thought.

"He was not too keen on it, but I was able to convince him." Marianne's smile turned a little devilish as she spoke, her eyes sparkling with pure happiness.

"Married life suits you." Elinor said quietly as she looked at her sister, the way she held herself, the joy that shone from her.

"It does." Marianne agreed. "It really does. Oh Elinor, I never could have imagined being this happy. I pray that your marriage is as happy as mine has started out."

"Yes, that reminds me," Elinor said slyly, "as now you are in a place to know. What exactly does happen on your wedding night?"

"*Elinor Dashwood*!" Mary's voice sounded like a firecracker through the small room, making both girls jump. "That is not a question one asks."

"But Mama, it is just us here, and both you and Marianne know but no one will tell me."

"It is for Edward to teach you, dear, not Marianne or I." Mary said sternly as she shot Marianne a look that would make even a royal obey her.

"Mama is right," Marianne said quietly, giving a small shrug when Elinor turned narrowed eyes on her. "It is something that Edward will want to teach you." The moment Mary turned to inspect the trunk Marianne mouthed '*I will tell you later.*'

"And Marianne, do not even *think* about telling her once I leave this room." Mary said sternly as she folded the clothing that remained on the bed and placed it in the trunk. "I know you are newly married, but there are some things that remain between the husband and his wife only."

"How did you…"

"I am your mother, Marianne." Mary turned with an eyebrow raised, a look eerily similar to the one Elinor sometimes wore. "Do not think I do not know the two of you."

"Yes Mama." The girls murmured at the exact same time, their eyes meeting in exasperation as Mary nodded and finished the folding.

"Now, is there anything else you would like to take with you to your new home?" Mary asked as she cast her eyes around the room.

"No Mama." Elinor responded.

"Good, then you are all packed." Mary turned to see her daughters standing side by side, and her eyes began to fill with tears. "Look at you, tomorrow you will both be married women, no time for your mother."

"Mama!"

"Do not say that, Mama!"

Both Elinor and Marianne started to protest their mother's comment only to go quiet as she held up a hand. "I am not saying you will not come to visit, but it will not be as it has been in the past. I know you will both visit, and I will surely come to visit you, but you will have your own families now, and I plan on spoiling all of your children as much as I can."

"Oh Mama..." Elinor whispered.

"None of that now, this is a happy occasion." Mary smiled. "Besides, you know full well that Mrs. Jennings and I will be terrors together, so do not worry."

"I worry more for those you turn your attention to." Marianne teased, making Mary throw her head back and laugh.

"That is true. But we will have a lot of joy with it. Now, I believe I hear Edward's horse coming up the way, let us get this trunk to him. Then I expect you both to get some rest, and Marianne to *not* provide you with information that she should not, as you need to wake bright and early for the ceremony tomorrow morning.

"Yes Mama."

"Yes Mama."

"Jonathan, could you please help us with this trunk?" Mary called down the stairs, stepping to the side when Jonathan made his way into the room, nodded to Marianne and then took the trunk.

"Do you need any help with that?" Elinor asked, concerned that it would be too much for him.

"I have it Miss Elinor, don't you worry about it." Jonathan smiled as he shifted it to his shoulder. "The feed bag for the horses weighs more than this."

"If you are sure."

"I am Miss Elinor, you just think about yourself and your wedding tomorrow. Goodnight Miss, Ma'ams."

"I'm a Ma'am..." Marianne whispered as Jonathan carefully moved down the stairs.

"That has just hit you?" Elinor laughed as Marianne's cheeks flushed.

"I just had not really thought about it." Marianne admitted. "It is not as if we really left our chamber during our honeymoon other than to eat. We were mostly..."

"Marianne Dashwood, I would recommend you not complete that sentence." Mary's eyebrow rose as she turned to glare at Marianne.

"That is not technically my name anymore mama." Marianne grinned, which made Mary's eyebrow rise even more.

"As long as I am still your mother and you are standing under my roof, I will call you Marianne Dashwood and you will listen, is that clear?"

"Yes Mama." Marianne pouted.

"Come now, I am sure there are lots of things you can tell me about your honeymoon other than what Mama has now forbidden us to talk about." Elinor shot her mother a wry glance, only to receive a wink back in return.

"Oh, I can tell you all about the villa Brandon took me too, oh the scenery was absolutely lovely and...

When morning dawned Elinor found herself wide awake. It was not nerves that woke her though, it was the happiness and realization that in a few short hours she would finally be married to Edward. She smiled at the soft snoring from beside her, Marianne had wrapped herself around Elinor as if seeking body heat, occasionally mumbling 'Brandon' as she slept.

"Marianne," Elinor whispered as she shook her sister's shoulder, "it's time to get up."

"5 more minutes..." Marianne muttered, burying her face in the pillow.

"Not today, Marianne," Elinor laughed as she began to tickle her sister, who woke up with a shriek.

"Elinor, I HATE YOU!" Marianne cried out as she laughed.

"No, you do not." Elinor smiled.

"Fine, I do not." Marianne giggled as Elinor eased her attack. "Are you ready to get married?"

"No." Elinor said simply, which drew a gasp from Marianne. "I am ready to be married. I now understand what you meant on your wedding day, that I am looking forward more to tomorrow than I am today."

Marianne smiled as she pushed herself to a sitting position. "And I pray he makes you always feel that way." She pushed her hair out of her face, revealing the small scar on her left wrist, the scar that now bound her to Brandon for his life, and not just hers.

In a small way Elinor was envious of Marianne for that scar, knowing she would have centuries with the man she loved, but Elinor also knew that she herself would cherish Edward for every day that she had with him.

The thought warmed her as she dressed in her best blue muslin dress, the same one she had first met Edward in. A smile curved her lips as she remembered that moment from so many months ago, her beating the carpet when he first arrived. Small moments of their times together drifted through her thoughts, their walks at Norland, his visit to the cottage, his shirt plastered to his chest through the rai...

Her cheeks flushed as she felt her body warm at the remembrance of that image. It had played in many of her dreams since then and now were paired with the kiss they had shared in the kitchen. While they had kissed in the weeks since, none had been that deep nor left her filled with that feeling of warmth, but in her dreams, she now pictured Edward, his shirt wet, revealing his chest, as his mouth pressed against hers, his hands holding her against him...

"Now what are you thinking about with that expression on your face?" Marianne teased as she tucked the last curl of Elinor's hair into place.

"Edward..." Elinor admitted shyly, only to sputter when Marianne laughed. "It is not funny Marianne."

"It is though," Marianne giggled, "and trust me, after tonight you will understand."

Elinor's mouth fell open as Marianne winked at her before quickly dressing herself, throwing her hair back into a simple bun. If a wedding night had to do with those thoughts, and that feeling then...

Elinor's eyes met Marianne's in the mirror, and Marianne gave a slow smile and nodded.

"Well let us get going, we do not want to be late." Elinor's voice was breathy as she stood, and Marianne just laughed at the sound.

"No, we do not."

Rather than use the church in town, Elinor and Edward had chosen to be wed in the Rectory that Edward had taken over, and a neighboring priest had come to oversee the marriage. The Rectory itself was small but felt intimate as Mary sat with Marianne and Brandon, Brandon's arm curled around Marianne's waist. Middleton and Mrs. Jennings sat opposite them, both their faces beaming as Elinor walked down the aisle.

Edward kept his back to the aisle as Elinor approached, and Elinor could see the slight tremor of his shoulders that showed his emotion. His black jacket framed his shoulders and chest well, a last remnant of his days as a "Lord" as he liked to call it, but it suited him. As she reached the end of the pews he turned, his Cobalt eyes capturing hers as he smiled. His hand reached out, and with an answering grin Elinor took it stepping up beside him. As the priest began the ceremony, they kept their hands intertwined, a physical reassurance that the other was there, beside them.

Edward turned to face Elinor; his eyes misty with tears as he repeated the words from the priest.

"I, Edward, take thee Elinor, to be my lawfully wedded wife. To have and to hold from this day forward, for better or for worse, for richer, for poorer, in sickness and in health, to love and to cherish, till death do us part, according to God's holy ordinance."

Elinor smiled as the priest directed her to provide him with her vows, and repeated after him, her eyes locked with Edward's.

"I, Elinor, take thee, Edward, to be my wedded husband. To have and to hold from this day forward, for better or for worse, for richer, for poorer, in sickness and in health, to love, cherish, and obey, till death do us part, according to God's holy ordinance."

Edward lifted her left hand, bringing it to his lips to place a gentle kiss on it before he slid a silver band onto her ring finger. "Elinor, I give you this ring as a symbol of my vow, and with all that I am and all that I have, I honor you, in the name of the Father, and of the Son, and of the Holy Spirit."

"By the power vested in me, I now pronounce you Husband and Wife."

The words washed over Elinor as her eyes drifted shut, and she could not stop the smile that formed across her face.

"You may now kiss the bride."

Her eyes opened to see tears falling from Edward's eyes and felt her own fill with tears as he stepped in, bending down to place a kiss on her lips.

"I now present to you, for the first time, Mr. and Mrs. Edward Ferrars!"

With a whoop of joy Edward took Elinor's hand in his, leading her back down the aisle and to the front steps of the church. There he paused, his eyes turning heated as he tugged Elinor's hand and drew her against him, his hand coming to splay against her back as he claimed her lips, finally revealing all the passion he felt for her in that one action. Elinor found herself adrift in a sea of heat as she wrapped her arms around his neck, burying her hands in his hair as she met his fire with her own.

"Elinor," Edward murmured against her lips, repeating her name like a prayer as his lips met hers again and again."

The applause that sounded around the two finally drew their attention from the other, and Elinor felt her cheeks flush as she caught the smirks of the women in the group. She stepped away from Edward to hug Marianne, neither girl commenting on the tears streaming down the other's cheeks.

With a sniffle Marianne stepped back, knowing Brandon would be there to wrap his arms around her as she settled against him. Elinor smiled as Edward came to her side, his arm sliding around her waist. As the two sisters' eyes met, their hands reached out, their fingers brushing, as they each smiled.

While they had been through hell and back that year, neither could say they would change any part of it. Each had grown and learned that they were more like their sister than they had originally thought, each now the embodiment of sense and sensibility, reason, and emotion. Their hands separated as their respective husbands held them close and they smiled.

And so, the years went by, with the sisters living almost within sight of each other, enjoying life without disagreement between the two, and their love with their husbands and later their families continued to grow as each day passed.